Anastasia

R.P.G. Colley

Novels by R.P.G. Colley:

Love and War Series:
The Lost Daughter
The White Venus
Song of Sorrow
The Woman on the Train
The Black Maria
My Brother the Enemy
Anastasia
Elena
The Mist Before Our Eyes
The Darkness We Leave Behind

The Searight Saga:
This Time Tomorrow
The Unforgiving Sea
The Red Oak

The Tales of Little Leaf
Eleven Days in June
Winter in July
Departure in September

**The DI Benedict Paige Crime Series
by JOSHUA BLACK**
And Then She Came Back
The Poison in His Veins
Requiem for a Whistleblower
The Forget-Me-Not Killer
The Canal Boat Killer
A Senseless Killing

https://rupertcolley.com

Anastasia

Rupertcolley.com

"October 23, 1956, is a day that will live forever in the annals of free men and nations. It was a day of courage, conscience and triumph. No other day since history began has shown more clearly the eternal unquenchability of man's desire to be free, whatever the odds against success, whatever the sacrifice required."

John Fitzgerald Kennedy, speaking on the first anniversary of the start of the Hungarian Revolution.

Part One

May 1949

Chapter 1: Zoltan

Zoltan Beke sat at his desk, his fingers arched in a steeple, eyeing the nervous youngster opposite him. The boy, nursing a bandaged hand, was only eighteen but, after a week in the cells, looked older; his skin had already taken on the sallow complexion of being too long away from sunlight. Above his right eyebrow, still fresh, a crescent-shaped wound.

'Well,' said Zoltan, 'I hope you found your time here of some value.'

'Yes, sir.' His nose was long and thin, a Jew perhaps, his eyebrows too thick for a boy of his age.

'*Comrade*, not sir. There are no sirs in the people's democracy.'

'No, I'm – I'm sorry, comrade.'

Zoltan, in a rare moment of charity, had decided to release him. He'd initially come to his attention when the boy's ex-girlfriend had informed on him – *"Dear Comrades, Jasper Szabo spends every night listening to the* Voice of America.*"* Their break-up must've been spectacular to go to such lengths to wreak revenge. *"He listens to their bourgeois claptrap and says how, one day, the people will rise against Comrade Rakosi and his Russian-loving cronies."*

'So,' said Zoltan, fixing his stare on the unfortunate Jasper Szabo. 'What is our opinion now of our esteemed leader?'

'Comrade Rakosi is our leading light, sir – I mean, comrade.' He looked furtively at the bull-necked guard standing to his side. 'He is the embodiment of Comrade Stalin and Stalin's greatest pupil; and through our beloved leader we will find the true way to a Socialist utopia.'

It was amazing, thought Zoltan, what a week's worth of rehabilitation could achieve. This young lamb, who'd strayed so far from the flock, had been successfully brought back to the fold. The first part of the process had involved tying his hand down to a table with a belt and smashing his knuckles with a mallet. If that didn't hammer the message home for the errant youth, nothing would. He smiled at his unintentional pun.

Jasper Szabo continued. 'Only through his teachings and his policies will we match our brothers in the Soviet Union and show the imperialist West that the communist is a worker free of exploitation.'

'And subjugation.'

'And subjugation.'

The initial phase of rehabilitation may have been severe but it was brief. Jasper Szabo was still a boy; Zoltan had only wanted to show him the error of his ways, not to break him. Another year or two older, he wouldn't have hesitated. The broken knuckles were but a trifle; the crescent-shaped wound nothing more than a scratch.

'And should we expect another visit from you at any point?'

The boy almost fell off his chair in his eagerness to respond. 'No, comrade. I have my future life to live among the happy people of our country.'

'And will you be listening to any more of that shit on the capitalist radio?'

'No, comrade. I shall be devoting my time to reading the works of Comrade Stalin.'

Zoltan laughed; he hadn't meant to but the boy was surpassing himself. Following on from the mallet, Jasper had experienced the hospitality of the Hungarian secret police, the AVO – two nights in a dingy cell without a bed or chair, with a ceiling too low for the average man to stand straight. Then transferred to the relative luxury of a regular cell where he'd been allowed to sleep, read and receive half-decent rations of food and cigarettes.

'Well, young man, you're at liberty to go.' Jasper Szabo stared back at him, his eyes agog. Zoltan continued, 'You will sign the pledge that forbids you to breathe a word to anyone about your time here. Understood?'

'Yes, yes, of course, comrade.'

Zoltan glanced up at the guard. 'Show him out,' he snapped.

Jasper rose unsteadily to his feet, clutching his bandaged hand. He seemed poised on the brink of saying something, perhaps even a thank you, but evidently decided against it.

As Jasper reached the door, Zoltan couldn't resist asking him one more question. 'Tell me,' he said, barely able to hide the smirk, 'will you be seeing your young lady friend?'

Jasper blinked, seemingly unsure how to respond. Zoltan obligingly filled the gap, 'I think you should. After all, in writing to us, she had your best interests at heart. You should seek her out and personally thank her for what she did for you.'

The boy glanced subconsciously at his bandaged hand and looked back at his interrogator, the corner of his mouth twitching in an attempt at a smile.

*

There were a number of arrested citizens awaiting Zoltan's consideration. Men and women plucked from their homes whose devious activities had been brought to an end by an informer – spies, fascists, counter-revolutionaries, deviationists, and a whole catalogue of reprobates whose business warranted the attention of the secret police. Thank God for the informers – an army of ordinary citizens; eagle-eyed comrades who were not prepared to see their country restored to the evils of capitalism, nor for their communist system to be perverted by devious, shit-stirring lackeys of the imperialists.

Zoltan and his fellow AVO officers were busy men and little appreciated. Suppression is a thankless task. He couldn't remember the last time he'd had a holiday. How little he saw of his daughter, Roza. He ran his finger down the glass of the framed photograph he kept of her on his desk – her eyes so wide, her hair so blonde, her cheeks so dimpled. In a week's time she'd be three years old. Petra was planning a party and he'd promised to be there to perform a few simple magic tricks (an old speciality he had – entertaining children with disappearing ribbons and card tricks). The hard work now was an investment for the future. With time, the work would bring promotion. And with the promotion, the greater privileges, the perks, the respect, and the holidays. It was only a matter of time – time, work and a fanatical devotion to the cause.

With a sigh, he plucked the top file from the pile of Category Xs. Everyone in Hungary had a category and the

Category Xs were the enemies of the people, the socially undesirables, whose arrest was only a matter of time. The telephone rang. It was Donath, his boss. Did he have a minute? As if there was a choice.

*

Donath's office was naturally larger and more opulent than his own. The desk was of a darker wood; the leather chair a deeper red; three telephones, not two; a larger bust of Stalin; a thicker carpet. On the desk, an overflowing ashtray; on the wall a portrait of Felix Dzerzhinsky, founder of the Soviet secret police. Donath sat behind his desk, his tunic decorated, as always, by his proudest possession – an Order of Lenin medal. His rubbery face flushed red, his fingers clutching a file – a priority, thought Zoltan, otherwise why the summons?

'Got one for you here,' said Donath, flinging the file onto the desk. A cloud of ash billowed up from the ashtray.

'What is it? What he's done?'

'Nothing yet. Your job is to ensure it remains that way.'

Zoltan peered at the photograph on the top page – a good-looking chap, dark eyes, strong cheekbones. He scanned the details: George Lorenc, aged eighteen, occupation – football player. 'A footballer?'

'A good one too, apparently, not that I would know.' He looked bored by it all. 'Who needs football when there's still so much to do in the real world?'

'The masses like it.'

'The masses like bonking and drinking – doesn't mean it's good for them.' He sneered slightly as he always did when he thought of the people *en masse*, the great working class on whose behalf they were fighting. 'Anyway, Beke, there's a game next week – one of the city teams against a visiting side from Moscow.'

'Moscow Lokomotiv – yes, I know.'

'Ah, well you know more than me. Message from Moscow is that the team need to win this game.'

'Why, is it important?'

'God no, it's only a friendly but they're having a tough time of it recently and a win here would set them up for an important cup tie next week or so. Apparently,' he added quickly, for fear he should sound like a man who gave a damn. But of course, the real reason hung unspoken between them – their political masters would not entertain the idea of one of their football teams being shown up by a bunch of feeble Hungarians. The Soviet Union led the way in football as it did in all spheres of life.

'So why this chap, this…' Zoltan glanced back at the name, 'this George Lorenc?'

'We've already nobbled their manager, Bordas, I think his name is, and he reckons if it wasn't for Lorenc, his team wouldn't stand a chance anyway.'

'Good then, is he?'

'Meant to be, yes. He's their centre-forward, a natural goal-scorer. So, a nice, easy job for you.' One of his three telephones rang and Donath grabbed it immediately. 'Yes? What is it?… Wait, let me get her file…' Resting the receiver on the blotting-pad, he pulled open a drawer.

'I'll get to it, then,' said Zoltan, not entirely sure whether his audience with the boss had come to an end.

'Yeah, do so,' said Donath, rummaging around in the drawer. 'A quiet word should do the trick. It's only a friendly after all, he won't mind.'

For half a moment, he thought he caught Dzerzhinsky's

portrait winking down at him. 'Dare say you're right,' he said, rising from the chair. 'It's only a friendly…'

Chapter 2: George

It was a definite dive, thought George. But what did he care; the resulting penalty provided him with a gilt-edged opportunity to bag his hat-trick. Kosak, the inside-left, had flown into the penalty area but the ball was already running away from him. The defender's shadow had barely encroached on his space when Kosak threw himself on the ground, clasping his ankle and screaming as if it'd been hacked off. The referee charged to the scene, his whistle clamped in his mouth and pointed to the spot. The Union players made a show of complaint, if simply for the sake of decency. The crowd cheered in anticipation of a three-goal victory and a hat-trick for their dashing rising star, now standing over the ball.

George placed the muddied ball on the penalty spot and took four carefully paced steps back. His first goal, late in the first half, was a far post header; his second, minutes later, was a low, powerful drive from fifteen yards out. And now the third beckoned…

The crowd hushed. Before him, stood the Union goalkeeper, his knees bent, his hands comically big in their oversized gloves. The image of his father flashed across his mind as it always did in life's big moments. There he was, standing between two piles of coats, telling his son to keep his eye on the ball.

The referee blows his whistle. One step, two, three… shoot! The goalkeeper dives the wrong way. He looks on helplessly as the ball almost trickles over the line and nestles in the far left corner, barely rippling the net. The 'keeper slams his fist on the ground in frustration but George doesn't notice: he's already halfway down the pitch, skipping with delight, acknowledging the crowd's rapturous applause. His colleagues slap him on the back and ruffle his hair. He looks up into the stands and sees his mother in her usual place, jumping with joy. There'll be tears in her eyes, tears of pride tinged, as always, with sadness that her husband wasn't around to see another momentous occasion in George's footballing career.

George's third goal takes the sting out of the contest and the last twenty minutes are played out as a formality. With ten minutes to go, Bordas, the manager, substitutes him. George is delighted – being able to exit by himself, secure in the knowledge that the applause is his alone. Sure enough, the crowd stand to show their appreciation, their smiling faces and cheers reflecting the joy in his heart.

Bordas welcomed him with a solid shake of the hand, the gaps between his teeth showing beneath his smile. 'Good lad, well played,' he said. 'Bring on the Soviets, eh?'

George laughed and, taking the tracksuit top offered to him, trotted off down the tunnel and down the stairs, his football boots echoing on the concrete steps. The dressing-room was empty but the noise of the crowd was still present, though dulled and distant, like the faraway crashing of waves. He rolled down his socks, removed the shin pads, and rubbed his calves. Three goals! What a feeling; his mind was still buzzing with the excitement, his muscles still tense with adrenaline.

'Bring on the Soviets,' he said to himself, repeating Bordas's war cry. 'We'll knock them for six.'

The game against Moscow Lokomotiv, a fortnight away, was nothing more than a friendly but the thought of beating the Soviet Politburo's third favourite team was the stuff of dreams. How his father would have loved it, seeing his son score against the country's political masters. Any snub against Soviet supremacy, even on the football field, was worth paying to see.

'Football is a game of psychology, a game where the confidence trickster wins.' He could hear his father saying it, his pipe in the corner of his mouth, the smell of sweet tobacco on his breath. George closed his eyes and leant back against the tiled walls, the noise of the crowd lapping in and out of his consciousness; his father's voice rising above the waves of sound: 'Show them even the slightest hint of fear and you're done for. Confidence in football, as it is in life, my boy, is the key to everything. Everything.'

George didn't hear the dressing room doors open or the soft-soled shoes as someone crossed the tiled floor. Nevertheless, something made him sit up and open his eyes. With a lurch, he noticed the dark figure approach. 'Sorry, you're not meant to be in here,' he said quickly, adding, 'you can collect autographs later,' although he knew full well that this short, middle-aged man with cat-like eyes, now standing in front of him, was no autograph hunter.

'George Lorenc?' asked the stranger. He had a round, moon-like face and a thin wiry moustache.

George's stomach tightened. The man, with his hands in the pockets of his long cream overcoat, looked every inch a secret policeman, an AVO. 'Yes?' said George, unable to hide the nervousness in his voice.

The man smiled, his moustache stretching across the width of his face. 'Mark Decsi,' he said, offering his hand. 'A good game today.'

George shook his hand. 'Yes, it was OK.'

'Ah, you're too modest. It's not every day one scores a hat-trick. May I sit down?' The man plonked himself on the bench so close that George had to fight the urge to inch away from him. Decsi looked at his watch. 'Final whistle in a couple of minutes. I'm sorry, I haven't introduced myself.'

'Mark Decsi.'

'I mean my responsibility and my reason for wanting to see you. You see, I am the player development officer for the Hungarian National Communist Football Team. In plain language – a talent scout.'

George's eyes widened. 'A talent scout?'

'Indeed. And you, young man, are on my list.'

'Really?' Amazing, thought George, how he'd assumed the man to be a threat to his future; instead, he had the potential to be the maker of dreams. Suddenly, the invasion of his body space seemed inconsequential.

The two men heard the eruption of a cheer. The game had finished; soon the dressing room would be full with his teammates. As much as he wanted to talk to this man, George didn't want the others to see him; this was his moment and he had no desire to share it.

'Your game in two weeks,' continued Decsi, 'against Lokomotiv – I'll be there, as will be Comrade Gusztav.' Had he heard correctly, wondered George, Sebes Gusztav, the national team manager? 'Play like you did today, my boy, and Comrade Gusztav cannot fail to be impressed and you'd have every chance of a place on his team. What would you say to that, eh? Playing centre forward for your country?'

'It – it sounds…'

'Quite.' Decsi rose abruptly to his feet, turned on his heel and marched quickly away, leaving the dressing room as George's teammates descended down the stairs and through the swing doors. No one seemed to notice the short man in the long cream overcoat who slipped away as quietly as he'd appeared.

*

An hour later, George was walking home, striding home towards Pest, his mind reliving for the umpteenth time the brief conversation with the talent scout. Following Decsi's exit, George's teammates had crowded around him, amidst whoops and cheers, and much handshaking and back-patting; jubilant in their own celebration and proud of their self-effacing, three-goal hero. Bordas was all smiles as he delivered his post-match dissection, congratulating George but emphasising the team effort. George tried to listen but his mind was too much a whirl to concentrate.

Following showers, the players dressed and talked excitedly of the coming evening and the bars they would crash and the girls they'd meet. But first, they had to "voluntarily" endure the half-hour lecture from the political advisor assigned to the team. After each game, they had to listen to another dirge on the glorious work being achieved by the Party, the need for vigilance, the supremacy of Stalin, and the wondrous future that lay ahead. Non-attendance was frowned upon but today George felt invincible. He slipped away before the lecture, asking the goalkeeper, Milan Ignotus, to vouch for him – a sick mother. He only hoped Kosak believed him. Kosak, the inside-left who'd won the penalty, was the only true communist amongst them, the only one who took his political obligations seriously.

George smiled as he crossed the Margaret Bridge into Pest. His teammates would be in the midst of the lecture now, stealing glances at their watches, desperate to escape, desperate for a drink. He stopped and gazed at the river beneath him, the city lights reflecting in the murky water, the occasional car passing behind him, the fumes hanging in the air. The names of the national players floated in his mind – Puskas, Bozsik, Kocsis. He added his own, slipping it between the familiar names as if trying it out for size. He imagined himself in the famous red shirt and white shorts, standing shoulder to shoulder with these Hungarian giants. 'This time two weeks...' he said to himself.

If only his father could see it. He visualised him, with his pipe and brown suit, teaching the ten-year-old George to play with his right foot. 'You have to play with both feet if you want to play for Hungary.' He'd spent hours in the local park learning to shoot and tackle with his weaker foot.

In the two years following his father's arrest, George lost himself in football. It was as if his very existence depended on it. He wanted to be as good as he could because one day, *one day*, his father would return, and he so wanted to impress him. He always had. His mother slowly began to embrace his enthusiasm, even learning the subtleties of the 4-4-2 formation and the offside rule. And as his proficiency improved, so the life returned slowly to her eyes.

The sound of a truck rattling behind him on the bridge brought George back to the present. His mother would be at home, preparing the evening meal, preparing to welcome home her conquering hero of a son. He couldn't wait to tell her of his meeting with Decsi. All that stood in his way from realising his dreams was one of the Politburo's pet teams, a bunch of over-hyped Soviets. This time two weeks, he thought, this time two weeks…

Chapter 3: Eva

I work as a history teacher. The school is close enough for me to be able to walk from our apartment. The school is large, about four hundred secondary school pupils, each classroom adorned with posters, proclaiming *Hungary is a strong bastion in the camp of socialism* or *For us work is a matter of honour and glory.* History is perhaps the most difficult of subjects, for the curriculum is constantly changing as the political fortunes of leaders past and present fluctuate. What was deemed politically acceptable yesterday is considered traitorous today. Of course, the history of Russia and the Soviet Union features large. At the moment, we are studying the recent Great Patriotic War. Until the end of the conflict, we were told to worship the genius of Marshal Zhukov. Now, his role has been marginalised and it is not Zhukov we have to thank for crushing the German fascists but the military expertise of Comrade Stalin.

My most able student is Tibor, a tall, strong boy of fifteen with floppish blond hair and bright green eyes. He has an absorbent mind and is slavishly devoted to his country and its socialist path. The girls adore him but he has time only for the heroes of communism. He likes to talk to me after class. He thinks we are like-minded, finding his fellow pupils politically immature. But recently, he has become withdrawn, a constant frown on his face. I worry for him.

Tibor tells me he's read Stalin's *Collected Works*. I am impressed. Now, he's reading his way through the writings of Lenin and trying to grapple with the principles of Marxist-Leninism. His enthusiasm remains undiminished. But so does the frown. After several days, I can bear it no longer and have to ask him what it is that's troubling him so. We are in the classroom after school, the other students have gone home but Tibor wants to ask me more about the political education of soldiers during the Battle of Stalingrad. I am always astounded by the ground he covers and have sometimes had to confess that he is two steps ahead of me. But when I ask him whether there's anything the matter he shakes his head and refuses to discuss it with me.

'Is it a girl?' I ask.

He looks embarrassed. 'No, Miss.'

With my chalk duster, I wipe away the day's lesson from the blackboard. 'You're at a vulnerable age,' I said, as I erased the names of Stalin and Beria. If only it could be that easy. 'I know I'm only a woman but because of that I know when something's wrong.'

He fingered the pages of his book on Stalingrad. 'Paulus surrendered, you know.'

'What?'

'At Stalingrad. Paulus. Hitler made him a field marshal right at the end because –'

'No German field marshal had ever surrendered before; yes, I know all that, Tibor.' I put down the duster. 'And today, four years on from the war, he is still a prisoner. Tibor, tell me, what's wrong?'

He did look at me but only for a moment. He wanted to tell me. 'Nothing's wrong. He can rot in hell for all I care.'

I turned my back on him and resumed my attack on the blackboard. 'Ok. I'll see you tomorrow then.'

'It's my parents.'

I stopped. Slowly, I turned around again. 'Your parents?'

'I don't know if I can say this.'

'Tibor, look at me… Whatever is on your mind, you can tell me and I promise it won't go any further. Just you, me and these four walls.'

He glanced around as if checking that the four walls were to be trusted. 'They don't believe.' He paused, wondering whether to go on.

'Believe?'

'They're traitors, Miss, they hate my love for Stalin, they say I'm mad.' He breathed out heavily as if relieved to have said it out loud. 'You should hear them, always criticising the Party, saying how they've messed things up, how they're ruining the country. They hate our brothers in the Soviet Union, and reckon the Hungarian leaders are simply puppets for the Politburo to do what they want.' He was looking at me now, his eyes burning with resentment. 'They don't understand what our leaders are doing for the working classes of this country, how they saved us from all the other parties, all those capitalist-loving imperialists. My father and I are… are ideologically irreconcilable.'

'And your mother?'

'Oh, she just thinks what he thinks.'

'What do your parents do? Do they work?'

'My father's an engineer.'

'A noble profession. Tibor, do you love your parents?'

He looked shocked by the question, his eyes widened. I don't think he'd ever considered it before. 'I don't know any more – I suppose I do...' He bit his lip and placed his book carefully on his desk. Then, looking at me with an earnestness only the young are capable of, he said, 'You're right, Miss, do love them. I mean, I couldn't say it – not to them. But yes, I suppose I must do.' He patted his book, smiled broadly and said, 'Thank you, Miss; you're absolutely right.' He turned on his heel and almost bounced out of the classroom. I wasn't sure what I had said or what I was right about, but it seemed to have erased all his doubts in a single stroke.

*

Today, I finished early at school. No post-school lectures for the staff on ideology or the need to remain vigilant, no meetings chaired by the head informing us of yet another change in curricula direction. So with a little free time on my hands, I popped into the local café, the clumsily named 'Café of the Revolution'.

It was another hot afternoon in late May. How I adore the month of May; when the sun finally appears and the summer months stretch ahead of one; when nature still feels fresh and full of optimism. The staff in the café know me by now, though not my name, but enough to exchange pleasantries and discuss the weather. The pretty young girl with her flushed cheeks and plucked eyebrows, and the old hag, with acid eyes and smoky voice, almost as round as she is tall. I wonder sometimes if the young girl realises there is probably less than fifteen years between them.

I took a seat next to the window with my coffee and cake. At a nearby table sat an elderly lady, her hair grey but her eyebrows surprisingly black, reading Chekhov's *The Three Sisters*. The two waitresses busied themselves behind the counter, the old hag occasionally remonstrating with her young charge. On the walls are portraits of Stalin and Rakosi, and a rather pleasant Alpine scene.

I flipped through the pages of *Free People*, the Party newspaper. I like to read of the Party's latest achievements, the exalted statistics, the rise and fall of the prominent, the promises of a bright new tomorrow, and our wonderful Soviet friends. Every invention, every innovation, every new design is Soviet: Russian technological and scientific advances surpass all else; in sport and the arts, they are supreme. Of course, it's all poppycock but no one dares say so. Not even the closest of friends, not even lovers whose whispers flutter to each other across their pillows.

Everyone lives a dual existence – the public persona and the private self. The public side keeps us safe – we repeat the Party slogans, we derive our opinions from *Free People*, and if the newspaper hasn't pronounced on a subject, then nor do we, we wait until we know what our opinion is supposed to be before we dare voice it. It's a bit like the joke about Trotsky. Trotsky wakes up one morning. "How are you?" an assistant asks. "I don't know," he says. "I haven't read the papers yet." We're terrified lest we should overhear a private thought – for one who listens without protest is as guilty as the speaker of such traitorous words. Idle conversation becomes a minefield as Party opinion constantly changes – we find ourselves criticising vehemently the very things that not long before we supported with gusto. We are all constantly frightened. And the more frightened we are, the stronger our commitment to the cause, the harder we work, and the greater our loyalty. But

I am no longer frightened. Fate has dealt me a blow crueller than even the state could devise.

I cannot think of a tomorrow; for me tomorrow doesn't exist. The weeks and months ahead are but a vacuum. Neither can I think of yesterday, for my whole past is simply one long series of events in preparation for tragedy. Whatever the recollection that flashes across my mind, be it a childhood memory or more recent, I cannot see it as an isolated incident but part of a gradual slide of time that ultimately finishes with the sixteen days a month ago. However long I live, my life will be divided by those sixteen days. And I don't know which is worse – knowing what's been or not knowing what's to come – like a blind man walking towards a cliff edge. I see myself as a little girl playing tag with my friends, laughing. But no pleasure comes from such images, because I believe that somewhere inside, I *knew* my life would be tainted by catastrophe. I'd always known, but sometimes I just didn't realise it. Whatever memory springs to mind, I find myself calculating how long I had left – x years and y months before the inevitable struck. My whole life hitherto has been but a tragic preface; the future now a mere aftermath.

On the radio, I recognised the deep baritone voice of Paul Robeson, the black American. As a communist sympathiser, he is one of the few American singers we ever hear. All our old favourites – the jazz players, the big bands – have been banned, along with all other things American, the 'vestiges of capitalism' as they call it – books, records, films. All but Paul Robeson.

The elderly lady with the black eyebrows was leaving. I noticed the generous tip she left on the table and, as she passed, she winked at me, perhaps acknowledging that the staff hardly deserved such a token of generosity. The young waitress cleared her table, saw the tip, turned round to check the old hag wasn't watching, and then deftly pocketed the change into her apron. I quietly cheered her triumph.

'Eva?'

A woman my age hovered next to my table, fair-haired, eau-du-cologne, lipstick, wearing a linen summer jacket. She knew my name; I recognised her because of her distinctive eyes. 'Yes?'

'You don't remember me – Karolina, my husband was your husband's assistant.'

Ah yes, I remembered his face but not the name: vain, lazy and self-important, I think that was Josef's summing up of him following his dismissal. 'Of course, Karolina, how are you? And…'

'Vida. Fine,' she said, in such a way it was obvious that he was anything but. 'Can I…'

'Yes, of course, take a seat, can I get you a coffee?'

'Thank you. White. No sugar.' She sat clutching the top of her handbag and didn't remove her jacket. Her eyes were of different colours – one brown, one green. It gave her the look of one who was very cunning – talking to her one had the feeling one was talking to a fox. I'd only met her on the odd occasion. The one time I particularly remembered was when Josef's workplace organised a party for the wives of bosses – a suffocating affair of empty conversations and poisonous smiles.

She talked quickly, pausing only briefly when the waitress brought her a coffee, skating over her words as she described her children, such lovely children, her new job, so wondrous and exciting, what a lucky girl she was. Then why are you talking to me? What catastrophe has befallen you to seek me out? I knew enough to know she wanted something; why else had she stopped to talk? What could she possibly want from me? I waited for her to finish extolling her life, waited patiently for the prelude to end. Not once did she ask after me or my life. But then I wouldn't want her to.

'Oh, Eva, I'm so pleased to have bumped into you, you see, I do have…' She glanced around and, lowering her head, continued, 'a bit of a problem.' She dropped two sugar cubes into her coffee. 'I'm trying to give up. You see, it's Vida.' Ah, I thought, here comes the rub. 'He's been arrested.' She'd said it so quietly and so quickly, I thought at first I'd misheard.

'Oh. I'm sorry to hear that.' I think perhaps I meant it.

'Last night. Well, the early hours of this morning.'

'How terrible.'

'I've been frantic, I can't tell you. Eva, I need your help.'

'Me?' The word came out louder than I'd meant, embarrassing us both.

'Yes, your husband liked Vida, and Vida worked hard for him, was always very loyal. Josef must've talked of him.'

'Yes, of course.'

'I was thinking if Josef could put a good word in for him.'

'I don't know if…'

'You never know, it could make all the difference.'

'But what could Josef do? He can't exactly approach the AVO.'

Karolina leant forward, her lipstick glistening. 'No, but he has contacts, you know, higher up. I'm desperate, I don't know what else to do.'

I shook my head. 'You don't understand; Josef never listens to me. I'll be frank with you – he's too concerned with his own self-protection to risk his neck for an ex-assistant. I don't mean that to sound rude but you know how it is.'

'So, you won't ask him?' There was an edge to her voice now.

'There's nothing he could do; there'd be no point.'

'Persuade him.' It sounded more like an order than a request. She looked away, unable to meet my eyes.

'What do you mean?'

'Vida told me things – about your husband.'

'About Josef? What sort of things?'

'Things to do with work. How shall I put it? Certain irregularities.'

I sighed, the poor, silly girl. 'And they would believe you?'

'Maybe. Maybe not. You know they take such things very seriously.'

She was looking at me now, with a concentrated gaze, waiting for me to give myself away. I didn't know what else to say. The poor woman was more desperate than I thought. Perhaps on no more than a few passing comments from her husband, she thought she had the means to blackmail me. Perhaps she was right, perhaps it was a weapon. The more I thought of it the more I realised I was on dangerous ground.

'Ask him, Eva. Ask him tonight.'

'Tomorrow night. He's out tonight.' It was a lie but I had to stall her, I had to have time to think.

'Tomorrow night then. God knows what they'll do to him by then. Come see me Saturday morning. Here…' She handed me a slip of paper with some writing on it. 'My address. Saturday, Eva. You must come to me on Saturday. Early.'

'OK, I'll try.' I wouldn't stand a chance. Josef never liked him and any amount of pleading wouldn't do any good. 'You'd better tell me everything; when was he arrested? And why?'

Chapter 4: Zoltan and George

Zoltan shielded his eyes from the sun and scanned the football pitch in front of him. Bordas, the manager, had his boys running around the field, a slow steady jog, interspersed with sudden bursts of speed. What an easy life, thought Zoltan – the occasional morning spent training and a game on Saturday afternoons. He knew it wasn't as simple as that; that most of these boys also had jobs or were students, but he preferred to dwell on his idealistic version of a footballer's life.

The players swung round the corner flag and were heading in his direction, their shadows preceding them. George was amongst them – the tallest on the field, his black hair stuck to his forehead, the circles of sweat under his arms. How fit he looked, how strong, how pronounced the muscles in his legs. As they passed, he noticed his eyes, fixed ahead, in full concentration; strong in mind as well as body. The boy was a true athlete, a thoroughbred. Only thirty himself, Zoltan envied George's youth, his vitality.

He looked at his watch – he'd been watching them for almost half an hour, time well spent, although initially he hadn't thought so. He resented it when Donath sent him out on these errand-like jobs; jobs he thought were better suited to those more junior than himself, like his new assistant, Fischer. Another new recruit, freshly out of Moscow's school for secret police, Fischer had returned full of the latest ideas and newest techniques for extracting confessions.

But Zoltan had enjoyed observing the array of footballing talent – the dizzying speed which some of them could muster with a ball at their feet, the strength with which they could kick a ball. And he'd been impressed by Bordas; for such a small, uninspiring-looking man, he had his players hanging on his every word, awaiting his nuggets of wisdom. Without having to ask, he had their total obedience and fulsome commitment. The man should be in government. Or the army. Only once had Bordas looked in his direction but if he'd thought of asking why Zoltan was there, he'd thought better of it.

Zoltan was aware that he looked like AVO. He'd spent years trying not to, trying to blend in with the populace, all the better to listen in to private conversations, to observe unnoticed. But something about working for the secret police blew your cover. People seemed to *know*. Some kind of instinct warned them. Perhaps it was the way he walked, the look in his eye. Perhaps because he looked like a hard bastard (at least, he liked to think so). And he took pride that when the need arose, he could act the part of a hard bastard. Only Petra, his wife, knew to what extent it was an act. And he couldn't deny it, he enjoyed it. He enjoyed the power, the look in the eyes of his victims when they knew they had nowhere to go, no one to help them. He enjoyed listening to their pleas, the reasons why they should not qualify for the severe beating that was

theirs to suffer. Did they never think he'd heard it all before –
hundreds of times: the dependent wife, their lovely children,
the fragile mother, their delicate health? He supposed that they
each thought they were alone in their special need for mercy.
But despite this, he knew he wasn't the hard bastard he wanted
to be. He didn't enjoy the violence; he could happily sanction
it, it was an everyday and necessary part of the job, but he had
no stomach when it came to actually applying it. That was
something he left to others more able than himself. Those who
derived some sadistic satisfaction from the application of state
justice.

The players had stopped running and were seated on the
parched grass, listening to their manager. Too far away to hear
what was being said, Zoltan wondered how long a strong lad
like George would survive before buckling, for buckle they all
did. Probably not long. Physical strength was no measure
when pitted against the AVO. No, it was the strength of mind
that mattered. Those with the psychological will lasted the
longest. Young women, old men. The ones that surprised you
by how long they lasted. But even they caved in in the end.
Just when they thought they'd survived the pain, the
humiliations, the degradation, the AVO played their final card
– to bring in their children for questioning. It never failed to
work.

He hoped George would never have to experience the
workings of the AVO. He was too young, too strong, *too
beautiful* to suffer such torments. It'd be like watching a tiger
shot – all that grace, that dignity stripped away. It wouldn't be
right. Beauty should not be sullied. But it wouldn't come to
that, there was no need. It was, after all, only a football match.
He looked again at his watch – it was almost midday, time he
was off, he'd spent too long here already. Bordas had finished

his pep talk, the players were back on their feet, awaiting their next instruction. This, thought Zoltan, was as good a time to interrupt as any. A quick word, a nod of compliance, and that would be it. They needn't ever meet again. And for some reason, Zoltan couldn't help but feel disappointed by the thought.

*

George had enjoyed the morning's training session – he'd trained as he had never done before. He was only ten days away from a match that could change his life, a performance scrutinised by the national manager. What better motivation did a man need?

Bordas's talk had been encouraging – Lokomotiv weren't the team of yesteryear, they were a shadow of their former selves. It was only a friendly but neither side would want to lose. For the Russians, it'd be akin to losing to one's kid brother.

George had been discussing their chances with the giant goalkeeper, Milan Ignotus, when he saw the stranger approach. 'Who's this, then?' asked Milan. George shrugged his shoulders. Despite the warmth, the man wore a long dark coat, his eyes fixed on George.

'George Lorenc?'

George smiled; it'd been the second time within a few days a stranger who'd known his name had approached him. Perhaps, he thought, he was a colleague of Mark Decsi, the scout.

The man offered his hand. 'Can I have a word?'

George took it. 'Yes, of course.'

Milan looked awkward. 'Yeah, I'll… I'll see you later then, George.'

The stranger watched Milan as he jogged back towards his team-mates. 'Perhaps we could…' He made to walk.

George followed. The man was wearing collar and tie, a bright red tie, and heavy boots – the type AVOs wear. His hair was nondescript brown, receding, cut short, but his neck was long – giraffe-like, thought George.

'My name is…' The man glanced over his shoulder, ensuring they were out of earshot. 'Zoltan Beke, AVO.'

The words AVO brought George to a stop, his heartbeat quickened. 'AVO?'

'Don't worry, you're not in any trouble.'

'Is it about my father?'

'I have no idea about your father. I'm here because we need your help.'

'You need *my* help?'

Zoltan grinned. 'Yes, your help.' He reached into his pocket and drew out a packet of Red Stars. 'Do you want one? No?' He paused to light the cigarette, cupping his hands against the non-existent breeze. 'No,' he said, blowing out the smoke, 'I don't suppose a man in your condition would smoke.' He coughed and, choking, added, 'Fact is, I don't really smoke myself.' They walked on slowly, following the perimeter of the pitch. 'I was watching you train. I'm no expert but I can see you're good. Your reputation precedes you, George. May I call you George? They say the team's a bit of a one-man show. Without you, they wouldn't stand a chance. Is that right?'

'No, of course not –'

'No?'

'No. It's a… it's a team effort and there are some good players –'

'Modest as well as talented. I like that. Modesty is a forgotten virtue these days. It's nice to encounter it every now and then. Too many people puffing themselves up, pretending to be things they're not. But not you – I can see that. You're the sort of man that this country needs. Strong, talented, forward-thinking. Are you forward thinking, George?'

'I… I suppose so.'

'Of course you are. And, I suspect, a man who knows that sometimes one has to sacrifice a little personal glory for the sake of the common good.'

George noticed Beke smile to himself, and a small shiver of discomfort ran through him. 'Sacrifice?'

'Yes, George, sacrifice. This game on Sunday week…'

'Against Moscow Lokomotiv?'

A loose ball lay in front of them and Beke kicked it back onto the pitch. 'Yes, Moscow Lokomotiv. You are to make sure your team loses.'

George stopped. 'Loses?'

'You're the hosts, the Russians your guests. It's customary, don't you think, for the host to make small sacrifices for the sake of his guest?'

Beke had continued walking and George had to stride quickly to catch up. 'But this is a game of football, not a dinner party. What's the point in playing to lose; what satisfaction can they derive from that?'

'They won't know. You see, none of your teammates will know, they'll be playing as normal. But you, George, you will know. Give yourself an off day; we all have an off day occasionally. If you play below your usual high standard, Lokomotiv should win.'

'You overestimate me.'

'I think not.'

'I'm only one man out of eleven, how can I influence the game that much?'

'You're the man who scores the goals. All I'm asking is that this time – you abstain. You see, we have a lot to thank our Russian friends for. Our liberators.' They had reached a corner flag. 'It's still only four years and our debt to the Soviet Union does not diminish with time –'

'So we must continue our subservience?'

'Subservience? Is that how you see it?'

For the first time, Beke was looking him in the eye, and George realised he'd said too much. 'Well, perhaps not subservience.'

'I think the word you're looking for, George, is gratitude. We, as a country, owe our liberty to the Russians.'

'To the extent of losing a football match?'

'Football is an honourable game, you don't need me to tell you that.' He looked up at the clouds. He threw the cigarette away and the two men stared at it for a moment, the red tip sizzling on the grass. 'I have to leave now. I've enjoyed our talk. You're an intelligent boy, George. Use your intelligence. You have plenty of more games ahead of you. Don't let this be your last one…'

George watched him walk away towards the pavilion, passing the ball he'd kicked earlier. This time, however, he ignored it. Milan and the others had gone in for their showers. He suddenly felt very alone.

Chapter 5: Eva

We were nearing the end of our lesson on the Yalta Conference and Comrade Stalin's magnificent role in the historical negotiations when Tibor suddenly asked if he could make an announcement. I gave my assent, but for some reason, I felt a terrible sense of apprehension about what was coming.

'Thank you, Miss Horvath.' He rose to his feet, looking every inch a politician with his thumbs hooked into his waistcoat. 'Comrades, I want to share my excitement at what I've done. Yesterday, I walked into the offices of the AVO and formally denounced my parents.' An audible gasp circled around the classroom. 'Yes, I know, on the surface it seems a shocking act but I know several of you are suffering the same agonies as I was until yesterday. My parents are harsh critics of our wise and benevolent leadership, critical of where they are taking our country and scornful of everything they say or do. Of course, I love my parents and still do. But I hated this…

this constant sniping at the Party, who do their best for us all; I hated the way my father, especially, undermined and even laughed, yes – laughed, at my political beliefs. For months, I grappled with the dilemma, trying to decide whether my loyalties belonged to the two people who brought me up or to the Party. It is to Miss Horvath I thank for making me see sense.'

My heart skipped – what part of our conversation had he misconstrued, what part had he managed to twist?

Tibor had warmed up to his oratory, drumming his fingers on his desk as he continued. 'She asked me simply whether I loved my parents. And in all truth, I hadn't really thought about it, I suppose I simply assumed. And then I realised I loved them so much that I needed to help them. It was then I'd made up my mind.'

I couldn't help myself, I groaned loudly with frustration. The class turned to look at me. Tibor looked puzzled. 'Are you all right, Miss?' he asked.

'Tibor, I see you believe in political re-education, don't you?'

'It is their only hope, Miss. If my parents are to play a part in the country's bright future, they cannot afford to dismiss it as some fancy fly-by-night fad. I know what I've done may seem a little drastic, but I hope you appreciate my logic. I did it for them and out of my love for them.'

His classmates looked at him as if in shock. He knew the effect he had had on them and glowed in his halo of self-righteousness.

I knew he would want to see me again after class. His curriculum questions were, by now, merely a disguise by which to see me. He'd become dependent on me; he saw me no longer as his teacher but as his mentor, possibly even his friend. Afterwards, once we were alone, he approached me. 'You think I've been rash, don't you, Miss?'

'I know you did it with the best intentions, Tibor.' I looked at him, with his long fringe of blond hair almost obscuring an eye, clutching a thick tome, and I suddenly realised I felt intimidated by him. He may only have been a schoolboy but that he was capable of such extreme measures made me conscious of my every word.

'I did. It'll be like a medicine for them. Horrible to taste but –'

'It'll do them good in the long run.'

'Yes. Exactly.'

'And your father's job?' I asked, stacking a few books in a neat pile.

'Well, he's… he's lost it for now.'

'For now?'

'He'll get it back; once they've been… you know.'

'Re-educated.'

'Yes.' He reached into his pocket and produced a packet of cigarettes. He offered me one.

I shook my head. 'I didn't know you smoked, Tibor.'

'I do now,' he said, lighting one.

'And are you OK? You're not regretting what you've done?'

'No, of course not. It's for their own good. Why should I be regretting it?'

A haze of smoke circled around us. 'No, no reason. So, where are you going to live?'

'With my uncle.'

'And what's he like, this uncle? Is he married?'

'He's all right. He lives alone. Why are you asking me so many questions? You think –'

'No, I don't. I'm sure you did the right thing. Don't you have another lesson to go to?'

He looked at me. I knew what he was thinking – that I wasn't the person he thought I was. He thought he could trust me and now he wasn't so sure. 'Yes,' he said, taking another drag on his cigarette. 'I'd better go.'

I watched him leave, his book under his arm; leaving a cloud of smoke in his wake.

*

In a moment of clarity, I decided I needed my husband back, the husband who'd emotionally detached himself from me almost a year ago. Our relationship had deteriorated to the point that we were husband and wife in name only. I decided to make a special meal; to play the part I had neglected for too long as I wallowed in pity, the part of a dutiful, socialist wife.

Using the coupons Josef acquired from his work, I had access to stores closed to ordinary citizens. As a man of responsibility, Josef enjoys the perks – the extra food rations, access to healthcare, access to better quality goods in better quality shops. And a whole apartment to ourselves – a real luxury at a time when families are forced to share with strangers. But Josef has no time to appreciate the perks. His fast climb up the promotional ladder came about, not through ability, but because his predecessors were, one by one, called to account. If they were lucky, they were transferred or demoted. Others, however, were not so fortunate. Poor Josef, how he has aged in the last two years, knowing it is only a matter of time.

It was time to make a change. I walked to the subsidised food store and, without having to queue, I was able to buy everything I needed for one of Josef's favourite meals – duck cooked in a mint sauce, runner beans and roast potatoes. I bought mushrooms for a starter and a bottle of red wine. Then, having left the store, I immediately returned and bought a second bottle. Once in ten days, he had a day off, half of which he'd spend in bed, catching up on his sleep. But this evening, instead of sloping off to read one of his reports in preparation for the following day, I insisted he sat down for a proper meal. I used a tone that would not accept no for an answer.

And so at eight o'clock, we sat down. I'd turned off all the lights bar one lamp in the corner. I'd lit candles; I'd covered the table with a tablecloth and laid napkins at our places. I wore my favourite chemise, a burgundy-coloured shirt I hadn't worn for a while, with a frilly collar and large buttons, and a knee-length skirt, slightly pleated at the hem.

'Sit, Josef, sit.'

'Is it my birthday?' he said, looking round.

'No.'

'Yours?'

'No.'

'Oh God, it's our anniversary.'

'No, Josef, it's not our anniversary.'

'So…' He waved his arms about. 'What's all this in aid of?'

'Do we need a reason?'

'Well. No. I suppose not.'

'Exactly. Now, if you would excuse me for a minute.'

I returned moments later bearing our starter – fried mushrooms with a dash of paprika.

'Oh my,' said Josef. 'This looks good.'

I poured us each a glass of wine. 'A toast. To us, Josef,' I said, lifting my glass.

'Yes. Yes. To us.' Our glasses clinked.

'Well, tuck in.'

'It looks good.'

'So, how's work?'

'Must I?'

'I'm interested.'

'Are you?'

'Yes, Josef, I am.'

He sighed. 'It's getting worse.'

'The five-year-plan?'

'The politicians order these huge projects and ask for advice from experts. When the experts try to point out the shortcomings in the planning process, they get chucked into jail. A second set is drafted in who of course are too frightened to tell the truth, so they say what the politicians want to hear. So when the project fails, and millions of forints are wasted, the second set of experts are punished because the first set was right. These mushrooms are delicious. We're walking into an economic disaster but ordinary civilians, people like you, have no idea. As far as everyone is concerned the country is meeting and exceeding every industrial target and, like the Soviet Union, will soon be the envy of the capitalist world. Eva, you wouldn't tell anyone any of this?'

'Josef – of course, I wouldn't. But what about you – are you safe?'

'No one's ever safe; you know that. The scrutiny is unbearable. I'm accountable for every aspect of the department's output, which means taking all the flak but none of the praise. It's the finger-pointing that gets me – the blame, the reproaches, the criticism, the liability moving like pass-the-parcel, all of us terrified lest it should stop with us. Well, that was very nice.'

'More wine?'

As we tucked into our roasted duck, I felt pleased with how the evening was going, that he felt able to unburden his woes with me. Josef rarely complained about work. The fact that he'd told me so much was a show of trust. If there was ever a time to approach him about Karolina, now was it. I began by passing comment on the weather, the building progress at the far end of our street, the patriotic fervour of our portly butcher. And all the while, I felt Karolina's presence at my shoulder, urging me on, threatening me.

'I met Karolina the other day.' I paused. No response. 'Do you remember Karolina? Pretty thing, different coloured eyes; she came to one of your work parties. Vida's wife?'

'Ah yes, Vida. Don't remember her, though.'

'He's fallen on hard times since he left.'

'Huh, no doubt,' he said, chewing on a mouthful of beans.

'Come now, Josef, he was a fine assistant, and you know it.'

'He was a fool to himself and rightly paid the price.'

How easy it is, I thought, to dismiss the past, to airbrush the inconvenient memories. The two men had been friends as much as two colleagues could be. Vida had saved Josef's skin over a slightly mistaken estimate, but once he'd slipped up himself, Josef was too afraid to stand up for him. The guilt lasted as long as Vida was still visible – which was not long. Out of work, out of favour, Vida disappeared from view. For a while, he was still a free man. But, according to Karolina, not any more.

'He's been arrested,' I said quickly.

Josef looked at me, his glass of wine poised mid-air, and for a moment his face displayed a flash of genuine regret. But his inner feelings quickly disappeared behind the mask as he recovered his composure. He sipped his wine, looked away and, with nonchalant effort, said, 'It was bound to happen.'

'Karolina's distraught, says he's innocent.'

'Innocent of what?'

This was a pointless conversation and we both knew it – people are usually arrested for no particular reason, hence, by default, they are innocent. It is only afterwards that they are charged with some immaterial allegation of which of course they are still innocent.

'Help him, Josef.' There – I'd said it, more directly than intended perhaps, but I'd said it.

'Me?' He pushed his plate to one side, a couple of roast potatoes still remaining.

'You like to pretend you don't remember but you remember only too well.' I was on unfamiliar territory, never before had I dared criticise my husband so directly. I knew I should have stopped; I was ruining the evening. This is not what I'd planned but I couldn't stop, I ploughed on with gusto. 'Your career would have died if it hadn't been for Vida. He saved you. But when he needed you, you turned your back on him. But here's your chance to make amends.'

'No.' His face was blank.

'You could use your contacts–'

'There's nothing I can do.'

'Josef–'

'Eva, stop it, just bloody stop it.' His face was not blank any more. Instead, there was a fear in his eyes I'd never seen before. 'OK, OK, I was in the shit and Vida pulled me out. Don't you think I know it; do you think I can ever forget it?' He rose abruptly from the table and paced to the window. Gazing out into the night and the flickering lights across the city, he said, 'But that was over a year ago when people could still talk. It's different now. You don't realise how much worse it has become. He wouldn't stand up for me now, he'd be too frightened, he'd have too much to risk. And I have too much to risk. I can't do it; it'd be suicide. You expect me to *use my contacts*, as you say, as if I could simply walk up to the director and say, *Listen, Comrade Director, a grave mistake has been made.* Can you imagine it? I might as well slit my throat now. I can't help Vida. I'm sorry for him, truly I am, and I'm sorry for Karolina, but there's nothing I can do.'

He ran his fingers through his hair, exhausted by his outburst.

'OK. I'm sorry. I shouldn't have asked.'

He sat back down with much weariness. 'Eva, listen. There's something I need to tell you.'

'About work?'

'No. It's not about work.' He took a deep breath. 'It's something else.' He fiddled with the stem of his wine glass.

'Oh no. Don't tell me what I think you're going to tell me.'

He nodded slowly. 'I'm sorry, Eva.'

Chapter 6: Zoltan

Zoltan Beke felt the need to undo his top button and loosen his tie. But he couldn't – he had an appointment to keep. Even with the window wound down, the heat in the Pobeda was suffocating, (these Soviet-made cars were the AVO's vehicle of choice). Fischer sat to his left, gazing out of the window. If his assistant felt hot, he certainly wasn't showing it.

'Shouldn't be too long a job,' said Fischer.

'As long as it takes,' replied Zoltan, hoping his reply sounded both offhand and authoritative.

The driver, a woman, glanced at him in the rear-view mirror.

But no, thought Zoltan, it shouldn't be too long. He'd spoken to the manager, to the centre forward, now it was simply a matter of nobbling the goalkeeper, and that'd be it. Not that it would make much difference, by all accounts. This goalkeeper, Milan Ignotus, was once a player to be reckoned with but his best years were far behind him. Liable to drink one too many, on a bad day he was as much use in goal as a sack of potatoes.

It still bothered Beke, however, that Donath was sending him out on these jobs. Surely, it was a job for Fischer and someone more junior in the department. Had he fallen out of his boss's favour? It rankled that he should work so hard, striving for the promotion he thought was his by right, only for Donath to send him out on these errands. It diminished his standing in Fischer's eyes; it wasn't right.

The car had stopped, halted by an overly efficient traffic policeman, who hadn't noticed the official car nor the distinguishable small-numbered licence plate. 'Just push through,' he said.

The driver beeped her horn, attracting the policeman's attention who, on realising his oversight, waved them through. The man saluted as they passed, the shadow of his peaked cap obscuring his eyes. Zoltan didn't salute back.

The driver laughed. He knew that she was relishing the power that came with the job. She'd once been a prostitute but after the Party had closed down the brothels, many of the girls were retrained as taxi drivers and used by the AVOs as chauffeurs *and* informers. No one dared hail a female-driven taxi any more – they drove terribly, too busy eavesdropping, and never knew the way.

Zoltan's thoughts returned to the job in hand. At least the consolation in this menial task had been meeting George Lorenc. The boy had prospects, not simply in footballing terms, but as a new man in Hungary's communist future – earnest, dedicated, and strong. You could see it in his bone structure. Zoltan believed you could tell a lot about a man by his bone structure. George Lorenc had a strong jawline and deep-set eyes. He had, Zoltan reckoned, a strength of character etched into his face that matched his undoubted physical prowess. He only hoped that the boy had the mental maturity to correspond.

'This is it, boss,' said the driver.

Milan Ignotus lived on the seventh floor of an apartment block on the outskirts of Pest, a relatively new but run-down affair, the street outside poorly constructed, littered with potholes and cracks. No one would dare complain, however. A small group of children played on the pavement, racing snails then cracking the shells. He thought of his own daughter. He'd never allow her to play such crass games, let alone out on the street with a rabble of children dressed like orphans straight out of Dostoyevsky. A child of about seven came out from the apartment block and Zoltan grabbed the door before it shut. The block was eight storeys high and he and Fischer began the climb to the seventh floor. There was no way he'd ever risk the lift. For such a new block, the stairwell was already in a poor state – the concrete steps chipping away, the paint falling off, half the light bulbs gone. Another child came racing down the stairs and shot at Zoltan with his wooden gun. He was in no mood to feign death.

On reaching the seventh floor, he paused to catch his breath and wipe his brow with a handkerchief. It was too hot a day to be climbing to the top of apartment blocks. Fischer looked as cool as ever.

He knocked on the door and straightened his tie. A young mother with a baby in her arms answered.

'Yes?' A wave of her hair obscured one eye; her clothes seemed surprisingly neat.

'Milan Ignotus, please.'

She eyed him for a moment, nodded and then stood to one side. After the bright sun, the apartment seemed depressingly dark. The goalkeeper was standing in the middle of the room, all six foot something of him, as if he'd been expecting them. In contrast to his wife, Milan Ignotus looked terrible – dressed in a string vest, unshaven, his hair unkempt. Not an image

Zoltan would associate with a top athlete; a far cry from George Lorenc. Zoltan introduced himself and Fischer. He noticed the sunken settee, the newspapers littered on the floor, an empty pack of cigarettes, a dirty plate on a chair, and, amongst the squalor, a sideboard decked with two glass footballers, some ten centimetres high.

'Have you come to arrest me?' asked Ignotus, as his wife came to stand behind him.

'No, no.' He tried to keep his tone light and realised he felt slightly intimidated. It wasn't a feeling he was accustomed to (except when in the presence of Donath).

'What do you want then?'

'A courtesy call, if you like.'

'Cut the crap.'

Zoltan exchanged a quick look with Fischer. 'I'll get to the point, then. May we sit down?'

'Whatever.' Ignotus sat on a hardback chair as his visitors sunk inelegantly into the settee.

Zoltan launched into his spiel – the visiting Russians, the role of the generous host, the need to stand aside for the greater interest. *No one would blame you if you let slip two or three through. We all have a bad day.* Ignotus listened carefully, leaning forward, stroking his stubble.

Zoltan finished, aware that he'd ended with his last word on the up so that it sounded less like an order and more like a request. Fischer, he knew, would be taking mental notes – how *not* to intimidate a suspect.

Ignotus did not respond. Instead, he opened a new packet of cigarettes and lit one without offering any to his guests. He blew out a puff of smoke and watched it dissipate. The baby stirred and Ignotus's wife held it up and sniffed its behind. Pulling a face, she disappeared into another room.

The smells interlocked and lingered, baby shit and pungent cigarette smoke. The olfactory assault and the silence seemed to mock Zoltan. He tried to rise to his feet but the settee sucked him back down. With greater determination, he hauled himself up, his face red with the effort and embarrassment.

Clearing his throat, he broke the silence. 'Well, if that's understood, we won't detain you any more. Fischer?'

Fischer too struggled to disengage himself from the smothering piece of furniture. But Zoltan was damned if he was going to humiliate himself further by offering his assistant a hand. Finally, on his feet, Fischer stretched his neck and pulled the creases out of his jacket.

Milan Ignotus still ignored them, watching a shaft of sunlight cut through the weaving strands of smoke. 'We will expect your full cooperation come Sunday then. Thank you, Comrade Ignotus, for your time.' He turned to leave, relieved to be escaping the fog of disgusting smells.

But Fischer, who rarely spoke, was speaking now. 'Answer him, you arrogant shit.' Zoltan glared goggle-eyed at his assistant.

Ignotus held his nerve. 'You expect me to play ball with your stupid games; get out of here.'

The shattering of the glass took Ignotus by surprise. Fischer had moved to the sideboard and now one of the glass football figurines lay smashed at his feet beneath his AVO boots.

Ignotus moved off his chair, stretching himself to his full height. 'You bastard, that was my –'

'I don't care what they are. You still have one left...' He ground his foot into the pieces of glass. 'For now.'

Ignotus stepped towards Fischer. Zoltan noticed his fists clenching at his sides. Neither he nor Fischer would be any match for the enormous goalkeeper. He had images of throwing himself onto the man's back like a child clinging onto the playground bully.

He knew he had to speak, to somehow take control of the situation. 'I think you should have the hint by now.'

'Fuck off, you,' yelled Ignotus over his shoulder.

Fischer held his ground. 'That's a lovely baby you have there,' he said. 'You have another, don't you, a girl, aged three?'

'So? What of it?'

'No doubt she dotes on you. Does she come to see you play, or perhaps she's a bit young? Still, she will one day, I guess. Unless of course…'

'Get out,' growled Ignotus, so deep that the floor seemed to vibrate. But Zoltan knew the sound came not from aggression but from fear. 'Get out before –'

'Before *what*, citizen?' said Fischer.

Ignotus's wife reappeared, still holding onto the baby. 'What was that noise?' she asked. 'Did something break?' She looked at the trio of men, Fischer and Ignotus only inches apart. 'What's going on?'

'Nothing to worry about, comrade, we were just leaving,' said Zoltan, nodding at Fischer that it was time to make a move. As they reached the door, Zoltan turned and said, 'We'll be there on Sunday, cheering you on, comrade. Make sure you don't fail us.' He winked at the goalkeeper but the man ignored him, his eyes still fixed on Fischer. 'Good day,' said Zoltan as they left.

Outside, the children had gone but the squashed snails with their shattered shells lay round and about. Twenty yards away, the ex-whore leant against the Pobeda, reading a paperback. She hadn't seen them yet.

Zoltan reached for his Red Stars in his pocket. 'That told him,' he said, circling his shoulders.

Fischer shot him a look designed to diminish.

And diminished is how he felt.

Chapter 7: George

The smell of burnt toast lingered in the air, swirls of bluish smoke dancing in the sunlight. George's mother skipped around the kitchen, throwing rashes of bacon into the frying pan, cutting tomatoes into two to grill, boiling a pan of water for coffee. George, meanwhile, sat at the table reading of the exploits of Moscow Lokomotiv in *Free People*. The team had recently beaten a visiting team from England, a team with a strange name he couldn't pronounce but written Wolverhampton Wanderers. It was only a week until the match; the match he'd hoped would change his life, and now knew for certain that it would, but perhaps not in the way he'd originally anticipated. He pondered on the two men who'd walked briefly and unexpectedly into his life and pulled him so forcibly in opposite directions. He wondered how much of it had been preordained.

His mother hummed a little tune he hadn't heard since his childhood as she busied herself preparing his breakfast. Why she should be singing it now he didn't know, but it made him smile inwardly. He remembered a family trip to the city zoo.

He must have been about ten before the war had come to Hungary. He'd been fascinated by a Bengali tiger, a huge brute, who seemed equally as fascinated by the podgy boy in long shorts. The tiger paced the length of his cage, his eyes fixed on George. Finally, it stopped and growled, exposing his fearsome fangs. Perhaps, in hindsight, it was no more than a purr, a greeting. But terrified, poor George burst into tears and ran for his mother. She held him and hummed the little tune quietly into his ear, wiping his eyes. George already felt too old for this and desperately wanted to pull away, as frightened of being caught in his vulnerability as he had been terrified by the tiger. But something held him there and wouldn't let him leave.

His mother was as excited by the prospect of Sunday's game as he was. The idea of Sebes Gusztav, the national team coach, being there in person to watch George play was quite the most exciting thing. In celebration, she'd opened a bottle of white wine she had kept hidden for years under the writing bureau. At last, they had the celebration worth opening it for. She toasted his future success and they sat quietly, sipping the wine, neither of them willing to admit it'd gone off.

But what George hadn't managed to do, was to tell her of the second visit. He watched her as she poured the boiling water into the coffee pot, a tea towel wrapped around her hand. He hadn't wanted to worry her, to burst her bubble. He didn't want to listen to her opinion in case it should be different to his. Not that he had an opinion, only a dilemma. Whether to play for football or for safety. It was as simple as that. And yet nothing had ever been so complicated. Would the Soviet masters really be that bothered about the result of a football game? Obviously yes, by the way the newspaper was revelling in the Russian victory against these English

Wanderers. Would the AVO forgive him if he played well but the team still lost? Or if he purposely played poorly and the team still won? Over the previous few days, he had thought of nothing else. He'd considered every possible permutation, every single cause and effect he could think of, and still, he was no clearer as to what to do. If only his father had been there.

'George, keep an eye on the bacon, be a dear.'

He poked at it with the spatula. He had to tell her; she had a right to know. But however hard he tried to rehearse, his opening words sounded wrong.

'Now, you're keeping an eye on that bacon, aren't you, George?'

'What was that tune you were humming earlier?'

'Was I humming? I've no idea. Does it matter?'

'No,' said George, watching the little specks of fat dancing in the pan.

*

Later that afternoon, George jogged home from a training session. It was gone five o'clock; the streets were full of workers winding their way home, with trucks and cars clogging up the streets, with mothers pushing prams, the sun still hot, shadows stretching across the pavement. Bordas had seemed agitated at training, short-tempered. It was unlike him. George began to suspect that he too had been approached by Beke. He'd downplayed Sunday's game, emphasising that ultimately, the game meant nothing – it was only a friendly. If only, thought George, if only.

As he climbed the stairs to the apartment, George made way for two grim-faced men coming down. Instinctively, he pressed himself against the spiral banister and avoided eye contact. Neatly dressed with smart, navy suits and red ties, thin lips and steely stares, George knew secret policemen when he saw one. Conscious of the amount of space he was taking up, he watched them descend. One of them glanced back at him. George quickly turned round and made his way up, hoping they wouldn't call him back. What were they doing here? Who were they after now? He shuddered. The AVO had been here and their presence lingered still as he climbed the last few steps to his apartment on the third floor.

He paused outside the door, key in hand, and felt a cold chill run down his spine despite the airless heat of the hallway. As he turned the key and pushed open the door, he tensed up, preparing himself for the shock he knew was awaiting him inside.

He heard the simpering first, breathless, almost apologetic. 'Mother?' A man was sitting on a hardback chair, his back to him. At his knees, his mother, her eyes swollen, her hand over her mouth. For a moment, George thought it was his father sitting there, the cause of his mother's distress. But as he circled round the chair, he realised it was an old man sitting there, with skin the colour of wax. Who was he? Only as the old man's slate-grey eyes locked onto his, did George realise. His heart fell with a thud as if one of the AVO men had thrown it down the spiral staircase.

'Hello, son.' The voice, reedy, delicate, was not one George recognised.

'No.' He shook his head, visualising the father he knew against the ghost of the man now sitting in front of him, this impostor who had the gall to call him 'son'.

His mother was at his side, linking her arms into his. 'They've just brought him back,' she whispered through a veil of tears.

The two of them stood, leaning into each other, staring at the delicate, grey being, who was now staring at the wall ahead of him. How thin he looked, how angular, as if his limbs could snap at any moment. How big his ears without the dark sweep of hair, how shallow the skin, stretched like parchment across his gaunt face; how pathetically ragged his clothes; and how he smelt, like a vat of rotting leaves.

'Any chance of a tea?'

Mother and son looked at each other. Somehow, the request seemed inappropriate, too mundane. 'I'll go,' said his mother, patting her husband's arm as she went.

George sat on the settee opposite him, conscious he was seeing his father not as a person but as an object of distaste; unable, unwilling to connect the memory of his father with the gruesome exhibit in front of him.

'How are you, son?'

'Erm…' Never had a simple question been so hard to answer. Never had bland politeness seemed so out of place.

'How's the football?'

'It's… it's fine. It's going well.'

'Good.' He nodded and George realised that it was all his father needed right then. Just a simple reaffirmation that life had gone on without him, that he was returning to a normal world. Not yet the details – that could come later. Yes, thought George, this man was not a ghost, but a man. And this man was his father. His father who had invested in George his dream, who had loved him as any father loves his only son, who had thought of him day and night during his time away, who had suffered unimaginable indignities, but who had come back. George was a man now but the hummed tune came back, the tiger who growled, the boy playing football in the park for hours on end. His father was an old man now, old before he needed to be, but he was back. Back in time to see his son fulfil his dream, for the dilemma that had plagued his thoughts for so many days was no more. His mind was made up. He knew what to do now; he knew where destiny would take him. The relief surged through him. For a moment he thought he was going to laugh. But when he opened his mouth, he burst into tears. Huge boy-like tears.

Chapter 8: Eva

I woke up alone. It was a Saturday. No school. Two nights ago, my husband left me. I hadn't seen him since. I had absorbed this new development in my life with a certain detachment. Already, within just thirty-six hours, Josef's sudden departure seemed almost inevitable. In a strange way, I was grateful that he'd left me so abruptly. No arguments, no lingering resentments. I often said he was the most matter-of-fact man I'd ever met. I missed him, but only in a way one misses a long-staying houseguest.

I replayed my conversation with Josef time and again. How my attempts to win back my husband had failed. Instead, I'd lost him for good. A colleague at work. That was all he said. But I could imagine the rest. A kind word from an attractive colleague, a shoulder to cry on. I couldn't blame him. We had drifted so far apart. By the time I noticed and decided to do something, it was already too late. I was angry, not with him so much as myself. The following morning, he went to work with a small suitcase of clothes and that was it. That evening, he didn't return. Where he was staying, he didn't say. Perhaps it was with the woman, perhaps a hostel. He talked of practicalities – my coupons, paying the rent. Everything was arranged. How long he'd been organising a life apart, I don't know. How long he'd been seeing this woman, I had no idea. I didn't ask. When I thought about it, I realised I didn't need to know the answers – what difference would it make? As he left, suitcase in hand, his coat draped over his arm, his last words to me were the ones that hurt the most. 'One day, Eva,' he said, 'you'll thank me for this.' And then he was gone. I listened to his footsteps echoing on the stairway while I tried to absorb his parting words. It was only after a while, after I'd closed the door, that I thought what a ridiculous thing to say. What presumptuousness. Why would I ever thank him for casting me adrift, to face the vagaries of life in isolation, the vagaries of a woman like Karolina, without support.

I had to call in on Karolina.

The day was warm but overcast, large clouds moved quickly across the sky. As I caught a tram and made my way to Karolina's apartment on Lehár Street, my mind wandered back to 1944. Josef and I had met a few weeks after the Germans marched in and reduced Budapest to a city of desperation and Hungary to a country of torment. Within these throes of suffering, I met a handsome, principled man who was soon to become my husband. Josef, an ardent anti-fascist, assisted in the protection and removal of Jews to safe houses. He worked with the Swedes, forging false identity papers, facilitating lines of communication. The number of Jews he saved from the camps can be counted in the dozens. And when the Russians entered the city, he welcomed them like brothers. He dismissed the tales of Red Army soldiers raping as an exaggeration; the Soviet Union was our saviour, communism the future. But the system that had saved my husband from the Nazis was now slowly destroying him.

*

Karolina and Vida lived in a salubrious area; Lehár Street was lined with trees, the buildings loomed tall. But prestige and influence in the People's Republic counted for nothing. As I strolled down the street, not in any hurry, I tried to rehearse what I would say. Surely she would understand. She and I were comrades-in-arms now – two women who, in the space of days, had lost their husbands. Still, I felt that nagging sensation in the pit of the stomach. I doubted that our common ground would make our encounter any easier or bring about a sense of female solidarity.

I passed a small parade of shops – a butcher, a bakery and a bookshop called Horizon. The first two were busy as housewives fought for space and things to buy. The latter was empty. I saw the young man inside, his feet up on the counter, reading *Free People*, smoking a pipe. He looked too young for a pipe. As I approached Karolina's block of apartments, the front doors swung open and there was Karolina, a man at her side. It took me a few seconds to register but the appearance of another man behind her confirmed it – she was being taken away. The first man was leading her by the arm. The men were AVOs. I stopped short, metres away. Parked on the curb, the car, the type driven by them, a female chauffeur waiting behind the wheel. Karolina saw me. Her fox-like eyes widened in acknowledgement. I felt myself shrink as her eyes then narrowed. She was still staring at me with a chilling look as the second AVO pushed down her head, guiding, almost pushing her into the car. The chauffeur revved the engine, indicated and glided off at a gentle pace. I stood and watched the car make its way down the street and out of view.

*

I decided to go to the café. The encounter with Karolina had unnerved me.

The café was unusually busy for the time of morning – the breakfast crowd had gone but it was still too early for the first lunches. Yet, on this particular May morning, almost every table was occupied. So, it came as no surprise when a figure hovered at my table. 'Can I take a seat?' The deep voice, I thought, had a Russian accent.

'By all means,' I said, gathering in my newspaper to make room on the table. Not that I meant it; I had no desire to share my space with a Soviet.

'Thank you, comrade.' He seemed too young to possess such a low growl. He'd bought a coffee and a white bread cheese sandwich. 'A lovely day,' he said.

'Mmm.' Equally, I had no desire to converse and concentrated my thoughts on an article about the AVO's unstinting devotion to duty. But my thoughts were full of Karolina. How vulnerable we all are. I realised I was in danger. If she was angry with me for not having come sooner, it would be so easy for her to denounce Josef and, by association, me. The central AVO office was at 60 Andrassy Street – everyone knew that. The address alone was enough to induce fear in the stoutest of hearts. I wondered whether I should try and visit her. The thought of stepping into the place made me shudder. And would it do any good? I tried to read.

Within my peripheral vision, I could tell the Russian opposite felt self-conscious eating next to me. He took small bites at a time and kept wiping non-existent crumbs from his mouth. He was handsome, dark with wavy black hair, and thickset eyebrows beneath which his eyes were surprisingly blue. I wondered what had brought him to Budapest. I began to feel annoyed with myself for giving him so much thought. But the more I tried to concentrate on the tiresome prose, the less I saw of the words.

It was almost a relief when I realised that someone was arguing at the counter. 'All I want is a cup of tea; is that so much to ask?' The irritated voice cut through the babble of conversation.

I couldn't hear the reply. My companion was facing the right direction to see what was happening but either he chose to ignore it or perhaps hadn't noticed. I wanted to turn around but feared I would appear nosey.

The voice at the counter was becoming louder. 'I can pay, I can't see the problem.' This time the Russian heard and looked up at the agitated man.

'Oh, this is ridiculous. A cup of tea, that is all.'

By now the café customers were silent, conversations paused, ears pricked, waiting. Now it would have appeared odd not to have taken an interest. I turned to see the red-faced young girl behind the counter say, 'I am not allowed to serve you.' Her voice shook as she spoke.

The old hag appeared next to her young assistant. 'Oh, it's you again. Don't you ever learn?'

'I want to see the manager,' came the retort. He was an old man with a long, white moustache wider than the width of his face, and a beard. He wore a large hat, black and battered, and an equally battered long coat. The man was a Jew.

But instead of the manager, out came two burly boys in stained white overalls.

'He's back again,' said the old hag, with a roll of her acid eyes.

'Get out,' said the taller of the two boys through gritted teeth.

'I will not. I demand a cup of tea.'

The boys looked at each other and then emerged from behind the counter from opposite ends. 'We've told you before, we don't want your type in here; now get out.'

'I will not; I insist –'

Before he could finish his sentence, the boys grabbed an arm each, lifted the man off his feet, and carried him to the door. 'Get off me, you bastards. Get off!' But the boys were strong and in no time had opened the door and dumped the old man unceremoniously on the pavement outside. The man sprang back to his feet with surprising nimbleness and resumed his protest. What happened next shocked me – the shorter of the boys punched him. The man's hat flew off as he staggered back. The boys re-entered the café, satisfied grins plastered over their faces for a job well done. The old hag nodded a thank you, and the pretty girl went redder still.

'They needn't have done that.'

I'd quite forgotten about my silent companion. 'No, I agree.'

'Look, he's coming back in.'

I looked back round and the old man, his hat back in place, was coming in, pulling on his moustache and shouting, 'How can you do this, eh? Me, an old man?'

With my back turned on my companion, I hadn't noticed him rise from his chair. Approaching the old man, he called out, 'Hey, comrade. Come join us at our table. I'll buy you your tea.'

The man eyed him for a few moments and then grinned broadly, first at the Russian and then at the young girl and her frosty old colleague behind the counter. 'Thank you, young man,' he said triumphantly. 'Thank you.'

Well, I thought, he might have asked me first for my consent. I had no desire to share my table with a misfit. What if word got around? Eva Horvath mixes with socially undesirable elements. People are routinely arrested for less. No, I wanted nothing to do with this. As the Russian returned to the table (*'our* table' he'd said), the old man behind him, I swigged the last of my (now cold) coffee, and quickly folded my *Free People*. I snatched my string bag from under the table and rose.

'You don't have to leave,' said the Russian.

I blushed. 'No, I have to… to go now.'

'Please…'

I paused and, despite my embarrassment, looked him in the eye. He held my gaze.

Sometimes one's fate lies in moments like this. I could have said no, could have stuck to my instinct and left, walked out of the Café of the Revolution and never seen him again.

But for some reason, I didn't.

Chapter 9: Zoltan

I, the undersigned, am willing and able to write a full confession of my crimes against the Party and the State. In admitting these heinous crimes, I confess to acts of betrayal and treason and that I freely admit my guilt and am prepared to accept the full and just consequences as decreed by law.

Zoltan re-read his introduction. He'd written these words on so many previous occasions, he could recite them by heart. He thought about the intended recipient of this document and tried to think about the sort of heinous crimes she might be guilty of – planning to sabotage the Party and re-implement capitalism was far too big a scheme for such a small-minded woman; that was the sort of confession they gave to the fallen politicians or economists. Her hands were too clean to be involved in direct action, such as industrial vandalism or transportation wrecking. No, hers was a more subtle kind of treachery. Spying. Yes, she'd make a good spy. And she had some distant cousin in America, Philadelphia, he thought she'd said. She could be guilty of passing secrets to the States, nothing grandiose, simply small but vital pieces of information over a number of years.

Zoltan enjoyed this part of the job – writing out full confessions of spectacular crimes, inventing the detail, the means, the elaborate self-flagellation, the grovelling pleas for full punishment. And he loved the expression on their faces as they read through his prose, their eyes widening with disbelief – *you expect me to sign this?* How tedious it must be, he thought, to work as a policeman or a lawyer in those democracies where there are so many rules to obey, where the accused stood innocent until proven otherwise. How much simpler it is here; where no one talks about rights.

Unlike so many of his colleagues, Zoltan enjoyed the paperwork, the desk jobs. Far preferable to being out on the streets, chasing men like Milan Ignotus. He still shuddered at the thought – how the brute had humiliated him in front of Fischer; how his assistant had had to come to his rescue. Fischer hadn't said anything; there was no need. But they knew. The goalkeeper had intimidated Zoltan; he'd been afraid. It wasn't meant to work that way – the secret police intimidated the populace, not the other way around. That was why Zoltan preferred writing out confessions – using his brain, not his brawn. Muscle power was why the AVO employed the Fischers of this world, Zoltan Beke was destined for better things.

It was ten minutes to eleven. At eleven, he had his weekly meeting upstairs with Donath. He hoped to get away early for once – today was Roza's birthday, three years old. He'd promised her, and Petra, he'd be home in time for the party. Nothing big – just a few of Roza's friends, all girls. Petra had baked the cake, bought the candles, the presents and the balloons. He sighed. Sometimes, he felt as if they belonged to a different world where everything was warm and comfortable, far from the routine brutality of the AVO offices. He saw so little of his wife and daughter; he sometimes missed them, so long was his working day. Not today, though; he'd made them a promise and he wasn't going to let them down.

*

'So, what's happening at your end?' Donath looked bored as usual, resting his face against his palm, the folds on his rubbery cheeks bunching up.

Zoltan briefed his boss on the previous week's events – the new and old cases, punishments meted out, cases he sent to the more formal court proceedings, amusing anecdotes, enjoyable confessions, interesting pleas for mercy. Occasionally, Zoltan heard an unusual plea, something beyond the wife and children or elderly mother routine. He remembered the old chap who was worried about the mice invading his apartment. He worried that if they sent him to prison for years on end, the place would be overrun with dancing mice. They reduced his sentence from five years to three, merely for the novelty value.

Donath half-listened, playing with an unlit cigarette, speaking only once, to urge Zoltan to speed things up on a specific case. But, as usual, thought Zoltan, no encouragement, no words of praise.

'Listen, tomorrow I want you to fetch me this kid.' He flung a file over to him. Inside, there were three photographs – a man, woman and a boy by the name Barat. Tibor Barat. Fifteen years old, according to the date of birth.

'I can't arrest a kid.'

'Who said anything about arresting? Take Fischer with you. Now, how are things going with the football match?'

'Fine. As well as Bordas, the manager, we've got George Lorenc, the centre-forward and now the goalkeeper, Milan Ignotus.'

'Any problems?'

'No.'

'Good. Fact is, we've had further communication from the Kremlin. They're saying that it's imperative Lokomotiv don't lose this game on Sunday.'

Zoltan peered up at the portrait of Felix Dzerzhinsky. 'We know that,' he said.

'Yes, but before it came across as more of a request, a recommendation if you like. But this, this is an order. Lokomotiv mustn't lose. Bordas has sent me a list of all his players and their addresses. Take Fischer and get the rest. Best do it straightaway.'

'All of them?'

'We can't afford to take any chances.'

Zoltan scanned the list of names, the addresses spread across the length of the city. The prospect of attending Roza's birthday party was already fading; another on his list of broken promises. 'But, boss, they're a crap team.'

'I don't want to leave anything to chance.'

'But with Lorenc and the goalie out of the picture, they're already as good as beaten, especially if Bordas employs tactics to ensure a stifled performance.'

'Well, you know more about football than I do.'

'Have you seen the names of the Lokomotiv players? They may be going through a lean patch but they'll still wipe the floor against our bunch of second-raters.'

Donath threw his hands into the air. 'OK, OK, if you say so, I bow to your better judgement, Zoltan. But you better be right.'

Zoltan nodded.

'I said, comrade, you'd better be right.'

Zoltan registered Donath's switch to *comrade*, 'Of course, boss, trust me, I know a bit about football.'

*

Outside, the city seemed smothered under a blanket of heat. Zoltan loosened his tie and swore. What if the team played beyond their means? He knew what people thought of the Russians – outwardly respectful, politically grateful, but inwardly seething. If someone saves your life, you say thank you but you don't expect to have to say it day after day for years on end. The football team would love nothing more than to beat the Ruskies.

He lit a Red Star. He'd made a promise – to Petra, to Roza. He'd prepared a few tricks that would impress a bunch of three-year-old girls. Roza would be hyping her friends up. He could visualise them sitting cross-legged in a semi-circle on the floor, staring at the space where they expected him to step into at any moment; their faces eager with expectation. And sitting at the front – Roza, her excitement ebbing away as concern crept in. And when finally the children lose their patience, Roza will feel humiliated, and ashamed that she'd let everyone down. Roza wore her heart on her sleeve – she'd be fed up for days and her mother would scold Zoltan with every disdaining look.

He'd hoped a bit of time outside would help him clear his mind but the heat simply made him feel more suffocated. He threw away the cigarette after only two puffs. He looked again at the names on Bordas's list. What did he know about these players? Nowhere near as much as Donath thought he did. *It's a team effort and there are some good players.* Lorenc's words came back to him. Was it pure modesty that'd made him say that, as Zoltan had suggested? Or was there an element of truth in it?

What was worse – Petra's contempt and Roza's tearful disappointment or the risk of the team playing well, and earning Donath's wrath and Fischer's smug satisfaction? He kicked a stone across the street and swore loudly, startling a well-heeled woman passing by.

Back in the office, Zoltan ordered Fischer to organise the ex-whore and her car to be ready in thirty minutes. It gave him enough time to walk to a toy shop he knew at the far end of Andrassy Street and buy the most expensive doll in the store.

*

Eleven o'clock. The end of a fifteen-hour day. He and Fischer had visited nine addresses but had only managed to speak to four players – all the others were out. The apartment was dark and empty. He saw the note on the kitchen table propped up against a vase of wilting flowers: *You bastard.*

In the living room, a pile of new toys stacked neatly on the armchair – scraps of wrapping paper on the floor, a red bow, a strip of ribbon, a couple of balloons slightly deflated. At least he'd managed to buy the most expensive doll in the shop… but where was it, it wasn't in his briefcase. Shit. Oh, *shit.* He'd left it in the whore's car.

Chapter 10: Eva

'Don't forget, tomorrow we'll be discussing Berlin and why exactly the city is divided between the communists and the imperialists. Don't be late.' The school bell had rung, signalling the end of the morning's last lesson before lunch. Outside the sun was shining and I looked forward to a sandwich in the park opposite the school. Unusually Tibor was getting ready to leave along with his classmates. As the children packed their satchels, I deliberated whether to call him over. The temptation was too much. 'Tibor, could I have a word, please?' He nodded, lit a cigarette, waving his classmates off as they dispersed, then came to see me.

'I just wondered whether you'd heard how your parents were getting on?'

'I don't know; the authorities don't send me progress reports.'

'Oh, yes. Silly question. And erm, how's life with your uncle?'

'All right.' He puffed on his cigarette. 'Look, Miss, I'm running late. I want to get to the library before lunch.'

'Yes, of course. I didn't mean to…'

But before he had a chance to go, there was a knock on the glass of the classroom door and in came two men in long coats. 'Miss Horvath?' asked the taller of the two. I nodded. Tibor stepped back towards the classroom window. 'Your headmaster told us you would be here. My name is Beke, Zoltan Beke, and this is my assistant, Fischer.' I nodded to the shorter man, Fischer, but received no response. The one called Beke continued. 'We're looking for one of your students, a lad by the name of…' He checked the piece of paper he was holding. 'Tibor Barat.'

'What?' muttered Tibor.

Beke turned to face him. 'Tibor Barat? Is that you?'

'Y-yes,' said Tibor quietly. I noticed he was holding the cigarette behind his back.

'Well, that saves us a lot of chasing around,' said Beke to me with a chortle.

'Yes,' I said, mirroring his little laugh.

Returning his attention to Tibor, Beke adopted a serious tone. 'Tibor Barat, your parents have been formally arrested as propagandists for the imperialists, charged with the intention of undermining, wherever possible, the proletariat ethics of the Party.'

'My parents have what?'

'You, as their offspring, are, by default, also deemed an enemy of the people.'

'A what? No.' Standing in front of the window, the trail of smoke behind him was caught by the beams of sun giving the impression that Tibor was on fire.

'You shall come…' Beke seemed momentarily nonplussed by the ethereal vision of the boy. 'You shall come with us, please, for further questioning under the Party's constraining orders.'

This young boy on the verge of manhood seemed to shrink in front of my eyes. How vulnerable he looked, reverting back to the boy he really was, the puzzled expression, the terrible realisation that he'd played an adult game and lost. He looked at me, imploring me to intervene.

'You're not arresting him, are you?' I asked, unable to disguise the tremble in my voice.

'We said nothing about arrest, comrade, he is too young for arrest; we are merely putting him, at his uncle's request, under constraint. What is all that smoke? Come on, son, let's go.' The AVO man gripped Tibor by his left elbow and shoved him towards the door, the second AVO taking his place on the boy's right.

As he was being led away, Tibor glanced at me over his shoulder. I had to try again, to save the poor boy. 'If his uncle doesn't want him, I...'

'Yes, comrade?'

'I'll take him in.'

The shorter AVO, Fischer, approached me at speed, a menacing look in his eye that immediately made me regret my rashness. 'A word in private, if you will, comrade,' he said, now taking me by the arm and impelling me to one side. 'A quiet word of advice. I wouldn't associate yourself if I were you. The whole family's for the chop. If you know what's good for you, you'll keep well away.'

'But what's going to happen to him? He's only fifteen.'

'Orphanage.'

'No...'

'Yes. Now, leave it.' He marched back to Tibor and, together with his colleague, led the frightened boy away. This time Tibor didn't turn around. On the floor, near the window, half a cigarette still alight, the smoke dancing in the sunbeams.

*

'So, you're a footballer?'

'Yes, is it so strange?'

Valentin and I were sitting on a shaded bench in City Park. 'Perhaps not strange but certainly unusual – I don't think I've ever met a football player before.'

As if on cue, a boy of about eight kicked a ball towards us. Valentin hesitated for a moment and then rose from the bench and gently passed it back to him. The boy tried to kick it back but scuffed his pass and the ball ended up too far for Valentin to run after it without appearing overly keen. The mother called after him and the boy collected up his ball and ran back to her. Valentin sat down with a sheepish grin on his face.

The previous day we'd spent a further half an hour in the café, listening to the old man with the walrus moustache as he talked about his life. A long, adventurous tale that ended with the café's persistent refusal to serve him, as if this last indignity surpassed all the deprivation of the Imperialist War of '14-'18, the Nazi occupation, and the Soviet bombs. Without pausing to ask our names, he talked and assumed, I think, that the Russian and I were a couple, if not husband and wife. Finally, he thanked Valentin for the tea and cake, poked his tongue out at the waitresses, and left.

Watching the old man leave, the Russian laughed. 'Perhaps now would be a good time to introduce myself,' he said, offering his hand across the table. 'My name is Valentin.'

'Eva.'

I'd been right – he was a Russian. A Muscovite. He was spending only a few days in Budapest, 'on business.' Yes, it was his first time in Hungary, in fact, his first time out of the Soviet Union, and what a beautiful city Budapest is, and how friendly the Hungarians are. At this last point, I pulled a face, knowing it to be false. He raised an eyebrow at me, acknowledging my scepticism. And yes, he said, the people in Moscow were equally as friendly. He told me that as a boy he saw a lot of his mother's cousin who was half-Hungarian, hence his ability to speak the language reasonably well.

I hadn't expected him to ask to see me again. But I was desperate for a diversion – my husband had walked out on me, I'd seen Karolina taken away, and my star pupil had misguidedly denounced his parents. And in the midst of this dismal merry-go-round, Valentin had appeared with his Russian accent and his confident ways. And here we were, the following day, in the City Park, sheltering in the shade, the sky free of clouds. The park is beautiful at this time of year – the flowers in full bloom, the trees so regal, the green of the lawns so vibrant they almost look artificial.

'Is that why you are here in Budapest – to play football?'

'Yes. We're playing against one of your local teams next week.'

'Where do you play?'

'Left midfield.'

'No, I mean, where does the match take place?'

He laughed. The team, he said, were playing in Budapest, then they had a couple of regional games, and then, after that, they were returning to the capital for two days of sightseeing.

'And then you go back to Moscow?'

'And then we go back to Moscow.'

I swallowed my disappointment. That this gruffly spoken Russian, almost a stranger, had caused such a reaction caught me by surprise. Why should I feel disappointment, of course, he had to return home; had I secretly hoped he'd say something different? I wondered what he'd be returning to. A girlfriend? A wife? I imagined a small, pretty Russian girl with blonde, plaited hair and painted nails, waiting for her footballer to come home. Why should he want to spend time with me, twenty-six but already so old? Neither of us spoke of our lives – our hopes, our triumphs, our struggles, but I felt he too had a story that lingered close to the surface, refusing to be buried in memory.

'So, what's life like in the Soviet Union?'

He shrugged his shoulders. 'Well, it's like a ride on a bus – one man drives and the rest of us cling on for dear life.'

An elderly couple ambled past, arms linked, both wearing long overcoats despite the warmth of the day. The man tipped his hat at us; Valentin nodded back. Again, the assumption – a young couple sitting on a park bench, enjoying the sun. Did it matter that he was returning to Moscow, that I wouldn't see him again? No, it didn't. I was trying to suppress my chaotic existence with something else, something superficial. I resolved not to be so silly.

'I think I should go now.'

'Would you care to see me play?'

'Play? Play what?'

'Football, of course. I could get you a ticket for the game.'

'Are you… are you inviting me to a football match?' I'd assumed women weren't allowed to attend.

'Well, I didn't mean hide and seek.'

'At least I would understand the rules of hide and seek. Tiddlywinks even better.'

'Tiddle-what?'

'You've not heard of… it doesn't matter.'

'So?'

'I don't know.'

He turned to face me and took my hand. 'Seriously. I'd like you to come… please.'

'OK, I'd like that very much.'

We smiled at each other before remembering he was still holding lightly onto my hand. The corner of his mouth twitched as if embarrassed by this sudden show of earnestness, and his hand slipped away.

Chapter 11: George

Despite the heat of the day, George's father shivered. George had given him a paperback to read, a Western, the sort of story his father used to enjoy, but the book lay unopened on his lap, half hidden within the folds of a blanket.

'You tired, Papa?'

'A little bit. That bath knocked me out somewhat. Lovely though. You don't realise how important the little things in life are until you don't have them.'

George nodded but at the same time, he hoped it'd be a while before his father wanted another bath. Once the old man was ensconced in the tub, he was too weak to get out, and his mother certainly wasn't strong enough to help him by herself. His father was sitting there, with the water drained, shivering and unable to summon the strength to haul himself out. With his eyes half closed, George placed a hand under his father's wet armpit on one side and clasped his arm on the other. Behind him stood his mother with a towel at the ready. Between them, they managed it but the sight of that scrawny frame, and his skin, flaccid and grey, was too much for George.

His mother came in with a cup of tea and a small plate with a couple of ginger biscuits on it. Placing the cup in her husband's hands, she said, 'It's a training day today, isn't it, George? Shouldn't you have gone by now?'

There was no point, thought George, if they were playing to lose. His earlier enthusiasm had already fizzled out. He wondered how many of the team knew, how many of them had been approached by Zoltan Beke and given their orders. Perhaps the whole team but no one would ever dare admit it. 'No, I'm not going today.'

'What do you mean you're not going? You can't miss training; what about this match on Sunday?'

'What match is that?' asked his father, through a mouthful of ginger biscuit. George had purposely not told him.

'They're playing Moscow Lokomotiv, aren't you, George?'

'Lokomotiv, eh? Now, that's something.'

'And… go on, George, tell him the rest.'

George told his father about his chat with Mark Decsi, the talent scout, about how the national team manager would be there at the game.

His father listened intently, his hands clasped around his cup. 'That's fantastic. But you don't sound particularly excited about it. Is there something wrong?'

No, thought George. He remembered, as a child, one Christmas, receiving a train from an uncle – a lovely wooden thing, painted dark colours with huge buffers and long funnels. He loved it. Within two or three days, one of the back wheels fell off, and however hard his father tried to fix it back on, it never properly worked again. It was that same feeling – the focus of excitement that quickly became a source of disappointment.

'He's been playing ever so well – tell your father about the hat-trick.'

George obliged.

'This is all wonderful.' His father held out his hand. George took it and tried not to wince at the effusion of bones. 'You've done well; I'm proud of you, my boy.'

'All the more reason, I should've thought, not to miss training,' said his mother, the irritation evident in her voice.

'He doesn't want to leave me, do you, George?' he said, chomping on his biscuit. 'But don't worry, I'm not planning to go anywhere for quite some time yet.'

George forced a smile and, retracting his hand, made an excuse about needing a glass of water, and disappeared into the kitchen. He'd forgotten how claustrophobic his parents could be when they were together, talking at him, talking for him, talking as if he was still a child. He could cope with one or the other but not both together. He couldn't do it two years ago and couldn't do it now. *It's wonderful to have Papa back again.* He repeated the thought two, three times but something wasn't quite right. The memory of the man outshone his physical presence. Perhaps because he expected him not to have changed. It was a naïve expectation, he knew that, but he couldn't suppress the sense of anticlimax. The presence of the shrunken man that was his father filled the apartment as his former self had before; but whereas then it had felt natural, now, somehow, it felt wrong. He'd become used to it simply being him and his mother and the memory of his father. And he'd expected something different in his mother as well – optimism, outpourings of joy. Instead, she seemed resigned and, at times, irritable, as if his father's return had upset her routine. Perhaps, she too was experiencing that same sense of anticlimax. *It's wonderful to have Papa back again.*

'I'm sorry, George, did you say something?'

'I was just saying how wonderful it is to have Papa back again.'

'Yes, isn't it.' Even her smile seemed forced. 'I was planning a special feast tonight – spicy goulash – one of his favourites.'

'It'd be too rich for him, his stomach can't cope with that sort of food yet,' he said, rinsing out the glass.

'Yes, perhaps you're right. I've got your kit ready; your boots look as good as new. I've put it all in your bag for you, next to the front door.'

'I've said already, I'm not going today.'

'You must, I insist.'

'Stop talking to me as if I was a kid, Mother, I've made up my mind – I am *not* going.'

'Now listen here, George Lorenc, you have a duty to yourself, to your team *and* to your father. You've got the sort of opportunity on Sunday that most boys of your age would die for. I will not have you cluttering up the apartment when you should be out there training for the most important game of your life. I simply can't understand why you're not more excited about it.'

'Mother, I…'

'Yes?'

He wanted to tell her, to share his burden, but he couldn't, the words wouldn't come; instead, he said simply, 'It's nothing. Nothing at all.'

His mother eyed him for a few moments as if wondering whether to push him into saying what he obviously wanted to say. 'I need to make a phone call.'

'A phone call? To whom?' he asked.

But she'd gone.

The communal telephone sat on a small table halfway down the hallway two storeys below. He'd never known his mother to make a call without having discussed it for hours beforehand. He wondered whom on earth she'd be wanting to call. Curious as he was, it was too far to follow her. Instead, he returned to the living room to find his father asleep in his chair, his mouth open obliquely, looking slightly grotesque. George sat and watched him. What sort of existence had he survived, what deprivations had he endured? Did they torture him, deprive him of food, of sleep, of company? How did he cope without his pipe? These questions and more floated through his mind; questions to which he had no desire to know the answers. He noticed that his father hadn't asked for his pipe since his return. It was a pity; whenever he smelled the sweet pungency of piped tobacco, he always thought of him in happier days.

His mother returned, her face flustered. Whomever she'd spoken to had obviously unsettled her. 'Did you get through?' he asked, timidly.

'No,' she snapped back. He watched her as she cleared away his father's plate and cup, plumped up the cushions, wiped clean the already-clean table. He refused to reply when she asked him whether he didn't have anything more interesting to do than watch her.

George was at a loss as to what to do. He noticed that the paperback Western had slipped off his father's lap and lay propped up against his feet. He picked it up and idly began to read the first few sentences when a gentle tap at the front door made him look up. 'Shall I get it?' he asked.

'No, no, it's all right,' she said quickly, her face suddenly drained of colour, her eyes fixed on the door.

The apartment was too small for anything grand such as a hallway or a lobby; the front door opened straight into their living room. His mother pulled the creases out of her apron and swept her hair back. But what she did as she opened the door took George by surprise – she opened it swiftly, then without pausing, stepped out into the hallway, her hand outstretched, literally pushing away the unseen visitor, before closing the door purposefully behind her. A strange way to greet someone, thought George.

He returned his attention to the paperback when, after a few seconds, something made him snap shut the book. Flinging it to one side, he rose quickly from his chair. He opened the front door, rushed down the corridor, down the stairs and outside. There, to his right, he found his mother leaning up, her arms round the shoulders of a tall man in a long cream overcoat, her face nestled into his neck.

George crept back, hoping to retreat unnoticed. But as she released her grip, his mother saw him. Letting go of the man as if she'd burnt herself, she turned to face him, her eyes agog, her mouth open like a fish on land. 'George…'

He shook his head, unable to say the words he couldn't find anyway.

'George, please…' She glanced up at the tall man in the long cream overcoat and George looked him in the eye.

'Hello, George,' said the man. 'We meet again…'

Chapter 12: Eva

The day was Sunday – the day of the football game and I felt strangely excited by it. I'd never been to a match before, indeed I didn't think women were allowed to attend but Valentin insisted that we were. Not wanting to go alone, I'd invited my friend, Agnes, and Ferenc, her husband – a rather dour man whom everyone but Agnes suspected of being a serial informer as well as a serial adulterer. I wasn't sure which was worse. We agreed to meet at the Café of the Revolution.

The stifling weather continued unabated, the heat melting the pavements, people fanning themselves with newspapers. I'd arrived at the café quite out of breath and had to order a glass of water to help me cool down. Settling into my usual place, I thought of Valentin and wished he was with me, sipping coffee, watching the people of Budapest hurry about their business.

Being a match day, Valentin had no time to meet me. How strange it would be to see him from a distance, watching him at work. The previous day, we met in the café and then took our routine stroll in the park. Usually, we talked but yesterday we were both subdued and walked in silence. We both knew it was possibly our last time together. After the match, the team will be whisked off for a few games around the country, then, unless called back to Moscow, the players will be permitted two days of sightseeing in Budapest. I had to cling on to that for I couldn't bring myself to think I might never have seen him again. How quickly we become dependent on another person, how strange to think that barely a fortnight ago I'd never known of his existence, that I had a husband, albeit a distant one. Now a future without Josef seemed bearable while a future without Valentin seemed incomprehensible.

I read *Free People*, re-reading the same short article again and again – about Moscow Lokomotiv's Hungarian tour and especially their visit to Budapest. Each player's name was listed, and there, amongst them, was Valentin Ivanov. I felt a twinge of pride at seeing his name as if he was already associated with me, as if I had the right to bask in his glory. The team had recently beaten the Wolverhampton Wanderers, one of England's top teams. The three-nil victory was another example of the superiority of Russian sportsmen and, by implication, the Russian system, a testament to the Soviet Union's breed of supermen.

'Hello, Miss,' said a vaguely familiar voice. Standing next to my table, circling his hat between his hands was the old man with the walrus moustache. 'On your own?'

'Well, I'm –'

'Don't mind if I join you? Phew, it's getting hotter every day. Where's your husband today? Or is he a boyfriend, or…' He leant towards me, lowering his voice, 'your lover, eh, eh?' He laughed raucously, not noticing how much he was embarrassing me. 'Look, couldn't buy me a tea, could you? See, I've been caught a bit short, if you catch my meaning...'

I caught it all right but still found myself buying him his tea. '...And a little cake, perhaps?' And a hefty slice of cake too. 'This heat, it's unbearable, isn't it?' The constant use of the rhetorical question, I noticed, was an intrinsic part of his conversation. 'Reminds me of the summer of '18. That was some summer, I can tell you, too hot to be stuck in the trenches with full kit, but I was a young man then, young and strong...'

He regaled me, for the second time, with the story of his life; of how he'd been a sniper during the Imperialist War; of how he'd killed two Nazis with his bare hands during the occupation; of how he'd saved the honour of his sister from the hands of a marauding Russian in forty-five. I shrunk in my chair, hoping to God no one could hear his blasphemous tale. He was a widower, he told me, his wife had red hair – like me, and how he still missed his dear wife, even if she never allowed him to talk. I couldn't say I blamed her. But perhaps it explained something –he was talking now to make up for thirty or forty years of marital silence. He didn't care whom he talked to or whether they were listening or not, as long as he could talk. It was like listening to a familiar record, knowing what to expect, knowing the good bits from the dull. There was something rather reassuring in listening to him. Perhaps because it reminded me of Valentin, the first day I met him when he rescued this harmless old boy from the clutches of the café's staff. How I wished Valentin were with me now.

The young waitress took the used cups and plates and then hovered at our table expectantly.

'Does she want a tip?' he asked me as if she wasn't there.

'No, we're obliged to order something else otherwise we have to leave.'

'Another cup of tea, then, please and…' he turned to the waitress, 'another of those delicious cakes.'

I sighed.

'Listen,' he said, 'this will cheer you up – three workers find themselves locked up, and they ask each other what they're in for. The first man says: "I was always ten minutes late to work, so I was accused of sabotage." The second man says: "I was always ten minutes early to work, so I was accused of espionage." The third man says: "I always got to work on time, so I was accused of having a Western watch."'

Despite myself, I laughed.

'You're a fine woman,' he said, wiping cake crumbs from his moustache. 'Where did you say your husband is?'

'I didn't –'

'So, where was I? Ah, this apartment they've put me in, it's a disgrace, I tell you; after what I've done for this country. No respect for the old, that's the problem. Now, when I was a young man we had respect for…'

'Eva.'

'Oh, Karolina.' Why did I say Karolina when I knew the voice to be Agnes's? 'I'm sorry, Agnes, I…'

'Expecting Karolina, per chance?' she said, leaning down to embrace me.

'Ferenc, hello.' We kissed cheeks, his beard scratching my skin. 'Please, sit down.'

'Yes, sit down, sit down,' said the old man, with exaggerated generosity. 'I was only saying to your friend here – Eva, is it? – how disgusting my apartment is, you wouldn't believe –'

I'd had enough. 'I think you were saying how you had to leave,' I said firmly.

'Well, no –'

'Your shout then, is it?'

'Er, yes, well, perhaps you're right.' He looked at his bare wrist. 'My word, is that the time already? Western watch, eh? Yes, I must be going.' He rose unsteadily to his feet. 'Well, it's been a delight. Thank you for the cake.' I resisted saying *or two*. 'Give your husband my regards.' And with that, he limped out of the café, raising his hat at the waitresses behind the counter.

Agnes and Ferenc watched him leave. 'He's met Josef?' asked Agnes.

'He's harmless,' I said nervously.

'He shouldn't be criticising his apartment like that,' said Ferenc. 'The State provides first-class accommodation for our senior citizens.'

'We should go,' I said, ignoring this blatant distortion of the truth.

I settled my bill with the young waitress, while the older one looked on, disgusted, I think, that I should have spent my time and money on the old man.

We had to catch two trams, with a short walk in between, to reach the stadium on the western side of Buda. We joined the throng of people making their way to the game, a snaking parade of young and old, fathers and sons, wearing green and white football scarves, hats and rosettes, twisting noisy rattles. The crowd was good-natured, emitting lively banter and rowdy singing. It was unusual to see people looking so happy; a far cry from the forced jollity of festival days. I couldn't spot any women amongst them and wondered whether Valentin had been right about women attending football matches. But I was enjoying the festive atmosphere, soaking in the joyous ambience. Only Ferenc seemed ill at ease, being in such close proximity to the masses, the very people he routinely denounced to the authorities. As we approached the stadium gates, the crowd bottlenecked and movement became laborious and slow. Agnes snatched my hand and we held on as we squeezed our way through, showing our tickets and pushing through the barrier.

I was surprised by the size and lush greenness of the pitch, and how small the people looked at the opposite end. Ferenc led the way to our seats, muttering under his breath, annoyed at having to squeeze past those already seated to get to our places. 'Kick-off's at three.'

'I expect the Russians will play a four-four-two formation,' I said with a grin, sitting down.

'A what?' asked Agnes.

'Or perhaps a five-three-two.'

'Stop showing off,' she laughed. 'So, were you expecting to see Karolina? Vida's wife?'

'No, not really. I bumped into her there the other day, that's all.'

'Huh,' said Ferenc, the other side of Agnes. 'You won't be bumping into her any more.'

'What do you mean?'

Agnes said, 'You haven't heard? You know Vida was arrested?'

'Yes.'

'Well, apparently, yesterday, she was arrested as well.'

'No.' I remembered the look she gave me as the AVO men led her away. 'On what charge?'

Ferenc spoke firmly. 'For being the wife of an enemy of the people. Looks like –'

He was interrupted by an eruption of cheers – the players were on the pitch. Twenty-two men milling about, kicking footballs to each other; on one side the green and white of the City team, on the other, the red and white of Moscow Lokomotiv. And yes, there he was, wearing number six, Valentin Ivanov, my Valentin, and how handsome, how strong he looked. I saw him scan the crowd, searching for me. And I felt special, wanted. He was searching for *me*, a single face amongst thousands. And for a few seconds, I forgot all about Karolina and Josef and forgot that within a few hours, Valentin might be gone from me forever. I found myself standing up and waving frantically, hoping to catch his attention.

'Eva, what on earth are you doing?' asked Agnes.

'Oh, I'm sorry,' I said feebly, suppressing the urge to laugh. I sat back down. 'I don't know what came over me. I think I feel a little overexcited.'

Chapter 13: The Match

The pitch feels suffocating under a blanket of heat. The referee blows his whistle. George receives the ball and passes back to Kosak who lobs the ball pointlessly forward into Lokomotiv's defence. The match has begun.

The Russians launch their first attack and George finds himself stranded on his own near the halfway line. How long had it been going on? Had their affair started before his father's arrest or after? Did he come along and provide her with a sympathetic word, a shoulder to cry on? No wonder she was so annoyed by his refusal to go to training, no wonder she ran off to use the telephone downstairs, no wonder she returned agitated because she'd missed him. And of all people – Mark Decsi, the talent scout. The ball comes his way. He runs for it but a Lokomotiv defender gets to it first and boots it upfield. Had Mark Decsi truly been impressed by his football? Was Sebes Gusztav really in the crowd right that moment watching him play? Did he really feature in the national manager's plans? Or was it all simply a ruse to impress his mother, to get her to… no, he couldn't think it.

Lokomotiv shoot but the shot lacks power and Milan Ignotus saves easily. The goalkeeper kicks the ball up the field. George jumps for it with a Lokomotiv defender and receives an elbow on the side of his head for his efforts. Losing his balance, the ball bounces off his head harmlessly to a Russian, who uses the opportunity to start another attack. The Russians are playing well.

Zoltan Beke stands in the VIP enclosure. To his left, stands Fischer, silent and grey as ever; to his right, is Donath. He hadn't expected his boss to attend but at the last minute, Donath had insisted on coming, despite Zoltan's best efforts to put him off. This simple job had, over the previous fortnight, gained a momentum of its own and now loomed large in the department's priorities. Hence Donath's personal attendance. He wanted to see Lokomotiv win for himself, knowing there'd be hell to pay with his superiors if they didn't. Zoltan couldn't believe how a stupid football match had taken over his life. Petra still wasn't speaking to him after the birthday debacle, Roza was still sulking, and Fischer, Zoltan knew, was secretly hoping for a Hungarian win to topple the immediate hierarchy and allow him a fast shot at promotion – at Zoltan's expense.

His heart feels heavy. God, it was hot. Never had he shown so much interest in football. Today, he is urging Lokomotiv on as if he'd supported them his whole life. He's desperate for a goal, for a Lokomotiv win. His career depends on it – and possibly more. But for now, at least, the Russians are playing well.

Gimes, the outside right, is making a run down the wing, making good progress. George sprints in parallel down the centre, careful not to run offside. Gimes crosses. Instinctively, George knows it's a perfect cross. He sees the goal ahead of him. He leaps but then subtly ducks his head a fraction. The ball skims off the top of his head and peters off the pitch for a goal kick. Gimes shouts at him, astonished that his ever-reliable centre forward should miss such a peach of an opportunity. George puffs his cheeks.

The Lokomotiv goalkeeper takes the goal kick, an imposingly large man, bald and broad, eyes too close together. George wonders whether the AVO man is in the crowd. Why should a friendly be of such importance to the secret police? Why should they care whether he scores or not, whether his team wins? Bordas, the manager, certainly seemed agitated, short of patience and quick to the criticism. It was unlike him; even before the most important games, he usually maintained a sense of proportion and of humour, motivating and encouraging by turn. Maybe it was the heat. And what if Mark Decsi was being straight and the national manager really is watching? Why had he ducked that ball? Because, he realises, he's frightened; frightened of the AVO, frightened because his life isn't what it seemed; because he hadn't expected to be so disappointed by his father's return.

Lokomotiv are on the attack. The winger seems set to cross the ball but instead turns inside and runs at the heart of the City defence. A short pass. A shot from the edge of the penalty area. The ball hits the post and ricochets out. Zoltan screams at the sky, pleading for some form of divine intervention.

Fischer claps quietly. Zoltan glares at him with more venom than he'd intended. Why was Fischer still looking so cool in this temperature, and why was he applauding? Because Lokomotiv almost scored or, as he suspects, because City got away with it? Even Donath shoots him a nasty look and Fischer desists from clapping.

Zoltan casts his eyes over the City players, counting off the ones he'd nobbled. At least two were missing but the big goalie was there, as was Lorenc. He hoped for their sakes, they played ball.

Donath has taken off his jacket, the circles of sweat beneath his armpits clearly visible. He looks at his watch. 'Almost half time, Beke.'

If the previous transition from his first name to *comrade* was ominous, then the transition to his surname was even more so. 'But it's still nil-nil, boss, and all the chances have fallen Lokomotiv's way.' He wiped his brow.

'Mmm.' But Donath wasn't convinced, that much was obvious. They still desperately needed that goal.

The referee blows his whistle. It is half-time. In need of an excuse to escape Donath's intense presence, Zoltan volunteers to buy a round of coffee. He fights his way through the crowd towards the refreshment stands. Donath and he take sugar. Fischer does not. He returns with three heavily sugared coffees. 'Oh, I'm sorry, Fischer, I forgot.'

The second half begins. The near side of the pitch is now in the shade – a striped oasis of relative coolness. George now knows for sure that the AVO had gotten to Bordas too. The manager's half-time pep talk was the most nonsensical, ineffectual one he'd ever heard. *Carry on playing as you are* was the basic message. Heck, thought George, normally if the team had put in a first-half performance such as that, Bordas would have something more to say about it. He would have blasted them and cajoled them by turns; dictated changes in tactics, picked up on specific points to dissect. But nothing of the sort today. Like the near side of the pitch, the man was a shadow of his usual self.

Milan takes a goal kick. Kosak runs onto it and simply blasts the ball speculatively towards Lokomotiv's goal. By sheer fluke, it hits the crossbar, bounces off and a defender scoops up the loose ball and clears. The crowd roars its approval – *this is more like it*, they think.

George's father is at home; too weak to attend. He wished George well, not knowing the rollercoaster of emotions George had ridden over this single game. But his mother was there, in her usual spot. Is this where she met the talent scout, watching her son play football? Were her post-match opinions her own or words taken from the mouth of her lover? The word *lover* sits on George's tongue like a distasteful scrap of food. He spits to clear his throat, to rid his mind of the word. Will his mother stop seeing Mark Decsi now that his father is back?

He realises that he's playing his worst-ever game. He hopes now that the national manager isn't in the crowd. Who'd take on a turkey like him?

At that moment, Lokomotiv's big number six shoots from ten yards out.

Later, when he thought back on that moment, Zoltan realised he'd never experienced such an intense rush of pure joy. When that ball hit the back of the net, he threw his arms up in the air, screamed as he had never screamed, and started jumping – again and again, knowing but not caring that he looked demented. He even threw his arms around Donath, who shrugged him off, disgusted at this unmasculine show of emotion. He realised he was crying – such was the relief surging through his body. By the time the match re-started, he felt exhausted, drained by the heat and the sudden intensity of ecstasy. He whipped a handkerchief from his pocket and dried his eyes, realising that he alone had cheered the Russian goal in a totally partisan crowd. Ten thousand pairs of eyes glared at him. But he didn't care. Glancing either side of him, he realised how embarrassed Donath and Fischer had been by his outburst. But still, he didn't care.

'Who scored the goal, boss?'

'Their number six,' said Donath, flipping through his match programme. 'Valentin Ivanov. You weren't the only one cheering like a maniac – there's that woman over there.'

Zoltan follows Donath's pointing finger and only a few rows away, he sets eyes on the attractive redhead with a huge grin, sitting next to a glum-looking man with a bushy beard.

The shade had inched across the pitch, slowly furthering the boundary between sun and shadow. George realises that the AVO man must've also got to Milan in goal. It was a good strike from Lokomotiv's number six but it was well within Milan's diving range. OK, he wasn't the 'keeper he used to be, but he was still capable of having stopped that one.

Kosak is deep in his own half but lobs forward a perfect cross-field pass for George to run onto. A Lokomotiv defender runs with him and attempts the slide tackle. George skips over the lunging boots and finds himself in acres of space with the ball at his feet. He sprints towards the Lokomotiv penalty area, thinks about the pass but instead shoots. It's a rasping shot that the Lokomotiv's keeper saves spectacularly, earning the crowd's sportsman-like appreciation. George turns, disappointed. But now he feels different. For the first time in the match, his mind is focused and all the external thoughts disappear. No longer the pawn in everyone else's lives, he is George Lorenc, the footballer, playing for his team, the supporters, and himself – and it feels fantastic.

Donath looks at his watch again. 'Still ten minutes left,' he said, in a tone that conveyed, *Don't count your chickens yet, Beke.*

If Zoltan thought he was nervous before, he now feels terrified. The last ten minutes would be the slowest of his life. He glances at his watch every few seconds, willing the second hand to move faster round the dial, for another minute to pass. Eight minutes. Between looking at his watch, he concentrates on the ball, silently cheering every time it ventures further into the City half, and filling with dread when it goes the other way. The Hungarian players had barely put together an attack the whole length of the game; surely they couldn't score now? Lokomotiv, satisfied with their one-goal lead, seemed content to sit back and soak up the pressure. It's a tactic Zoltan finds difficult to comprehend.

Seven minutes. That wonderful number six, Valentin Ivanov, is loitering outside the penalty area, the ball at his feet. A quick side-step around a defender, and a shot. Somebody in Row Y caught the ball.

Six minutes. Zoltan would happily fall to his knees and pray for another Lokomotiv goal. He'd give up his possessions, halve his salary, work double the time, whatever it took. City's centre-forward, the majestic George Lorenc, takes hold of the ball and runs at the Lokomotiv defence – his first display of skill of the game. He takes a pot shot but the ball is easily gathered by the bald-headed Russian goalkeeper. Thank you, God, thank you.

Five minutes. Another Hungarian attack – they seemed to have decided to give it a last throw. The inside left, Kosak, Zoltan thinks is his name, sprints into the penalty area, but the ball is running away from him. A defender slides in, misses the ball, and catches Kosak, bringing him crashing down inside the box.

The referee blows his whistle and, running, points to the penalty spot. Zoltan feels his knees buckle. Donath, fanning himself with the match programme, glares at him. 'You did nobble the ref, didn't you, Beke?'

'Erm…'

He'd never given it a thought.

Another dubious penalty, thinks George, remembering the previous game when his spot-kick sealed his hat trick, when life was so much easier. But this time, George doesn't want to take it. Kosak's getting up, wiping himself down. 'Do you want to take it, Kosak?' asks George. 'After all, you earned it.'

'No, you take it, it's your job.'

Yes, it's his job. Someone throws the ball at him. He drops it and someone quips that it's a good job George is the striker and not the goalie.

He places the ball on the penalty spot and wipes the sweat from his eyes. Four carefully paced steps back. His heart is beating furiously. He feels weak.

He looks round – the referee is ready, his whistle poised at his lips; the Lokomotiv goalkeeper is on his line, his close-together eyes on the ball, the sun reflecting off his scalp. A gaggle of players from each side gather on the D of the penalty area; the crowd are hushed – in full anticipation of another Lorenc goal. But it is those George cannot see that crowd his mind – his mother, up there in the stands, the talent scout with his cat-like eyes, the national manager – if he's there at all, his father of old with his pipe, and the father of now sitting pathetically at home, dreaming of happier times, dreaming his son's dreams.

The referee blows his whistle.

It feels as if the whole world is holding its breath.

He shoots.

The roar of the crowd fills his ears, but everything is as black as the darkest night. He realises he's retching, the bile clawing in the back of his throat. Nauseating. The noise is getting louder, suffocating, a ceiling of noise he can't escape from. He opens his eyes for a moment, a flash of light, a circle of men looking down on him; he thinks perhaps he's dying as the blackness returns and descends like a curtain. And then the silence. Nothing but the silence.

Chapter 14: Eva

I almost felt embarrassed that the gap left in my life by Josef should so easily be filled by Valentin. I knew Valentin was no more than a distraction, a means to escape the every day, that soon I would be engulfed by the certainty of loneliness, having only the demons of my failures to keep me company, but like a drunk drinking more to delay the inevitable hangover, I was determined to postpone the inescapable and enjoy the moment, to relish the sensation of infatuation, to wallow in the rapture of this fantasy I found myself in.

Today is the day I hope to meet Valentin. It is ten days since Moscow Lokomotiv's game against the team from Budapest and since then they have been touring the country, playing a number of games. If they have done well, the players will be permitted two days sightseeing leave in the capital. I have been following their progress in *Free People* like an avid supporter, hoping each time for a victory. And I haven't been disappointed – five games: four wins and a draw. I just hope that the Soviet authorities don't cancel their leave on account of that sole draw. I couldn't bear not to see him again – one last time.

Today the heat is as intense as ever. I have forgotten the meaning of rain or cold. Valentin and I agreed that if all things went well, we should meet at the Café of the Revolution at ten. It is now half past nine.

The café is busy today. I hope this time we don't meet the old man. I couldn't face hearing his life story for the third time; I think I'd scream. I wave at the old hag waitress as I enter but receive only a glare in return. I order my coffee and cake, and open my newspaper, not that I can concentrate, my heart is in too much of a flutter. My palms are wet and I feel almost sick with nerves. Realising I'm not hungry, I push the cake aside.

For the first time, I allowed myself to think what I might do if he didn't show. It is a possibility. Such are my nerves, I think in some ways I'd be relieved. For then, at least, I'd be spared the agony of parting, for whatever happens today, it must end with a parting. Not this time for ten days, or a few weeks or a year, but forever. Despite the warmth, I shudder.

I think of Karolina and her futile attempt to save her husband, whose circumstances she now shares. Karolina's situation has brought home to me the precarious position Josef and I are in. The responsibility of his work is such that he won't survive unscathed for much longer. One day, he will stand accused of a mistake, real or fictional, it won't matter. And, like Karolina, if my husband falls, separated or otherwise, I will fall soon after. If not arrested, I'd be ejected from the apartment and left with no means by which to live. Unless, of course, we were divorced.

I need Valentin to do the impossible, to save me, to take me away. But to take me away to what? I still have no idea how he lives in Moscow. He hasn't told me and I haven't asked. I don't want to know, don't need to know. Anywhere is better.

'Eva, hello.'

Oh, how I melt at the sound of his Russian accent. 'Valentin. Oh, Valentin.' We embrace, not as friends, but in an indiscreet manner that I know will have the waitresses talking.

We sit, refusing to let go of each other's hands. 'I've missed you,' he says.

'And I've missed you.' You don't know how much I've missed you, how much I've waited for this moment.

'I've forgotten quite how beautiful you are.'

'Oh.' I feel almost faint. I feel beautiful because you make me beautiful.

I ask him then because I have to: 'Today, is it your last day?'

'Yes,' he says quietly. 'It is our last day.'

We had to five o'clock, the time of the team's evening meal together in the hotel restaurant.

We sit in silence for a while; thankful we had this day, this final day.

'I've thought of you my every waking moment.'

I try not to giggle; how love reduces us to the silliest of thoughts. If only life could always be so wonderfully silly; why must our lives be so complicated when the most important things are so simple?

'Even when you were playing?'

'Especially when I was playing,' he says, picking up on my slightly mocking tone. 'You were my motivation. I dedicated my goal to you.'

A goal dedicated to me. I held the words in my mind, frightened of letting them go.

'Eva?'

'Sorry, I'm sorry, I… I don't know.'

'Shall we walk?'

'Yes, let's walk.'

*

We strolled through the park in silence, gently holding hands, breathing in the warm air, the smell of freshly cut grass, of the blooming array of flowers – the snapdragons, busy lizzies, geraniums, and roses plentiful, white, yellow and pink. We were both too frightened to talk, worried that if we talked, we might talk the day away. Each moment had to last, each second treasured.

When I did finally speak, I said words I would once have believed impossible but my feelings for him were so acute, my trust so absolute, and our parting so imminent, I did not even hesitate. 'Valentin, I want you to take me to your room.'

He smiled the faintest of smiles, took my face in his hands and kissed me.

*

The Hotel Astoria near the city centre is an ancient Gothic-style building; large, imposing and ugly. The square in front of it was a mass of cars and nearby the privilege shop or simply stroll around, wanting to be seen in the fashionable part of the city.

'I share a room with a team-mate but he'll be out sightseeing,' said Valentin, as we approached the foyer. 'But we may have a problem.'

'Oh?'

'We are not permitted to entertain guests in our rooms.'

This, I concurred, was potentially an obstacle.

The effort of getting me into his room was the stuff of pantomime. We had to enter the hotel together, otherwise, I would never have got past the doorman. We sat for a while in the lobby bar and, for the sake of appearance, ordered water. After a while, I followed Valentin's instructions and, alone, walked confidently to the lift and asked for the fourteenth floor. I was to go first in case I ran into trouble. I was then to walk slowly down one flight of stairs by which time; Valentin should have caught the lift to the thirteenth floor and made his way to his room. If the door was ajar, I could go in; if not, I was to wait for him back down in the lobby.

Fortunately, when I got there, the door was ajar.

The room was large with two single beds and an adjoining bathroom. The curtains were thick, the carpet lush, the bathroom spotlessly clean. Obvious things perhaps, but not to me; I'd never been inside a hotel room, never seen such luxury.

'Welcome,' said Valentin as I entered, closing the door behind me.

'He reached for my hands. Pulling me towards him, we kissed, delicately, nervously; our first private kiss.

'What if your roommate comes back?'

'He has a lot to see in Budapest; he has never left Moscow before and he wants to see everything before dinner.'

'Five o'clock?'

'Five o'clock.'

'Lock the door.'

'It is locked.'

*

Valentin is half-asleep, a small smile fixed to his lips, his hair slightly dishevelled. He lays there, one arm beneath my shoulder and one hand resting on his torso, his fingers caught in the mesh of his chest hair. With my head resting on his shoulder, I watch the steady rise and fall of his chest. My body tingles; I can feel it reaching down to the ends of my fingers and toes. But satisfaction is denied me, for I can't think of what has been but what is to come. I can't bring myself to believe that what is now, will soon be confined to a memory; that what is in the present, will all too soon belong to the past. I can't believe that what is so real will gradually dim with the passing of the years, that one day all that will remain of this wondrous moment will be fragments of remembrance – the scent of this, the touch of that. It frightens me how quickly memory evaporates the details.

Valentin opens his eyes and looks at me with such tenderness I could cry. I have never experienced this sort of love. Josef's love, when it existed, was a trickle compared to this torrent.

The small alarm clock on his bedside table reads three o'clock.

'We haven't long,' he says, stroking my cheek with a gentle finger.

'I know.'

'One day we will be together again. You know that, don't you?'

'Yes.'

'Do you believe it?'

I am close to tears. 'Yes, Valentin, I believe it.'

But I don't believe it. How can it be? We both live under a system that restricts and suffocates. We have no future; we won't be allowed a future. We are together now; but our lives are a mystery to each other, for we exist for one another only in this moment of time. A moment of time that is perfect, but which has no past and no future. We have but the two hours ahead of us. It is all we have.

And then there will be nothing more.

Just me and a love that could have been; a husband that was no more; and, born three months before, a little girl…

Chapter 15: Eva

Anastasia was born in Budapest on the second of February 1949. She died on the eighteenth of February 1949.

She was just sixteen days old. Poor thing, she never stood a chance. Born eleven weeks early, she never left the hospital. Josef never had the chance to hold her. Nor did I, not properly, never had the chance to feed her. Everything inside her tiny little body was underdeveloped – her kidneys, the lungs, the liver, her heart. Nothing worked as it should; the odds were against her from the first. I spent sixteen days and nights just staring at her, secretly praying that God would help her build up the strength to live, to survive. I cursed my womb for not providing for her.

Sick day and night for the first three months of the pregnancy, I became thin and lethargic, barely able to move, unable to nourish myself, least of all the baby inside me. After the period of sickness, came the pain, the muscular pain which seemed to permeate into the bone. A sudden movement and it would traverse through me. For weeks on end, I was unable to move. Josef ate at work, bringing me home small scraps of dinner, which I would heat up and stare at, unable to face swallowing such tasteless and uninspired offerings. It was a life of misery, compounded by the thought that the baby was suffering as much as myself. The birth itself, eleven weeks too early, was relatively easy; Anastasia slipped quietly into the world without a murmur. How I wished to hear her cry, to see evidence of lungs full of air. It was never to be; she fell silently into a coma and never woke up. She was conscious long enough to see me and her father briefly before her eyelids closed, never to open again.

I slept at the hospital. The hospital staff provided me with blankets which I would spread out on the chair to make myself as comfortable as possible, wrapping myself against the cold draft. I didn't dare grumble, the hospital was a hospital only in name. It lacked virtually all essential supplies, and medicines were precious, used only in cases where the patient was important enough or ill enough to warrant it, but not sick enough to make recovery unlikely. My body seemed thankful to be rid of the torment that it had to endure all those months. I spent hours watching her, burdened by guilt, apologising for the inadequacies of my womb. I would make up little tunes, slow tunes in time to her laboured breath as I watched her delicate chest move up and down. My mind would repeat again and again the words plastered up on the wall of the delivery unit – *To give birth is a girl's glory and a wife's duty*. How those words mocked me.

One night I dreamt of horses, grey horses galloping riderless through dark forests, zigzagging past trees, jumping over fallen branches and exposed roots, their manes and tails blowing dramatically in the wind. When I awoke, Anastasia had died. It was the final betrayal. Just as my body had failed her during gestation, my consciousness had deserted her at the point of death. I never saw her slip away, never held her match-like fingers to comfort her as she drifted from this miserable world into the next. I'd barely had the chance to say hello and now I'd missed the opportunity to say my farewell. I prayed that God would accept her and give her the love and security I'd failed to provide. Once, believing myself to be a good communist, I had tried to deny my God, pretended that I didn't need religion. Sometimes I believed I *had* renounced it for the illusion that the Party said it was. But if I didn't need it, Anastasia certainly did. I couldn't bear the thought of her going from one darkness to another in such a short space of time. I needed her to have an afterlife to make up for the miserable sixteen days spent in a cold bleak hospital in Budapest. I'd expected to cry and yes, I mourned for her, but the tears did not come. Whatever grief I had was tempered by the relief that her troubles were over.

The staff removed her from the cot where she had spent her short existence, and carefully placed her in a small wooden box, lined with a faded shawl. They were about to take her away into the depths of the hospital but I insisted on taking her home with me. I wanted to save her from the indignity of the hospital's incinerator. Josef hired a car from work and came to pick me up and drove me home, disgusted that I should want to bring Anastasia back. I remembered how delighted he was when I first became pregnant, thankful that at last I was doing my patriotic duty. But he soon lost interest when it became obvious that things were not as they should have been. He spent longer at work, unable and unwilling to face his miserable wife at home. After the birth, he came to see me three, maybe four times and would pace up and down asking if I was ever likely to give birth to a normal child, a future communist. I was a disappointment to him, and I don't think he ever looked at Anastasia; she was too much of an embarrassment, lying there oblivious to the distress she caused him. I was always relieved when he left and found myself apologising to her for his abruptness. My only other visitor was Agnes – she came every other day, bearing fruit and a sympathetic word.

As Josef drove me home, I sat silently in the back with the wooden box on my lap. I stared out of the window, watching the huddled figures going about their business, the long pointless queues, the shop fronts with nothing to sell, the blocks of flats, bleak and grey. Everything seemed so damn grey. And so I brought my baby home, back to our tiny apartment. It wasn't, of course, quite how I imagined it to be.

*

'A Christian burial, eh? That's a rarity these days,' said Father Aczel, looking at me through his spectacles perched precariously at the end of his nose. 'You're very lucky I haven't renounced the cloth, I'm a dying breed you know. Literally.' I felt sorry for him – the Party ridiculed the church, depicting the clergy as sexual perverts or money-grabbing thieves.

I had rung Father Aczel the day after coming home from the hospital. I waited until Josef had gone to work before phoning him. Before leaving, Josef declared he wanted to see that "grisly box" gone by the time he got home from work. I had no intention of doing otherwise. I opened the lid and peered at her and stroked the strands of bronze-coloured hair – she would have been a redhead, like me. It was the first time since her birth that I'd looked at her without cursing God and begging His intervention at the same time. Now, I just cursed Him. But if I had been unable to provide her with life, at least I could oblige her with a proper send-off.

And so I rang Father Aczel and told him about Anastasia and my desire to grant her a proper Christian burial. I feared it was short notice but, as he said, he was in little demand and was glad to accommodate me. I then rang Agnes and asked whether she would accompany me. Together, in her husband's car, we drove the five or so kilometres towards the east of Pest and a small church beyond the City Park. The three of us stood beside the church altar, the small box resting in a nearby pew. At the back of the church kneeled an elderly woman dressed in black crossing herself ceaselessly, otherwise the church remained deserted. 'You sure it won't compromise you, Father?'

'Just being here is compromising enough, Eva. There's fewer of us by the day.'

'But you're still here, Father,' said Agnes. 'Your church is still standing.'

'Yes, and for every day it survives, I thank the Lord, but sometimes I wonder how long I can go on. It's only a matter of time until they come for me. Shall we go? I've arranged for a grave to be dug and I've got a small wooden cross. Well, Eva, what did you say the infant's name was?'

As Father Aczel wrote out Anastasia's name on the cross, I smiled at Agnes – she'd tied her hair back into a bun, accentuating the roundness of her face. I wanted to thank her for coming but I knew I couldn't express how grateful I was that she was there. How pathetically grateful.

Outside, the dark clouds swept across the sky and the wind whistled in the trees. We stood beside the grave that had been dug next to the churchyard wall, the spade still standing in the mound of fresh earth. Father Aczel clutched his bible, his robes blowing in the breeze, his honeyed voice washing over me. 'We pray, O Lord, that Anastasia may be taken into the

Kingdom of His Almighty God and that there she may find peace in the company of angels. We pray that God in His mercy may take her into His realm and deliver her the peace she was so cruelly denied in this mortal world…'

As Father Aczel lowered Anastasia into the ground, Agnes took my hand and squeezed it. And finally, I was able to cry for my precious little daughter, the daughter who had only caught sight of her mother for a few brief moments before resigning herself to the darkness; whose passing existence I shall always remember. I cried for her blighted life, her sixteen days on this earth, her frailty, her helplessness. She never heard me call her name, never tasted her mother's milk, was never held by her father. I cried for myself, as a mother denied the opportunity of seeing her daughter as a proper being, denied the sound of hearing her baby cry, denied even the tactile presence of her lips against my breast. My baby, my poor little baby. May we meet again, my darling.

Part Two

**Four years later:
March 1953**

Chapter 16: Zoltan

She simply sat there, a look of determination in her eyes, ignoring the pen and sheet of paper on the desk in front of her.

'You have to sign,' said Zoltan.

'I will not.'

He slammed his palm on his desk. 'Just sign the sodding piece of paper.'

'I will not put my name to this pack of lies.'

'Yes, we both know it's a pack of lies but that's not the point, surely you must see that. We need your signature on this confession and if you don't sign it now, I'll have no option but to…'

'But to what?'

'You know damn well.'

'I shall never sign it.'

Zoltan slumped on the desk; he felt exhausted. He couldn't bear the thought of her pretty face being pulped, of her innocence shattered. She was quite the most beautiful girl he'd ever seen, with her blue-grey eyes and her little upturned nose and perfect lips of natural vermilion. She reminded him of a young Petra when they'd first met. This girl was prettier still but there was something about her, the way she spoke, the way she conducted herself that drew him to her, that was very Petra-like.

Her crime – to have had a grandfather who'd invested carefully and bought a huge country house, a few miles south of the city and had left it to her mother. The mother had already been arrested as a bourgeois speculator and now, this girl, Elizabeth Vas, was being made to suffer for her grandfather's unfortunate provision. Her second crime was to have an older cousin who'd escaped the 'People's Democracy' and now lived in Connecticut. She maintained she hadn't spoken or written to this remote cousin and had forgotten all about him until, that is, the AVO reminded her of the fact and accused her of using her cousin as a recipient of the information that she gathered as a spy.

'Look, I'm begging you. I don't want you to get hurt–'

'In that case, you can use your authority to inform whoever needs to be informed that I am totally innocent of these charges, that you don't have a single piece of evidence to show that I am a spy and that I should be released from this… this mockery.'

'I haven't got that sort of authority,' he said quietly as her words impacted on his self-esteem.

'I thought you were important.'

'I am. It's just that…' He didn't know how to explain, perhaps because she was right. Five years in the job, an early run up the promotion ladder and then what? A bloody football game. 'For Christ's sake, just sign the bloody thing.' He jumped up from his chair, circled around the table, and sprang in front of her, clasping the back of her chair behind her, his face inches above hers, as she shrunk back from him. 'You think you can beat the system, don't you? You think you can stand up to us? But you're wrong, they'll destroy you, they'll have you so that death can't come quickly enough. God, you're beautiful but it means nothing here, nothing.'

'You think because I'm beautiful I'm vulnerable.'

'Stop being so stupid, you're vulnerable because you're here.'

'I'm not signing it.'

He slapped her. He hadn't meant to but the frustration got the better of him. Her head twisted to the side, her eyes clamped shut. Immediately, he regretted it. 'I'm sorry, I'm sorry, I didn't mean to do that.'

'Do you think I give a shit for your apologies?'

He paced to the window, fighting back the hurt she'd caused him, a pain he knew ran deeper than the sting on her face. The red imprint of his hand was clearly visible on her cheek. Couldn't she see he was trying to protect her? He stormed to the door, swung it open and summoned a guard.

As the guard took her away, he pleaded one last time. 'I'd ask you to think very carefully about what I said.'

She ignored him.

*

The morning was cold; a fresh breeze blew into their faces. The park was deserted, a sheet of newspaper floated around their feet. Roza paced ahead of them, her slight frame wrapped in a pink coat with a matching woolly hat, stamping her boots into puddles and squealing at the splashes. Petra slipped her arm through Zoltan's. 'How's it going at work?'

'Hideous,' he said.

'We hardly see you.'

'I know.'

She had cut her hair, her curls hacked away; she looked younger for it, more boy-like. He saw Elizabeth Vas in her, the confident smile, her still-fresh skin disguising the vigorous determination within.

'How's Roza been?' he asked. On hearing her name, Roza skipped back to them.

'Roza's a little upset today, aren't you, love?'

'Why, what's the matter?'

Roza shook her head and grabbed her mother's hand.

'Are you cold, sweetheart?' she asked, rubbing her gloved hand. 'Her friend Marika won't be coming back to school.'

'Oh.'

'And we're a bit sad about it.'

'Maybe she'll come back,' said Zoltan, realising that for a policeman it was an incredibly naïve comment to make.

Petra pulled a face and withdrew her arm from Zoltan's. 'Do you want me to tell Papa?'

'Her Mama and Papa have to leave,' said Roza.

'Twenty-four hours' notice,' added Petra.

'Why do they have to leave, Papa?'

Zoltan sighed. He knew his daughter held him personally responsible for every piece of bad news that happened at her school. The other children knew what he did for a living and tended to avoid Roza as a result. 'Sometimes, love, it's for people's own good.'

'But they were nice people.'

'Yes, but sometimes even the nicest of people have secrets that aren't so nice…'

'It's unfair,' she said, stamping her feet on the gravelled path. 'Marika was my friend.'

They'd come to the artificial lake and stopped at the low wall to gaze across the water rippling in the wind. 'No boats today,' said Petra.

'Pity,' said Zoltan. 'It'd be good with this breeze.'

Someone called out Petra's name. She turned and waved at a friend who was on the path, twenty yards away, a woman Zoltan didn't recognise under her layers of coats and scarves. 'It's not that cold,' he muttered.

'I'd better go say hello. Back in a minute.'

Roza had climbed onto the wall and was tiptoeing across, her arms outstretched. 'Roza, get down from there,' said Zoltan.

She did as she was told, picked up a stone and threw it into the water. 'No ducks today,' she said.

'No. No boats, no ducks.'

While Roza found bigger stones to throw, he turned and looked at the two huddled women. He wondered who Petra's friend was but, when he thought about it, he realised he hardly knew any of his wife's acquaintances. They preferred to socialise while he was at work. He knew why – they all thought it wise not to mingle with someone who had the power of arrest over them. He couldn't blame them. He drew out his packet of Red Stars and lit one.

The splashes behind him were getting louder with each stone. He drew heavily on his cigarette and wished he could relax but he couldn't shake Elizabeth Vas from his mind. He only hoped that while he was here on a rare day out with his wife and daughter, she was using the hours to reflect carefully on what she was letting herself in for. How could a young girl like that truly believe she could beat the system and come out unscathed? He could picture her eyes; that look of innocent ruthlessness, a contradiction that only the young are capable of. A ruthlessness borne out of conviction but not yet dulled by disillusionment. Conviction, he thought, is a worthy attribute but not when it merges into stupidity.

Zoltan's mind was still full of Elizabeth Vas when Roza, who'd climbed back onto the wall, lost her balance, slipped and fell noiselessly into the lake. Afterwards, when he thought back to those terrifying moments, he wondered why, despite being so close, he never realised a thing while his wife, twenty yards away, turned at that very moment. He put it down to a mother's intuition. It was only the sight of Petra running down the slope, almost in slow motion, screaming something garbled that Zoltan knew with heart-stopping fear that something was amiss. Dropping his cigarette, he turned and scanning his eyes, searched frantically for the figure in pink. Now, Petra was next to him, screaming *the water, the water* but how distant and disconnected her voice seemed. But he knew what he had to do and as he stepped over the wall and into the cold water, the greyness of the lake suddenly looked as fearsome as the angriest ocean.

There she was, his daughter, on her back, her arms circling, fighting for breath, unable to scream, a flailing sludge of pink. He waded through the knee-high tide, the sharp coldness of the water biting into his calves, his shoes heavier by the moment. Four huge steps and he was there, scooping her out, surprised by her weight, her arms drooping down. Petra stood on the grass, shaking, her face etched with terror. Her friend had come down the slope and held her still with a protective arm around her shoulders. Zoltan lay Roza on the grass, tilted her head back, and blew into the mouth; his hand gently pounding her chest. With every blow he asked God, then begged, then demanded, that she should be spared. Roza grimaced and he felt the first stirrings of hope; then with a strength he didn't think possible from one so small, she threw up, her chest caving in as the bile erupted from her mouth. Zoltan could have drunk it as champagne; his daughter was alive!

The push was so severe and so unexpected Zoltan found himself lying on the grass, unsure what force had propelled him there. He looked up to see Petra, her arms wrapped tightly around Roza, squeezing her into her chest, her whole body, it seemed, emitting a terrible wail, earth-like and primaeval. A thrusting blade of jealousy pierced him.

Like a tidal wave, exhaustion crashed over him but, summoning a strength forged through the need for reassurance and to reassure, he got up. He could hear Roza crying now beneath her mother's wailing and it brought the tears to his own eyes. He reached out an arm, desperate to touch his family, to reassure them of his presence, to be as one with them.

But Petra, sensing his presence, flung out her arm to repel him. 'You buffoon, she almost drowned,' she said, with a look that grieved him.

'But… I saved her.'

Her words came out as a growl: 'Get out of my sight.'

'Petra? Please…' I saved her, he thought, I saved her.

*

Returning to work that afternoon, Zoltan felt sick. His head thumped, his stomach churned but it was in his heart that the sickening manifested itself. He'd never felt so alone, so at odds with the world. Often, his work compensated for his home life or *vice versa*. But now, whatever way he looked, he could find no escape from his misery. Beyond home and work, there was nothing, no third option, no escape route. He was a weak father, he knew that, and that, in turn, made him a weak husband. However hard he worked, the promotion never came; however hard he tried to love her, the gap between him and Petra never shortened. There never seemed to be any light to lead him forward, no promise of a brighter future. He knew now why he took Elizabeth Vas's case to heart; not only did she remind him of a younger Petra but she reminded him of the Petra who'd loved him; the Petra who didn't hold him responsible for all the shortcomings in her life.

He looked at Petra's clock that still, after all these years, sat on his desk. Next to it, the photograph of Roza from four years ago. For some reason, he never got around to replacing it with a more recent one.

Three o'clock; he had a meeting with Donath. Although they didn't know it, Donath and Petra had much in common – a disappointment that the young man who promised so much had delivered so little. For Donath, Zoltan's nadir came with the football match, and in his boss's eyes he'd never really recovered from that. Zoltan had suffered as a result and he still shuddered when he thought back to that horrendous time. Donath and his seniors squarely blamed him for Moscow Lokomotiv's failure to win an unimportant football game and devised what, in their minds, was a simple but devastating punishment for Zoltan to suffer. They gave Zoltan Fischer's job, and Fischer Zoltan's. A simple swap, designed to humiliate. But they hadn't expected it to backfire. Fischer was as uneasy with the arrangement as Zoltan and, as a result, failed to deliver. Eighteen months later, Fischer was transferred out of the department and Zoltan got his old job back. His delight was soon tempered by Petra's wry observation that a promotion that merely cancelled out a relegation was not truly a promotion.

'Sit down, Zoltan.' Donath, still wearing his Order of Lenin with pride, lit a cigar, which, as if in evidence of his rising status, seemed to get bigger with every passing year. 'So, this Elizabeth Vas case, she's finally signed the confession.'

What a relief; Zoltan smiled.

'No need to look like that, it has nothing to do with *your* powers of persuasion. We had to take her to the second stage.'

Zoltan moved to the edge of the chair. 'But why, I almost had her.'

'Oh, for goodness sake, *I almost had her.*' This was a new habit of Donath's; to cruelly impersonate those who caused him displeasure. 'Sure you did, but we thought we'd save you some time. No point hanging around.'

'Where is she now?'

'Waiting transfer. Five years hard labour.'

His heart sank. 'Oh.'

'Indeed.' The two men contemplated the gulf between them. Felix Dzerzhinsky stared down at him. 'What's happened to you, Beke? You're weak; that's your problem and you're getting weaker.' Donath puffed on his cigar, a spiral of blue smoke obscuring his face. 'Fact is, I'm losing patience, I can't keep covering your tracks; you need to mend your ways – and fast.'

Zoltan coughed, the acrid smoke sticking to the back of his throat. 'I've got a lot on my mind, boss, you know, at home.'

'Who hasn't? Tell me something new. Now listen, you remember a youth we had in a few years back, lanky chap by the name of Szabo; Jasper Szabo?'

Zoltan thought back. Yes, he did remember, grassed up by his girlfriend for furtively listening to the *Voice of America* on the radio. They'd hammered his knuckles, threw him down for a week, then told him to get lost.

'Well, he's back,' said Donath. 'Sabotage; caught red-handed stealing from his factory, tractor parts, that sort of thing. Doesn't get much easier than this, Zoltan. Sort him out and this time…'

'Yes, I know.'

'No pissing around.' He tapped his cigar into the ashtray. 'Full confession or the body-grinder. Got it?'

'Yes, boss,' he said firmly. 'Got it.'

*

'What cell is Elizabeth Vas being held in?'

'Let me see, now.' The secretary leafed through a file, running his finger down the last sheet. 'Here we are,' he said, 'one-fourteen.'

One-fourteen, thought Zoltan, as he strutted off towards the stairs, that's a holding cell, means she'll be carted off to prison within the week.

As always, the line of bright light bulbs dazzled him as he entered the first basement floor; the iciness seeped from within its thick damp walls, cold condensation dripped down the huge metal doors. He flashed his pass to the duty guard even though the guard knew him well by sight. Cell eleven, twelve, thirteen… each one host to a miserable specimen of humanity. Cell fourteen. He flipped open the Judas hole and peered in. She must've heard the scrape of the metal because she clambered to her feet, her back facing the door. The prisoners were meant to remain on their feet for hours at a time. The job of the guard was to check regularly that his charges were behaving.

'Open this,' he said to the guard.

The door closed behind him, its slam reverberating through the cell. Elizabeth Vas stood facing the wall, a threadbare blanket wrapped around her shoulders. She was shivering, her feet bare and blackened with dirt. He noticed on the back of her head, the patches of scalp where clumps of her hair had been yanked out.

'Elizabeth.' He said her name quietly, apologetically. It was, he thought, probably the last time anyone would address her by her first name; from now on she'd be known only by a number. 'Elizabeth?'

Slowly, she turned around, shuffling her feet step by step. He tried not to let his shock show but they'd gone to town on her – her face was a mess of black and blue, her nose misshapen out of recognition, her once-vermilion lips now glued together with dried blood, her eyes lost within the swellings. Her wrists, twisted and puffy, had been broken. Her clothes too were ripped, her skirt speckled with blood, her blouse stripped of buttons. They would have raped her, possibly many times over.

Now he'd come, he had no idea what to say. An apology seemed pointless, any promises futile. 'I… I tried to warn you,' was all he could think to say.

She stood like a statue about to topple over, comatose, beyond help. But then she opened her mouth and tried to say something.

'I'm sorry?' he said, relieved that she could still attempt to talk. He stepped towards her, hoping to catch her words. But with a quickness that took him unawares, she rolled back her head, stretched open her lips and, throwing her head forward, spat at him. Her spittle landed squarely on his cheek. He didn't move, conscious of the warm phlegm creeping down his face, and felt the pain of yet another humiliation. He could have wept for her but he hated her at the same time, hated her for reminding him what a ridiculous man he'd become. Even this broken woman was capable of reducing him to nothing.

He'd had enough. The AVO thugs had already taken a swipe at her and, as far as he was concerned, they could do as they wanted with her now. Flinging open the cell door, he stormed down the corridor, ignoring the guard, and ran back up the stairs.

He'd tried to warn her. He'd saved his daughter but still, they blamed him. Even Roza blamed him. Six years old but she still held him responsible for the disappearance of her friends. A *buffoon*. Petra's voice came back to him in all its mocking glory, *you buffoon*, she'd said as she pushed him away, not wanting him to touch her or their daughter. What a word to use, as derisive as a mouthful of spit. And Elizabeth Vas, beaten to a pulp yet she managed to find the strength to exhibit her contempt for him. Contempt – that was the word etched on all their faces – Petra, Elizabeth, Roza and Donath. *You're weak, Beke, and you're getting weaker.* Fuck them. Fuck them all; he'd show Donath what he was made of. His job, he thought, was to interview, to intimidate. It wasn't for him to apply the physical, that was for the employed thugs. But if that was what Donath expected, then that's what he'd get.

*

Jasper Szabo was waiting for him in his office, another guard standing behind him, beside the door. Szabo hadn't changed much, thought Zoltan, the crescent-shaped scar above his right eyebrow gave him a distinctive look. His left hand was deformed, the broken bones had set badly leaving his buckled fingers at odd angles to each other.

He stood above him for a few moments, the two men silently re-familiarising themselves, the breath coming from

Zoltan's nostrils like a bull in the ring. *Buffoon. Weak. Always to blame.*

The first blow hit the cheek, his fists impacting the bone. The second on the mouth, the third, the fourth… It all became a blur. Szabo cowered in the chair, his arms trying to divert the blows. Blood splattered his clothes, the grunting became louder but still, the blows rained down, one after the other, while all the time the voices mocked him, belittled him. He'd show them, this wasn't the act of a weak man; Zoltan Beke was not a man to be toyed with any more. Things were going to change. Blood smeared across his knuckles. He felt fantastic. Yes, things were going to change. No one would ever mock him again. No footballer was ever going to inflict a career reversal like that again. He'd kill him. If he ever saw him again, he'd fucking kill him.

'Comrade… comrade.' The guard had his arms on Zoltan's shoulder, trying to prise him away from the battered Szabo. 'Comrade…' Slowly, the guard's voice permeated his brain. 'Comrade, I think you ought to be questioning him first.'

He stopped as suddenly as he'd started, exhausted but elated. 'Yes!' he said, between breaths. 'Yes, thank you, comrade, I'm well aware… of that.' He looked down at Szabo, whose eyes peered up at him from behind a shield of arms.

'Jasper Szabo?' said Zoltan, 'I think we've met before…'

Chapter 17: George

'Sign here.'

'What is it?'

The squat man with a peaked AVO cap too small for him handed George a pen. 'Your pledge that you're not to say or write a single word about your time here,' he said, leaning back in his chair.

George duly signed his name on the line, not bothering to read the lines of text above it, and realised he hadn't held a pen for almost four years. How cumbersome it felt, yielding this pen, how spindly his writing.

The AVO receptionist glanced at his signature and filed the sheet of paper into a manila folder, George's name writ large on its cover and the ominous X engraved in the box denoting his category. 'One thousand, three hundred and seventy days.'

'What?'

'How long have you spent here – three months short of four years? Less than most, you're a lucky man.'

George felt far from lucky. He took his crutch that had been leaning against the office wall.

'Right then, you're a free man,' said the receptionist, folding his arms and grinning with self-satisfaction, as if he was the one responsible for granting George his freedom. 'Show him out,' he said, nodding to a typically burly security guard.

'Can't I have a belt or something?'

'What for?'

'My trousers; they're too big for me now.'

'Do I look like a gentleman's outfitter? Sod off out of here.'

Two minutes later, George found himself on the pavement outside the prison walls. *You're a free man*, he said aloud, repeating the receptionist's words. But, he knew, he'd never be a free man while that *X* remained pinned to his file – excluded from work, accommodation, or any form of state help.

He was coming out in the same set of clothes as when he went in, one thousand, three hundred and seventy days previously – a cream-coloured, linen summer suit. (He remembered how the AVO men had allowed him to change after he'd been stretchered off the football pitch.) He held onto his trousers for fear they'd fall down, the jacket hung around his shoulders now like a shawl, his shirt ballooned at his waist with loose fabric. The cold breeze bit into him. The linen suit was not designed to withstand the cold March wind. How strange the world looked – the buildings looming high, the cars and trams whizzing past on the roads, the length of the streets stretching into the distance, the hoards of people going about their business, a blur of strangers, no one sparing him even a second glance. How strange and how frightening. Part of him wanted to run away, to escape back to the confines of his cell, to hide behind the thick steel doors. It was all too much, too bewildering all at once. He wondered how he must look to all these people – a gaunt man in a filthy linen suit, leaning on a crutch, his hair bedraggled, his beard scraggy and unkempt, his trousers falling down. Budapest's answer to Robinson Crusoe.

He searched his pockets, remembering the few florins he'd left but of course, the money was not there. He hadn't expected it to be. He had no choice but to walk across town to his parent's apartment in this cold.

Adjusting his crutch, he started to walk holding onto his trousers. After only a few minutes, he had to stop, exhausted. The crutch was a crude thing and the unfinished wood left splinters in his hand. He leaned against a garden wall and tried to steady his breathing. This was going to take longer than he'd thought. Summoning up his will, he focussed on the pavement in front of him and started again.

After an hour and a quarter, he arrived at the foot of his parents' apartment block. He sat down on a step shivering, less from the cold and more from the physical effort of getting here. His fingers bled, the sweat on his forehead seeped into his eyes, his fringe was plastered onto his skin. But he felt no self-pity. For he was outside, going where he wanted to go under his own free will, this was freedom, this is what he'd dreamt about for over three and half years – for one thousand, three hundred and seventy days. He would have smiled but for the effort of doing so. He was now only minutes away from his mother, his father, a bath, a shave, proper food, and a bed. These were the things that dreams are made of. He only hoped the lift was working.

As he stepped out of the lift onto the fourth floor, his nose was hit by the various cooking smells emanating from behind the closed doors; a mish-mash of ingredients and aromas; an olfactory assault that left him feeling faint – how rich it all smelt, so overpoweringly strong, so beautiful.

He knocked on the door and braced himself for his mother's screams. He braced himself too for the shocked sense of anti-climax – he remembered all too well the day his father came home. The door swung open but instead of his mother, a tall, thin man in a vest stood there, unshaven, a cigarette stuck to his lip. The two men gaped at each other; George noticed the tuft of chest hair poking out of the man's vest. 'Well?'

'I… I was looking for my parents.'

'Bit old to have lost your parents.' He laughed at his own joke.

'Lorenc. Mr and Mrs Lorenc.'

'Never heard of them,' he said, closing the door.

'No, wait, please. I… I used to live here –'

'Well, I live here now, along with half of bloody Budapest –'

'Who is it, Thomas?' The woman's shrill question came from within.

'Some…' He eyed George up and down, 'some bloke looking for people called Lorenc.'

A moment later, a woman with a thin, swan-like neck was standing behind the man in the vest, peering over his shoulder at George. 'Lorenc, you say? They lived here before but got booted out. Exiled out East. Maybe Russia. Some even reckoned Siberia.'

George swallowed, his eyes fixed on her but saw nothing.

'This is their son,' said the man by way of explanation.

'Oh. You've been away too by the looks of it.'

He appreciated her interpretation. 'I couldn't bother you for a piece of bread, could I?'

The man stepped out into the landing, pulling the door half-shut behind him. 'Sorry, pal,' he whispered. 'Don't take it personal but if the others in there see us talking to you… well, you know.'

George nodded. He knew his appearance stuck him out as a Class X: he was untouchable, unsafe to be seen talking to. 'Thank you anyway,' he said.

He returned to the lift, the sound of his crutch echoing down the corridor, his mind as numb as his body. As he waited for the lift to ascend, a hand touched his arm. 'Here, take it, quickly, put it in your pocket.'

He turned as the swan-necked woman ran barefoot back to her apartment. 'Thank you,' he mouthed, clutching in his hand a large chunk of bread.

*

Back out in the street, he sat down on the same step as before and hungrily tore into the bread. To his surprise (and gratitude) he found a small hunk of cheese in the middle. He sighed with pleasure as the food hit his stomach – what a relief. He chewed slowly, making the most of each morsel – a habit he picked up in prison.

How strange it was to be away from it all – the endless hours of cold and darkness without books, cigarettes or company, forced to remain standing for eighteen hours a day, the continuous glare of the light bulb. How liberating not to be spied on every few minutes through the Judas hole, not to feel one's brain rotting away.

Two trains of thought competed in his mind – to ponder the fate of his parents, or to work out what to do next. A fresh gust of wind cut through his suit. What about his teammates? Kosak – now where did he live? He'd once been to his place but couldn't, for the life of him, remember where. Bordas? No. Ignotus? Yes. Yes, he couldn't recall the name of the block but he knew the street, and it wasn't far.

Twenty minutes later, he was standing outside Ignotus's door. The block had been easy to identify once he'd found the street. He just hoped for better luck this time.

To his relief, the giant goalkeeper answered, his hair longer than George remembered, his beard almost as unkempt as George's. But it was Ignotus all right. 'Milan?'

'Yeah, what of it?'

'It's…' He felt faint, the exhaustion of so much walking, the heaviness in his feet.

'By George, it's George…'

*

George had no idea how long he'd slept for but when he opened his eyes, he saw that the darkened room was full of people. Perhaps he'd interrupted a party. But no one seemed very gay. In the corner, on a ragged settee, a woman breastfeeding; next to her a bald but young-looking man sat smoking a pipe and reading a newspaper. A number of others milled about, an older man with a toilet roll; a woman carrying two mugs of tea.

'Your friend's awake,' he heard someone say.

Milan was staring out of the window. He approached George with a smile, 'Welcome back,' he said. 'You've been asleep all day and night.'

Heck, thought George, he could feel it in his back. 'What happened?'

'Guess you must have fainted, or something. You seem to have a habit of doing that.'

'It's good to see you, Milan.'

'And you, my old friend.' He shook his head in a paternal sort of way. 'Look at you,' he said. 'Come on, you need a bit of a clean-up.'

*

It felt incredible to be wearing a fresh set of clothes and a proper coat, to be properly washed, to have a full stomach and to feel clean-shaven. A week later and the ex-centre forward and goalkeeper were sitting on a park bench, away from the apartment, away from flapping ears.

'It's hell. You think it was bad when you were around but it's a lot worse now. There're not enough places to go around any more, not since Rakosi's Five-Year-Plan kicked in. We've had a whole migration from the countryside, people with no work because of collectivisation. But they know they'll find jobs in the cities with Gero's huge industrial drive underway. OK, it pays peanuts but it's better than nothing. So the bloody communists simply allocate people to places. No matter you've already got ten to a two-bedroom apartment.'

'Couldn't you appeal?'

'What and get kicked out altogether? No, too risky.' He paused to light a cigarette. 'When did you get out?' he asked, blowing out a cloud of blue smoke.

'The day I knocked on your door.'

'You poor sod, you looked awful. Still do, really.'

'They deported my parents. Don't know when. You remember the last game? My father had only just come back from a stretch. He was in a dreadful state – far worse than me. I only have to contend with the leg. But he was ill – ill from the inside, you could see it. He wouldn't have survived exile. The train journey alone would have killed him. My mother was strong. I only hope she was strong enough.'

The thought occurred to him that he had nothing to remember them by – no photographs, no letters, nothing at all. He remembered when Kosak's mother died, how he'd spent hours going through her belongings, sorting things out, things to keep, things to donate or pass on to relatives and friends. How cathartic a process it must be, thought George, allowing the memories to come back, breathing in the familiar smell still so clearly impregnated in her clothes, reading her thoughts committed to paper, seeing her handwriting. But George had none of this, not a single memento to latch onto, or souvenir to treasure. Nothing. They may as well never have existed. They lived only in his mind and once he was gone, there would remain not a single trace of them, save some disparaging AVO file – not much to show for two lives.

'What's happening to the country, Milan?'

'They're squeezing us, that's what's happening. No one talks, no one writes, no one thinks; in fact, no one dares do anything; we all do as we're told. All their promises, these promises of a utopian future, it's all bull; they know it, we know it. Our wages have gone up by fifteen per cent – they put great store by that but what they forget to say is that at the same time, food prices have gone up some eighty per cent. It's impossible to buy anything now, even if you've got the cash because there's nothing in the shops to buy. The country's broke. We sell our exports to the Soviets at ridiculously cheap prices and import stuff back at the highest rates. I'm telling you, George, it's a mess, one big fucking mess.'

'It can't go on like this.'

Milan threw his cigarette on the ground. 'What do you propose?'

The two of them sat on the bench, huddled in their warm coats, and watched as the cigarette end fizzled out on the gravelled path. The park was empty, no couples walking by, no boys playing football, simply a grey expanse of manicured grass and forlorn-looking trees. Somehow, George had expected more from freedom. 'What happened after the game?' he asked.

'You scored from the penalty and then fainted. They came on, carried you off on a stretcher and we never saw you again. After that, we carried on with the last three minutes, the ref blew and that was it – one-one. Bordas also disappeared.'

'Anyone else?'

'No. One by one we were hauled in for a chat and that was scary enough, but I don't think they could be bothered with all of us. I was all right; I'd let in that goal, after all. It was a good shot but I had it easily covered.'

'So, they'd got to you as well?'

'Yeah, chap called Beke. You don't forget things like that. He came round to the apartment once, with his assistant. Face like a lemon. They were the good old days when there were just the two of us. All that space to ourselves, what luxury; problem is, we never appreciated it at the time.'

'What happened to your wife?'

'She upped and left one day. About two years ago. Took the kids and disappeared. Haven't heard from her since. So, what are you going to do now?'

'I don't know.'

'You need a job. Category X?' George nodded. 'I reckon we could get around that. How old are you now?'

'Twenty-two.'

'Yeah but the body of an eighty-year-old. How's the foot?'

The memory shot back into sharp focus – the dingy office with the one light bulb, the threadbare carpet, three heavies pinning him down on the ground, a fourth towering over him, mallet in hand, a devilish grin plastered on his lips, positively salivating at the prospect. He remembered being unable to control the shaking fear, knowing there was no one to help, that his cries would go unheeded. How terrifying it is to be totally at the mercy of men who mean to do you the utmost harm. Then the whoosh and the almighty pain as the hammer smashed into his calf bone, the sickening sound of splintering bone, his screams unrecognisable to his own ears. Then the second blow, further down the leg, the third, the fourth, each blow lower until the mallet reached his foot and a hundred delicate bones smashed. The tears soaking his face, the all-encompassing pain, the utter helplessness of not being able to move, not knowing when the terror was going to stop, whether it would ever stop. 'Not so bad,' he lied.

'How long will you need the crutch?'

'Not long. Some days, I can do without. The cold doesn't help, though.'

'It was the foot that scored the goal?'

George nodded. *Doubt you'll be scoring any more goals for a while, comrade.* And with that they'd left him, whimpering, wishing to be dead, the cheers of the football crowd echoing in his mind, teasing him in its adulation, Bordas slapping him on the back, the gaps between his teeth showing beneath his smile, *Good lad, well played, bring on the Soviets, eh?*; Beke's voice, *Give yourself an off day; we all have an off day occasionally.* So many voices, so many cheers, so much pain.

'Come on, George, you look pale all of a sudden, let's get you back.'

*

Three months later, George was ready for work. A connection of Milan's found him a job as a lathe operator in a munitions factory; a thirteen-hour day spent under a banner that proclaimed *Our five-year-plan is a great blow to the capitalists*. He needed to work, to repay Milan's kindness, to prove to himself that he was ready to slot back into life and face the world. Milan had shared all his food, his wardrobe, and had been willing to forgo his bed but George preferred to sleep on the floor, a bed was too soft for him. It was a prison habit that was never to leave him. After his first month at work, George received his first pay packet. He almost wept with joy. Even though it was barely enough to feed himself, it was something, a start.

The work was hard, the conditions hot and unpleasant. One didn't dare think at work in case someone saw into your thoughts – the factory workers were outnumbered by a multitude of trade unionists, administrators, foremen and factory policemen. For weeks no one spoke to him – it was unusual for an ex-convict to get a job so quickly after release, so his fellow workers assumed George was in the pay of the AVO, a stooge sent to spy on them. Once, when he turned up late, he faced the army of bureaucrats who took great pains to admonish him for his tardiness. By late morning, a picture of a stone-age man had been plastered up on the work's notice board with George's name under it, and with a speech balloon coming from the caveman's mouth: *Today I helped the Imperialists*. But George didn't mind because it earned him the trust of his workmates. Another time, he donated the entire contents of a monthly paycheck to buying 'Peace Bonds', a voluntary contribution that brought the threat of arrest if one didn't comply.

Each day, after fighting his way home on the perpetually crammed tram system, he returned from work covered in grime, his nose blocked up, his hair plastered with dried sweat.

He returned to an apartment that was akin to a never-ending rush hour, with people he hardly recognised coming and going, queues for the bathroom, squabbles over food, constant noise and unpleasant smells. If this was cooperative living, he'd rather take his chances and live the life of a hermit. At least, prison offered silence, even if it was sometimes crudely interrupted. But George never complained because however bleak it seemed, the AVO receptionist had been right after all – he was a lucky man. When he thought of so many of his prison friends carted off for forced labour, working sixteen hours on empty stomachs for nothing but survival.

One evening when the apartment bustled with so many people it seemed the floor might give way, George decided he couldn't bear it for another minute. He needed a drink. Milan was on night shifts so he went alone. The self-sufficiency he had learned from years of incarceration was proving to be a plus. The first bar he tried was beyond his price – full of high-heeled women in pretty frocks and men with glistening hair and bulging pockets – this was the sort of place for AVOs and their devious associates.

Lowering his sights, George found a smaller, cosier bar in a backstreet behind Rakosi Avenue. Ducking his head under the low door frame as he entered, the heat hit him. A fog of smoke gathered under the low ceiling, a pianist played gently in the corner, glasses clinked as people drank and laughed under the red-tinted lights. At the far end, away from the street, he found a couple of empty tables. Ordering a red wine, he sat back and opened a packet of cigarettes. The smoking habit was new to him and he still felt a bit of a fraud whenever he indulged. The waiter plonked his wine on the table. The tangy taste pricked his tongue as he gulped it down. He wiped his mouth with the back of his hand. He ordered a second and by the time he'd drunk half of it, he already felt a little dizzy.

He remembered the bottle of wine his mother had saved and opened on the day Mark Desci had appeared.

He often found his thoughts wandering back to his parents. They would have been arrested as a direct result of his own downfall – he knew that but every time the thought passed through his mind, he felt a familiar tightening in his stomach. How long did they have before they came for them? His mother must have known. Had she tried to protect her husband? And what happened to her man, the talent scout, the provider of dreams, the deliverer of nightmares? Were they still alive? His father, he knew, couldn't be, but of his mother, he didn't know. How hard it is to live with so many questions. But they were gone and nothing was left of them, not a single hint of their existence. He never had the chance to say goodbye – no forwarding address, no funeral, no headstone. Only the memories and the questions. Too many unanswerable questions.

The pianist had increased his volume, playing jaunty tunes George didn't recognise. The wine had lost its novelty. He took another sip but decided in future, he'd stick to the beer. Rising from the table, he wondered where the toilets were.

Glancing over his left shoulder for the gents, he didn't see the woman approach from the right. The squeal of pain as she stood on his battered foot brought the bar to a halt – the piano stopped mid-song, voices broke off conversations.

'Oh my word, I'm terribly sorry,' she said, her face creased in sympathy. 'Are you all right?'

'I… yes, fine.'

'Did I hurt your foot?'

'No, no, it's just a bit delicate, that's all.'

'Well, if you'll excuse me…'

'Can I buy you a drink?' He'd said it quickly, not thinking about it. He certainly didn't expect her to say yes.

Chapter 18: Eva

Once a month or so on a Thursday night, I meet Agnes for a drink and a chat at the *Lenin Bar*, a small tavern behind Rakosi Avenue. The bar is small, the lighting subdued and the ceilings low. With the tables separated by wooden and glass screens, one can relax and talk in relative privacy. After my divorce from Josef, the few friends I had disappeared from view. Only Agnes remained faithful. We have little to talk about yet the hours pass, Agnes smokes, we drink and whisper our secrets, secrets we've swapped numerous times before. Men look at us but we are rarely disturbed. Two thirty-year-old women, unaccompanied, drinking in public, smoking with abandon is not something any sane man would want to associate with. Agnes is still married. Ferenc is still the denouncer, denouncing neighbours and work colleagues alike. His habitual denouncing has brought them benefits and a degree of protection but, Agnes knows, it is a dangerous game he plays. His marital indiscretions are not quite so numerous or varied, but in his position of seniority, he still attracts the young girls whose ambitions override their reservations about copulating with such a man as Ferenc.

Tonight, the seventh of March, we are still coming to terms with the shock. The whole nation is in shock. No one knows quite how to react. Agnes and I talk of the future and ask ourselves what is to become of us, will it signify the start of a new beginning? It is a conversation being had across the breadth of the country, from the highest echelons of power to the factories and farms. We are all in shock. For two days ago, Comrade Stalin died.

Agnes and I may be the closest of friends but even we know there are limits. We talk of our disbelief and our upset that Stalin is dead, whereas I know that in her heart, as it is in mine, we are leaping with joy. In a moment of rashness, I suggest we go pay homage to the great leader, and visit his statue in the City Park. A fine idea, she says, gulping down her glass of wine. Let's go now. She stubs out her half-smoked cigarette. Even Agnes knows that it's pushing the boundaries of decency too far to be seen, as a woman, smoking in the street.

It's approaching ten o'clock yet the park is abuzz with activity. Half of Budapest seems to have had the same idea. We make our way through the park, joining throngs of people, shoulder-to-shoulder in reverential silence. The evening is cold; no one looks at anyone. Beneath our thick coats and hats and behind our vacant expressions, we are one large anonymous mass, paying respect to the man whose distant voice held sway over us for so long.

Large circles of people stand around the steps of the monument. Some make their leave, pushing back through the crowd silently but politely. Others take their place. Many, those who had come prepared, carry candles. Those at the front place their candles on the steps that lead up to the tribune of the statue. Dotted around, watching us carefully, a number of AVOs with their rigid postures and steely stares.

Agnes and I gaze up at the eight-metre-high bronze effigy which, upon its plinth and the tribune, dominates the night sky. We all know its history – erected in 1951 as a present to the great leader on the occasion of his seventieth birthday from us, the 'grateful Hungarian people', as it's inscribed. How we all hate it – being watched over by this oppressive foreigner. Yet, here we all are, placing candles at his feet. To think he was dead – we thought he'd live forever.

Agnes nudged me in the ribs. 'Come, let's go,' she whispered.

I nod and follow her out of the mass of mourners.

'Didn't expect there to be so many people,' said Agnes, once we were free to talk.

'Rather macabre when you think about it.'

'Well, we were part of it.'

'I'm cold.'

We were walking towards the park exit. Still people were coming through. The atmosphere was quite strange – that of a subdued festival. More AVOs lined the entrance to the park, the street lamps reflecting in their buckles and shiny boots. As we made our way out, I heard my name being called. My heart leapt; the natural guilt reflex. I looked around but saw no one.

'Eva,' came the voice again, a woman's voice. Agnes gripped my wrist, looking straight ahead at the line of AVOs. I followed her gaze and sure enough, an AVO was walking towards me. I stepped back – again a reflex. I couldn't see the face under the peaked hat. But then I saw her eyes – her different-coloured eyes. 'Eva, it's me – Karolina.'

'Karolina?' My word, Karolina.

'Hello, Eva, how are you? Come to pay your respects to our most esteemed leader?'

'Y-yes.' I couldn't believe it was the same Karolina, wearing the blue uniform of the AVO, her hair tied back, sporting a peaked cap.

'How strange to bump into you after all this time. We should meet for coffee.'

'Erm… yes, that'd be nice.' I couldn't think of anything worse.

'Tomorrow, Sunday. That café you used to go to. Is it still there? Ten o'clock?'

'So soon? Well, yes. Why not? Ten o'clock.'

'Excellent. See you tomorrow.' With that, she spun on her heel and rejoined her colleagues.

I could tell that Agnes was suppressing the urge to laugh. '"So soon?" You didn't expect that, did you?'

'No.'

'Why did you say yes? You didn't have to.'

'I don't know. She caught me off-guard. Anyway, perhaps she has something to tell me.'

*

And so I was back at the Café of the Revolution. I don't come so often now, only very occasionally. I sat down at a table to the side of the counter. The window seats seemed too exposed. Karolina hadn't shown up yet but I was almost fifteen minutes early. I wanted a few minutes to myself, perhaps to compose myself. I didn't order anything – I said I was waiting on a friend. The café is much the same as it was four years ago. The only thing to have changed is the staff – gone is the old hag and her young assistant with her flushed cheeks and plucked eyebrows, instead two middle-aged women serve behind the counter. One slim, one plump. I prefer to be served by the plump one; the slimmer one always has dirty fingernails. The portraits of Stalin and Rakosi are still there, as is the Alpine scene. A radio, barely audible, plays a collection of brass band music. I think of Karolina as I saw her in her shiny AVO uniform, so different from the Karolina who came to see me in this café four years ago. I'm dying to know how she became an AVO, one of *them*. But it's the memory of her being arrested, or perhaps just being taken away, that is implanted most firmly in my memory. The look on her face – a mixture of anger and fear. Although I am thinking of her, I still jump a little when, suddenly, she appears in front of me.

'Have you not ordered?' she asks. 'Here, let me.' She approaches the counter and speaks to the slimmer one. She's not wearing her uniform, but a jacket and skirt, drab in colour. Her hair is loose, stray strands held in place by hair grips.

So, with our coffee and a slice of cake each, she asks about my job and my life as a teacher, she asks about where I live, and what I do. She tries to ask as subtly as she can whether there's a new man in my life. Instead, for some reason, I find myself talking about Ferenc.

'You may be wondering,' she says, 'how I came to be working for the AVO.'

'The question did cross my mind.'

'Well, they arrested me – as you know. And I'll admit, Eva, I've never been so scared. I told them everything they wanted to know, and then some more. I sold poor Vida up the river in order to save my own skin. I wasn't proud of myself but what could I do? They asked me to become an informer. I did. They were impressed. And one day they offered me a job. So I took it. That's it.'

'As easy as that.'

'As easy as that. This cake is awfully dry.'

'So, what's it like – working for them?'

'It's changed my life – made me into a stronger person. It's given me a purpose.'

'And Vida?'

'Ah, poor Vida. Perhaps if we had children, I might have tried harder. So I survived and Vida was defeated.'

'Poor Vida.'

'That's what I said.'

'I thought you might have turned on me – for not being able to help you.'

'No. I knew I'd put you in an impossible situation. And I'm sorry about that. Anyway, I've got something to tell you; I thought you'd be interested to know. Do you mind if I smoke?' She rummaged in her handbag, pulling out a lipstick, a compact…

'Karolina?'

'Yes?' She lit her cigarette.

'You're about to tell me something?'

'Yes, I'm sorry. Vida is in prison. He got ten years. As did Josef.'

I gasped. 'Josef is in prison?' I asked, leaning towards her.

She nodded. Turning on her chair, she gazed around at our fellow customers. 'Ten years also.'

'Oh.' I poked at the remains of my cake with the dessert fork. This, at least, was new – they never used to supply dessert folks. We used to have to use our fingers and afterwards wipe them on a napkin. Ten years. A flood of questions crowded my mind. Yet I couldn't speak.

Finally, Karolina broke the silence. 'Do you want to go see him?'

'I can go see him?'

She stubbed out her cigarette, grinding it into the ashtray. 'I can arrange it.'

'Oh dear. I'm not sure I could face it.'

'Perhaps not. But you should, Eva. You have to go.'

*

And so, three weeks later, I sat waiting in a large, dingy room full of tables with a chair on either side of each, stone floor, no windows, just the single light bulb, and a faint unpleasant smell akin to dirty socks. Yet despite all the tables and chairs, there were only four of us waiting – all women, one with a child, a young girl. Watching over us, four prison guards, each with a revolver in a holster, and one with a rifle slung over his shoulder. We all waited in silence. Even the little girl, clutching onto a rag doll, sitting on her mother's lap, had been awed into silence. There were two iron-clad doors leading into the room, the one we came through, behind us, and one in front. It was on this door we all focussed, waiting for it to swing open. My stomach groaned; I hadn't eaten breakfast; my nerves had suppressed my appetite. I had Karolina to thank for this. But gratitude was far from my mind. I'd brought a little present. Karolina had suggested it; said it would be OK to bring one item. After some thought, I settled on a jar of honey. Josef always liked honey. I'd wrapped it in a brown paper bag, tying it together with string. Colourful paper, Karolina told me, was not permitted. A reception guard had inspected it, a woman with a huge bust and hefty shoulders holding it up to the light, opening it, sniffing it. Deeming it acceptable, she screwed the lid firmly shut but confiscated the string. I wrapped it back into the paper, screwing it at the top. My mind went back four years; to the day Josef left my life to start anew with the 'colleague from work'. How my efforts to renew our marriage had failed at the first hurdle. I never saw him again. One day, on returning from work, I found he had been and taken the rest of his possessions – his clothes, a few books and a bust of Lenin. That was about it. He'd left a note – a single sheet of paper anchored down by an empty vase. Just two words – *I'm sorry*. And that was it. It was a Friday and for the next two days, without school to distract me, I sat in the apartment and festered, reliving our time together. Of course, I knew what had caused our marriage to fall apart. I glanced at the little girl, sitting quietly on her mother's lap, twisting the doll's plaits around her finger. The woman caught my eye. 'How old is she?' I whispered. 'Four,' she mouthed. One of the guards cleared his throat. Four years old. The same age. In the autumn of forty-nine, five months after Josef had disappeared out of my life, I received the notification of divorce. My consensus was not necessary, my signature not required. Josef had merely to fill out the necessary paperwork, sign it himself, ask the registration bureau to notify me and that was it. And so there it was – in black and white. Stark and soulless. The end of a marriage. What puzzled me though was the date stamped on the divorce certificate – 1st October 1946. It was 1949 – why had they put the wrong year? I missed him. I'd got used to living without him very quickly but I still missed him awfully. I felt sometimes as if my memory was full of the missing – Josef, Valentin and of course Anastasia. I often wonder too what happened to Tibor. He'd be nineteen by now. A man in his own right. I wondered what sort of life he was leading now; whether the state had forgiven his adolescent *faux pas*. I hoped so. I think once I may have prayed for him. And now, sitting in this dank room, four years on, clutching my jar of honey, I was about to meet my former husband. A foreboding prospect. I tried to plan what I wanted to say but my nerves prohibited any semblance of rational thought. The silence of the room was oppressive. I tried to control my breathing. My palms, I realised, were damp. The little girl whispered something to her mother but was cut short by a shush.

The door in front of us opened. Into the gloom, stepped one then another guard, anonymous beneath their uniforms. Then a short parade of ambling men, stooped, diminished beings, handcuffed, all in grey, jacket and trousers, like pyjamas but coarser. Glancing at each of them, it took a few seconds to discern which one was Josef. He stood at the end of the table, stock still, looking down at me. I tried to stand but my legs, sapped of energy, prevented me.

'Sit,' barked one of the guards at him.

He did so. 'Hello, Eva.'

His voice. It sounded different. Deeper. Slower. 'Josef.'

A guard spoke. 'OK, you have five minutes,' he announced. 'Guests may offer their packages now. No touching. No standing. No smoking and certainly no fornication.' His colleagues guffawed at his little joke.

'I… I brought you a little something. Here.' I pushed the package across the table. I realised my hand was trembling slightly.

'That's very kind of you. What is it?'

'Open it.'

I watched him as he opened up the paper and pulled out the jar with its golden contents. His skin, how grey it was, the same grey as his jacket. His hair had lost its colour too. How pronounced his Adam's apple, dotted with grey stubble, how thin his fingers.

'Honey. That's lovely. I haven't had honey for years. I can't open it though, the lid's too stiff.'

'Here, let me.' He passed it back. I couldn't do it either. The reception guard had screwed it too tight. 'I'll try again in a minute,' I said, placing it to one side and patting the lid.

'It's wonderful to see you again, Eva.'

'And you, Josef. How are things? Or is that too difficult a question?'

'I'm fine, actually. I'm past the worst. They do say that – once you've survived the initial arrest and interrogations and the first few weeks inside, then it gets easier. You just have to keep a low profile. I'm good at that. I've been here three years so I'm already almost a third through. And what about you, Eva? Tell me all about yourself.'

'There's not much to say, really.' But I tried. Speaking almost in a whisper, I told him about my life without him, about my job, how we survived, the shock from Stalin's death, the uncertainty of the future post-Stalin.

'Two minutes,' said a guard.

'Already? Josef, I have to ask you this… what happened to the woman, the other woman?'

He chortled, shaking his head. I felt a knot of tension tighten within my stomach. 'Oh, Eva. There was never another woman.'

'What? I… I don't understand. I…' I felt a prick of tears in my eyes. 'Oh, Josef, I never knew.'

He nodded, almost imperceptibly, a wry smile. 'I had to.'

'You did it to protect me.'

'Yes.'

'You did it for me.'

Leaning forward, he spoke. 'I knew my time had come; that I'd be arrested any minute. You would have been arrested too, of course. I survived longer than I thought. A whole year. By the time they came for me, I was able to say, "I have no wife. We divorced many years ago."'

'Many years? The certificate – the date said nineteen forty-six.'

'Did it? Excellent. He was good to his word.'

'You got them to change the date?'

'It cost a little. The longer we were divorced the safer you were.'

We stared at each other. How we assume. How I believed his story about the other woman. And yet… And yet.

'Thank you, Josef.'

He smiled.

I asked, 'Do you ever think of Anastasia?'

'Not now, Eva; not now, eh?'

I had to swallow my disappointment. I wanted to ask him why; why not now when the shrill voice of the guard declared, 'Time's up.'

'Will you come again? Next year?'

'Prisoners to their feet.'

'Next year?'

'I'm Class A,' he said, collecting his crutch. 'It's all I'm allowed. One five-minute visit a year.'

'On your feet – now.'

'Oh, Josef.'

'It was good of you to come.'

'Silence. Talking is now prohibited.'

'To next year then.'

He smiled. A guard, a more junior one, poked him in the back. He turned around and faced the wall behind him.

'Josef, your honey.'

He didn't turn around. The guard held out his hand. I passed him the jar. 'Can you open it?' I said. 'The lid – it's too stiff for me.'

The guard raised an eyebrow, perhaps surprised at my affront, although certainly less surprised than I was myself. I smiled weakly. He twisted and realising it was more difficult than expected, looked at me, then tried again, putting in an almighty effort while pretending he wasn't. And off it came. A small smile of satisfaction flashed across his lips as he passed the jar to Josef. Josef nodded his thanks.

'Right,' said the guard in charge. 'If we're all ready?'

And with that, I watched my ex-husband be marched out of the door.

*

Anastasia. Josef's bravery in divorcing me had been tempered by his refusal to discuss her. Now I would have to wait another year. She would be a month short of her fourth birthday now. I can't imagine a time when I won't know exactly her age. The pitiful sixteen days diminish with each passing day as it recedes further into the past. Every morning, I awake and her face is there, smiling down at me. I experience a few moments of joy before the reality of the day reasserts itself. Each morning I die. In my dreams, I have lived her whole life for her, a life that stretches ahead through the years, the distant decades to come. And it's a life full of joy, full of love; a life that transcends my own in its beauty. It is a life destined by God, His guiding hand leads her through, showing her the strength of her love, the way it radiates on everything around her. See how it touches all those she meets, how they leave her with a smile on their faces, a lighter beat in their dismal hearts.

And through the years of her long, happy existence, I am never far away; for it is I she loves the most, the first point on her compass. And as each night passes, it is I who becomes dependent on her. She needs me less and less but she never leaves me, never ventures too far away, keeping her presence near, her reassuring attendance. And then she is a baby once more. And it is at night she calls me Mama, it is at night she suckles, it is at night I smell her hair, that fresh odour, so indescribably beautiful that I want to bottle it and die with it filling my nostrils, filling my every sense, my whole being.

I still visit her plot in the cemetery and the wooden cross battered by the elements, her name all but invisible now. Oh, my pretty little Anastasia, how I still miss you. I always shall.

Each morning I die.

*

Tonight, three weeks after seeing Josef, I am going out again for a drink with Agnes. It is still early evening when we meet and make our way to the *Lenin Bar*. Tonight, a pianist is playing, which means Agnes and I can sit at our table protected by the screen and talk quietly without fear of being overheard. The pianist launches into a series of Hungarian folk tunes as we clink our glasses.

I told her about my meeting with Josef, about his efforts to protect me, about the prison and the guards. 'I'm having to reassess my relationship with Josef, my ex-husband. The problem is I've grown so accustomed to not being in love with him, it's difficult to feel different.'

'It may come – with time.'

'Oh, Agnes, I don't know what to think. I still feel as if my heart belongs to another man.'

'Your gorgeous Russian?'

I laughed. 'Yes. My brief time with him was like an island of joy in a sea of grief. I still think of him. I wonder what he's doing now, whether he still plays football; if he's married and has children, whether he thinks of me as I think of him.'

For months I yearned for him, his touch, his smell. I think back to those dreadful days so soon after Anastasia and remember fondly our walks in the park, our coffees in the Café of the Revolution, and our last afternoon together in the Hotel Astoria. I remember the football match, and Valentin's wonderful goal, dedicated to me. How important the result seemed – to me, who'd never been to a football game before nor since. It finished one-one when the home team scored through a late penalty. And the poor chap who scored the goal and then fainted, so happy to have equalised. I think back to the café and remember too the man with the walrus moustache. I never did find out his name. I wonder whether he is still alive, telling his life story I got to know so well to other unsuspecting strangers.

'Eva – are you all right?'

'I'm sorry, I was miles away. So, how's Ferenc?'

'Well… oh…'

'What's the matter?'

'I'll be damned, I know that woman,' said Agnes.

I turned and followed her gaze. A woman in purple caught Agnes's eye and the two of them waved at each other. 'I'd better go say hello,' said Agnes, leaning towards me. 'She's a colleague of Ferenc's. Will you be all right on your own for a minute or two?'

'Yes, go ahead, I'll be fine.'

I sipped my wine. I needed the loo and caught Agnes's eye and mouthed, *back in a minute.* As I crossed the bar the sight of the barman spinning a bottle in the air and catching it diverted my attention. As a result, I walked straight into someone and didn't realise I'd stepped on his foot until the shriek of pain and the sudden silencing of music and voices.

'Oh my word, I'm terribly sorry,' I said. 'Are you all right?'

'I… yes, fine.' What large brown eyes he had, and such a long, thin face. But somehow he seemed younger than he looked.

Conversations and music resumed. 'Did I hurt your foot?'

'No, no, it's just a bit delicate, that's all.'

'Well, if you'll excuse me…'

'Can I buy you a drink?' he said it quickly and then flashed an embarrassed smile.

His clothes looked too big for him, his hands disappearing up the sleeves of his jacket. I suppose, looking back, I said yes out of pity. 'Well, I did stamp on your foot,' I said. 'So really I should be buying you a drink but yes, a red wine would be nice, thank you.'

He waved at me as I returned from the bathroom. My wine sat on his table for me. His name, he said, was George, and he worked as a lathe operator in a munitions factory. The pianist had taken a break and the sound of muffled voices and the clink of glasses surrounded us. Agnes was still with her friend in purple so reluctantly I stayed and we talked in automated tones of Rakosi's industrialisation, of teaching and the state of schools, both of us skirting around anything that could be construed as controversial. It was a typical, insubstantial conversation and I was thinking how to politely extricate myself, when he said, 'I used to be a football player.'

'Really?' I asked. 'Were you any good?'

He smiled ruefully. 'I think so. I used to score the odd goal.'

'I once knew a footballer.'

'Local?'

'No, Russian.'

'I miss it. Life seems so mundane now. Sebes Gusztav came to see me play once. At least, I was told he'd be there.'

'You never spoke to him?'

'No. Never had the chance.'

'You don't play any more?'

'No, I broke my foot.' He nodded towards his crutch, propped up against the table.

'Oh dear, that's not the foot I stepped on, is it?' He raised his eyebrows in mocked pain. 'My word, I'm sorry. How sad. When did it happen?'

'Four years ago.'

I thought it strange he still had to have a crutch after four years but thought it tactless to pursue it. Instead, I said, 'I went to a football match about four years ago.'

'To see your Russian friend play?'

'Yes, that's right. He scored a goal. It was one of the happiest days of my life.'

He laughed. 'Football can do that. Would you like another drink?'

I glanced back at the table and Agnes was now sitting there, probably wondering where I'd got to. 'Thank you but I'd better get back to my friend.'

'Oh, OK,' he said, not hiding his disappointment. 'Well, it was nice meeting you.'

The pianist had resumed his playing. Returning to our table, Agnes pretended to be shocked that I could so brazenly accept a drink from a strange man. 'Tell me next time and I'll come with you,' she said, indignantly.

'What – as my chaperone or my nosy companion?'

'Oh, listen to you, such ingratitude. No doubt, he tried to get you drunk.'

'Don't be silly. In fact, he was rather nice. A bit lonely, I think. He used to be a footballer.'

'Well, watch out, here he comes again.'

Sure enough, the man approached with his crutch, looking rather sheepish. 'I'm really sorry to interrupt…'

'It's OK.' I introduced him to Agnes, who smiled a toothy grin at him.

'Did you say four years ago – a Russian?'

The look of intensity on his face sobered me in an instant. 'Yes, what of it?'

He slid into a chair without asking and glanced round his shoulder. 'I have to ask,' he said, his voice almost drowned out by the piano. 'His name – was it Ivanov? Valentin Ivanov?'

Chapter 19: Valentin

Valentin Ivanov had never cried so openly. He wandered down Moscow's Gorky Street in a haze. All around him, people looked shocked, many had tears in their eyes. Strangers embraced and consoled each other. Soviet flags hung everywhere at half-mast, loudspeakers played Chopin's *Funeral March* repeatedly. Trams and cars drove slowly as if embarrassed to be still going about their business on such a day as this. The whole world seemed to be in mourning. The unthinkable had happened and now life would never be the same again. What would become of them; what did the future hold? But it was too big a question, too daunting a prospect and not one to be dealt with today, or for the foreseeable future, not while the shock still pained their souls, not while the grief seeped from every pore. Valentin knew he would remember this day forever more. 5th of March 1953 – the day Comrade Stalin died.

The day seemed to highlight the other disappointments in his life – the day his mother died, the day he left love behind in Budapest, the day he knew his footballing days were over.

Years of existence, punctuated by these days of disappointment. And now this. For thirty years Josef Stalin had been their guiding light; for thirty years their father and saviour. And now he was gone. It was inconceivable. The man who'd been at Lenin's side at the forefront of the revolution; who'd succeeded the Soviet Union's founding father; the man who'd fought so hard to rid the country of enemies; who'd exposed sabotage and counter-revolutionaries at every turn as he sought to protect socialism; the man who'd guided the nation to victory against the Nazis, who'd out-thought and outmanoeuvred Hitler; who'd brought harmony to the Soviet Union. Yes, people had suffered, families torn apart, but no one said revolution was easy when there were so many with evil intentions and selfish motivations. You can't make an omelette without breaking eggs. Everything the country now stood for was down to the one man. And now that man was dead. No wonder people cried, no wonder they looked at the future with uncertainty. Life without Stalin was unimaginable.

Valentin was a soldier now, a sergeant in the Red Army and he wore his uniform with pride, but never with such pride as on this day. As a young lad, he'd managed to avoid national service by virtue of playing for one of Moscow's premier football teams. He'd been the envy of his friends but his moment of glory was short-lived. The game in Budapest, four years ago, had, in effect, been his swansong. On their return to Moscow, he was reprimanded for missing too many training sessions whilst in Hungary, for too often turning up late. When they demanded an explanation, he wouldn't tell them. He couldn't tell them it was because he preferred to be walking in the park with Eva; he didn't want Eva's name written in their grubby files. Then, soon after that, a youngster, a 'name for the future', had risen through the ranks and was waiting for his turn to play in the first team. His chance came at Valentin's expense. Valentin remembered too well watching the team play, wanting them to win out of a lifetime's loyalty while desperately wanting to see the usurper fail. But game after game the team won and the usurper played better each time until even Valentin had to stand back and admire his pernicious talent. The end wasn't long in coming. Called in for a quiet word – greeted by sympathetic voices and heartfelt gratitude for three years of service, and then 'goodbye'.

The barren years, as he liked to call them, followed. Years of mundane jobs disguised as doing one's duty as a proletariat that sapped his energy. Feverish attempts and applications for a transfer to Hungary were rejected out of hand. He could provide no reason or justification for such a move. Finally, he gave up, as he knew he would do all along.

Then, the previous year, in a moment of patriotic ardour, he volunteered. No conscript was he, but a volunteer. There was kudos in that, and when added to his illustrious past as a footballer, it resulted in a fast promotion to the rank of sergeant. He was liked, his companionship sought, his opinion respected. Unlike the *dukhs*, the young conscripts, Valentin never suffered the bullying, the habitual violence meted out by the longer-serving boys while the officers too readily turned a blind eye. He was never forced to clean toilets with a toothbrush, or made to spend hours cleaning one pair of boots. Officers and recruits furnished him with books, writing paper, cigarettes and respect.

He'd joined with a grin on his face, happy that he'd made the commitment and given himself some direction in life. They shaved his hair and gave him his uniform, trained and drilled him, and finally accepted his oath of loyalty to the People's Army, promising to serve their beloved leader and the motherland with honour and dignity, prepared, if necessary, to forfeit his life for the greater good. He spent his spare time in the barracks' Lenin Room, reading his history, learning military science and polishing up his political theory. The officers appreciated the good example he set to the younger boys, and verbally patted him on the back. He purposely kept his distance, refusing to join cliques, maintaining a jovial comradeship with all but aligned to none.

By chance, his regiment had been ordered into Moscow a month before Stalin's death. Amongst their duties was guarding visitors through Lenin's Mausoleum, the most sought-after and easiest of duties, guiding the daily streams of visitors past Lenin's waxwork-like figure, ensuring no one stopped or tried to take photographs. The day of the fifth of March was a rare day's leave. Never did he think he'd spend all of it in tears, his ears devoid of all sound but Chopin's *Funeral March*.

Often, during his idle moments, he would think of his days in Budapest. It felt like another lifetime, a memory that by right belonged to someone else. He'd had many affairs during his time as a footballer; the players attracted women, and his affair with Eva was amongst the most short-lived. They'd only made love the one time, the rest consisted of coffee in the café and genteel strolls in the park. But it was Eva with her beautiful bronze-coloured hair, and Eva alone, who'd stolen his heart, and she alone who remained indelibly fixed in his memory. There'd been a sadness about her, a part of her life stained by some event too raw to mention, too real for words. But he'd never been tempted to ask. Her past belonged to her and he had no wish to interfere; he didn't want to associate her with any catastrophe he had no control over, just as he knew that he could never exist in her future, nor her in his. Theirs was a time spent in the present for each other. That present now survived in the past but the smell, the touch of it still belonged in his memory as a living thing. He found himself capable of reliving their conversations, their sideway glances, the gentle brushing of hands. He remembered too the old man thrown out of the café, the two waitresses, the boy and his football in the park, the little details, the small components that made up the whole.

He remembered vividly the goal he scored, the goalkeeper who should have saved but fumbled. He wasn't a player who scored often but that was his most prized goal because she'd been there to witness it. It was also quite the strangest game he played in, something had upset the Hungarian players, something he could never pinpoint, culminating in their goalscorer's fainting fit following his penalty goal (the most doubtful of penalties he'd ever witnessed). The boy looked like death, fear written all over his face, as if scoring that goal was the biggest mistake of his life. Strange game, football.

He wished he could relive those times for real, to touch her, to smell her breath; to relive that final afternoon in the hotel room, her nakedness, her desire. He'd call it love but love seemed too big a word for so short a time. But, he knew, in his heart, there was no other way to describe it.

But for now, he was a soldier in Stalin's army and Stalin was dead. It was impossible to comprehend that a man who'd been such a huge part of everyone's life, should now be gone. Impossible and frightful. The world would never be the same again. And at that moment, on the afternoon of 5th March 1953, the future looked bleak.

Very bleak.

Part Three

**Three years later:
October 1956**

Chapter 20
Day One – Tuesday, 23 October

1.

The morning was warm, a hint of autumnal sunshine. Wandering down Andrassy Avenue in Budapest, I wondered why there were so many crowds congregating everywhere. A car roared down the street beeping its horn. People waved at it, shouting and cheering. There was excitement in the air. People ran past me, shouting, laughing. Something was happening. I joined a small group of workers dressed in dungarees jostling around a tree. What were they looking at? It was a piece of paper with writing, a poster. Looking around, I saw similar groups gathered around other trees and lamp posts and shop fronts. The sheet of paper seemed to be everywhere, causing much elation.

'What is it?' I asked a man sporting a trilby with a flower incongruously peeking out of the ribbon.

'Demands.'

'Demands?'

He laughed. 'The students – they've printed up a list of political demands, sixteen of them.'

I gasped. I tried to squeeze through. 'What does it say?'

As if to answer my question, someone at the front began reading them out: 'We, the honest and law-abiding citizens of Hungary demand a new government constituted under the direction of Comrade Imre Nagy, and that all criminal leaders of the Stalin-Rakosi era be immediately relieved of their duties.' The gathering cheered. 'We demand that general elections, by universal and secret ballot, be held throughout the country to elect a new National Assembly, with all political parties participating…'

I staggered back. It didn't seem possible. We did as we were told; we didn't make demands. More people were pouring into the street, smiling faces, walking with a new-found purpose. Words filtered through – revolution, uprising, reform. It didn't seem possible. I expected to see AVOs restoring order, putting an end to these frightening words. But there were no AVOs. I had to get home; I had to tell George and Milan. They were due to go to work at eleven; they'd still be in bed. But they wouldn't want to miss this. The thought made me laugh aloud – they'd never forgive me if I allowed them to sleep through a revolution.

It was as I was scurrying home that I saw it for the first time. The sight of it made me stop in my tracks, leaving me open-mouthed with shock and no small amount of admiration – a boy, no more than thirteen, was leading a group of excitable men and women. He was holding a flagpole bearing a large Hungarian flag – but the Soviet emblem that adorned the tricolour had been removed, leaving a large gaping hole at its centre.

2.

Zoltan Beke was less enthusiastic about the turn of events. It was now dark; the time approaching nine o'clock in the evening. An hour earlier, he'd been dispatched as part of a detachment of about two hundred AVO men and women to the Radio Building. At first, he'd been comforted to see so many of them armed with Kalashnikovs and that, dotted among them, were a few AVO machine-gunners. But not now. Now, they seemed hopelessly outnumbered against the sea of angry faces filling the cobbled square in front of them; a huge mob baying for the right to broadcast from the Radio Building. He'd never felt so frightened. The noise, the stamping of boots, the jeering. Even with his rifle trained on the crowd, he knew that if they charged, he and his colleagues didn't stand a chance; his detachment would soon be overrun.

The rebels had marched from the Parliament Building where Ernest Gero had addressed them, told them to go home, and referred to them in unflattering terms that only managed to make things worse. When someone lit the Soviet electric red star adorning the building, the crowd booed and hissed until it was turned off again. Nagy addressed them too, the man they wanted as leader, but even that had done nothing to diffuse matters. This lot had gotten their blood up and if someone didn't take control soon, things would only get awkward. The hum of hatred filled his ears. Zoltan felt a little reassured that, parked in nearby streets, were lorry-loads of soldiers waiting to go in. But would it be enough?

The demonstrators nearest them began shouting at them. 'Are you going to fire on your own people?… You should be ashamed of yourselves.'

A lanky AVO boy, pale as mist, whom Zoltan knew vaguely as Paul, began muttering next to him. 'Shut the hell up,' snapped Zoltan; the boy was making him feel worse.

'We've had it,' said Paul. 'They're going to kill us. There's millions of them.'

The crowd drew menacingly nearer, edging forward, pushed in from the sides; the taunts becoming progressively louder, more aggressive. 'Traitors… Death to the AVO!'

'Oh, mother, what are we going to do?' The boy's rifle was trembling, the whites of his eyes looming in the dark.

At that moment, one of the AVO gunners let rip a round of machine-gun fire into the sky. The mob immediately backed away but their jeers only increased in intensity. Windows clattered open above him and the hiss of tear gas descended onto the crowd. Huge holes suddenly appeared before him as the canisters fell amongst the crowd and bounced on the cobbles. Immediately, the air stank of the sharp smell of gas, stinging eyes and catching in the back of throats. Amongst the screams, shots rang out. The boy next to him followed the example and fired three shots into the dense mass. Zoltan couldn't tell whether he'd hit anyone as people fell over themselves to avoid the gas and gunfire. A gap would appear, only for others to stumble in and fill it again.

His eyes stung as the gas drifted across the street. He pressed his finger against the trigger, wanting to fire, but couldn't bring himself to shoot randomly into the groping mass that now surrounded him. He had to escape; his life depended on it. He forced his way back, knowing that the gas and dark were providing enough of a distraction for him to break out. Where had all the AVOs gone? Tears streamed down his face as he fought for space, tripping over a body writhing on the cobbled ground.

He found himself in a side street with high buildings on either side, lit by dingy street lamps. The sound of gunfire echoed from the Radio Building square, wisps of gas had floated across. He'd lost his rifle and cap but had no idea how. People ran in all directions, some, like him, clasping handkerchiefs to their eyes. Coming to a junction, he could see a line of army trucks parked along the wider boulevard. A moment's relief was soon shattered – the soldiers were freely handing their guns to the rebels. The bastards, he thought.

'AVO!' someone shouted. Zoltan almost fainted. He turned and people had stopped in the street, staring at him. *This is it*, he thought, *my time has come*. 'AVO.' His very own mob began to close in as the tears from the gas smarted his eyes. But then a siren pierced the air, screeching above the sounds of chaos – an ambulance trying to get down the boulevard, heading towards the Radio Building. Only yards away, it was enough to distract his tormentors. 'Let us get through.' The driver was leaning out of the window, yelling at the mass blocking his way, slamming his hand rhythmically against the ambulance door. The ambulance lurched forward and then braked. One of the back doors swung open and shut, and a gun fell out onto the road. Zoltan's mob were the first to see it.

'Hey, wait,' shouted one of them.

Zoltan edged away as they darted towards the now stationary ambulance, swinging open the backdoors. 'It's full of weapons. Look at all this!'

'They're AVO.'

The driver and his mate scrambled out but too slow; the mob pounced on them and they disappeared under a shower of blows. Zoltan could still hear their screams as he sprinted back down the narrow side street, unsure of where he was going but relieved to escape the brighter lights of the boulevard.

Amidst screams, shots and sirens, Zoltan ran.

And ran.

3.

Meanwhile, three miles away in City Park, George was enjoying the spectacle. It was ten o'clock and the excitement of this momentous day showed no signs of letting up. Eva had wanted to go home, complaining of a headache, and Milan volunteered to take her back and rejoin George later. Hundreds milled around, chatting incessantly. Comrade Stalin's statue loomed high in the night sky, his brooding presence surveying the city, a constant reminder of their servility. A group of youngsters had climbed onto the plinth and flung ropes around Stalin's neck. But however hard they pulled, the statue remained stubbornly in place. Stalin wasn't prepared to be toppled. Suddenly, the rope snapped and the huddle of boys fell laughing into a heap. George and his fellow onlookers clapped. Amongst the spectators, stood a group of local soldiers, the Soviet five-pointed stars ripped from their caps. One of them stepped forward and shouted, 'You'll never pull it down; you'll need proper cutting gear.'

George had never seen such entertainment, never felt such a sense of freedom. One thousand, three hundred and seventy days, followed by three years of mundane jobs in filthy factories. However hard they worked, it was never enough. If they, the workers, exceeded the quota, then the quota was upped and still they were expected to exceed it. The award for greater output was the demand for even more. Wages continued to rise but at only a fraction of the spiralling costs of food and basic amenities. Such bleak times.

He remained friends with his old team-mate, Milan; the two of them speaking for hours on their favourite subject – football. George had never mentioned the talent scout – there was little point. And over the years, he'd come to doubt Mark Decsi's legitimacy, believing that it had all been a ruse to impress his mother. He'd persuaded himself now that his talent would never have been good enough to interest Gusztav, the national manager, not because he truly doubted his talent but because he couldn't bear to think of the things he'd missed out on. In 1952, the Hungarian football team won Olympic gold in Helsinki; and then, in '53, doing what no team had done before – beating England at Wembley, Puskas inspiring the team to a historic 6-3 victory. And then, in '54, they played the World Cup only to be beaten in the final by the West Germans (although rumours persisted that the government had 'sold' the game to the Germans for hard currency).

What could have been in a life of could-have-been's. But amongst it all, he had found perhaps not love but certainly companionship. Eva had been there – back in '49 at his final game, his final performance. Like so many Hungarians, they shared a history of disappointment. But it was their shared experience of a football match that had brought them together following his release from prison. After that first meeting, they agreed to meet, to share a drink and talk football and the what-could-have-been's. But when he asked if they could meet again, she said no.

A year later, she was back, a small suitcase in hand. She'd lost her apartment – requisitioned.

Their relationship was based on mutual need. Him with his dodgy leg; her with her dodgy past. But they were never *that* close, however much George would have wished it otherwise.

Someone had driven a van into the park and, with the help of others, unloaded bottles of gas. Now, they were busy with the blowtorches, working away on Stalin's knees, just above his jackboots, the intensity of fire illuminating their faces. Minutes later, satisfied they had sufficiently weakened the bronze, they flung the ropes around the legs and neck, and, with the van, pulled. More people came to help, a whole team pulling on the rope in a tug-of-war contest; the Hungarian youth versus Stalin. George joined in the cheering and laughed at the catcalls, *Bring the old bastard down; we'll give you the People's Democracy*. Bit by bit, Stalin's resistance weakened, His legs slowly giving way. Then, with an enormous groan, He lunged forward and tottered. He was coming down! The tug-of-war team scattered in different directions, whooping with delight. And then *He* fell, the bronze figure crashing to the ground to thunderous applause. Then they set about Him, smashing the metal to pieces with sledgehammers from the van, pieces of bronze ricocheting across the path, picked up by onlookers as souvenirs.

Three and a half years after his death, Comrade Stalin had finally fallen.

Chapter 21
Day Two – Wednesday, 24 October

1.

The noise started as a low rumble, slowly pushing its way into my subconscious. As it became louder, I awoke and wondered what on earth it could be. It seemed to be getting nearer and nearer and suddenly from my drowsy state, I was wide awake. It was still dark. Despite the now-monstrous roar, George and Milan were still asleep; George, as usual, on the bedroom floor. I rushed to the window and swept aside the curtain. Dawn was beginning to rise. But the sight that hit me sent a shiver down my spine. 'George, Milan, wake up.' After some prodding, they too were alert and staring with disbelief down onto the street.

'The bastards,' said Milan.

'T-54s,' observed George, matter-of-factly. Snaking its way along the narrow avenue was a long procession of Russian tanks with the hammer and sickle painted on the sides, dozens of tanks, rolling boldly past our apartment and towards the city centre.

'How dare they?' I asked, as if their presence was a personal affront.

'What time is it?'

'Four thirty.'

'Put the radio on.'

The announcer's grave voice talked of counter-revolutionaries attacking public buildings. Milan turned the radio off incensed. 'How dare they call us *counter-revolutionaries*,' he said, indignantly.

2.

An hour later, I was alone. George and Milan had dressed and shaved (both wanting to appear smart for the revolution, as they called it), and had had breakfast. I had the place to myself, which in itself, was a rarity. I picked up the fragment of bronze that George had so proudly brought home last night – a piece of Stalin's tunic, he'd said. How heavy it was, this small piece of metal, and how bright it shone.

The sight of the Russian tanks made me think of Valentin so many miles away in Moscow. I pulled out Milan's old copy of Stalin's *Collected Works, Volume One* – old but still in pristine condition. He'd bought it so that it'd look good if the AVO ever came to him. Not that they had for many years, so he told me. And there, hiding beneath the back flap was Valentin's blank postcard. On the front, a picture of a parade of Red Army soldiers, marching erect, their heads facing left, acknowledging a podium of dignitaries, perhaps even Stalin himself; and the back addressed to Mr *and* Mrs Horvath – but no message. But I knew, of course. Valentin had joined the army and, what's more, he still thought of me. He still thought of me. I lived in a bubble of joy for weeks after that. It was as if he'd sent me a ten-page letter. But my thoughts, these days, are more with Josef. I realised now that my infatuation with Valentin was no more than that – an infatuation in the midst of such difficult times. Josef had just left me, supposedly for another woman, and Valentin provided a distraction in the grey world I inhabited then. I visit Josef once a year – every March. Five minutes. Each time, he sounds a little more cheerful but still he dismisses me whenever I try to broach the subject of our daughter. And each time I come away more frustrated. It's left me questioning why it is so important to me that not once, not once, has he mentioned the fact that for sixteen days he and I had a daughter. I need to know why.

I lived now with George and Milan in Milan's rather chaotic flat, although, from what he says, it's certainly less crowded than before when, as a ruse, he hinted to his housemates that he was an informer. Three years ago, I was obliged to move out of the apartment I had shared with Josef – it was needed for a new star of the party and his wife. I stayed with Agnes and Ferenc for a few months until Ferenc got bored of having me around. I took the hint and sought out George, almost a year after our meeting in the bar. They made a strange pair. George with his kind heart acts as a foil for the brash Milan. I sometimes worry that George likes me a little too much. But he respectfully keeps his distance – he knows I am waiting for my husband to return. For return, he will one day.

'Eva, turn on the radio quickly.' George was already returning, rushing into the still-deserted apartment. 'Quickly, there's going to be an announcement.' He stopped to catch his breath, then added, 'There's already been some fighting with the tanks, some Ruskies killed, and still disturbances going on round the Radio Building. Quickly, Eva, the radio.'

The announcer's voice crackled severely from the wireless set: *"The Central Committee of the Hungarian Workers' Party announces that Comrade Imre Nagy is the new Prime Minister and Comrade Ernest Gero, the First Secretary, Janos Kadar, Secretary. The members of the newly appointed Politburo are…"*

'Sod that,' bellowed George, drowning out the announcer's voice. 'Gero's still there, and Kadar; what damn good is that?'

'But Nagy's Prime Minister,' I ventured.

'Window dressing; he's only there to be Gero's puppet. They say Nagy called in the Soviets and Kadar's talking of our "Soviet brothers" defending the nation against counter-revolutionaries. It's sickening.' He reached for a cigarette.

'George, not in the living room, please.'

'He's turned out no better than the rest of them and now they're threatening to cancel the international against Sweden on Sunday week.'

'Can they do that?'

'Of course. Why don't you come out with me?' asked George, the unlit cigarette in his mouth. 'You should see it out there, it's mayhem.'

'No, I don't want to. Anyway, where's Milan?'

'Roaming the streets with a rifle he picked up. Come on, Eva, it's history in the making –'

'I said no, I'd rather not. Thank you.'

He threw his arms up in the air and looked at me goggle-eyed, unable to comprehend my reluctance to venture out. I couldn't tell him, he'd be suspicious, but the fact was I didn't want to see any Russians killed.

One of them might be Valentin.

3.

The rain splatters on the trees around him. It is pitch black in the forest. Some of the men sit in huddled groups, talking, smoking. He ought to get some sleep, he'll need it, for goodness knows what they'll encounter tomorrow and it could be days before they can sleep again – if at all. But they've been told it'll be an easy operation. Go in and restore order. That was about it. Then get out. Not too difficult – not against an unarmed, disorganised mob.

Most of the men don't know why they're here, or even where they are. But Valentin knows. He knows all too well. It is something he's dreamt about for a long time. He'd never expected it to happen nor for it to happen in this manner. His mind wishes it wasn't happening at all, but in his heart he is pleased. After he'd left with the tears welling in his eyes, he never thought he'd see the city again. But tomorrow he will. For tomorrow, they enter Budapest.

Chapter 22
Day Three – Thursday, 25 October

It was a terrifying sight; Zoltan had never seen so many people crowded into a single space, a solidified mass of humanity with a life of its own. The young AVO with the pale face, Paul, had attached himself to Zoltan and, like some nursery rhyme, it felt that wherever he went, Paul was sure to follow.

Word had got to them that something was going to happen in Parliament Square, and every AVO man and woman was ordered straight there. Now, from the rooftops of the Agricultural Ministry, directly opposite the Parliament Building, they gazed down on this seething sea of proletariat resentment, with their slogans and banners and songs. Zoltan now understood the meaning of fear. For years, he and his many colleagues and their army of informers had induced a state of permanent fear in the population. Never had they expected the tables to be so swiftly turned. Never had the AVO expected to be shaking in their boots. And with his rifle at hand, Zoltan was certainly shaking.

At the very moment they needed the government to react, it dithered, unsure what to do; whether to crush the uprising or yield to it. Rumour had it that the Kremlin had sent in some of their top brass to give the shaky ship a guiding hand. God, it needed it, especially with the chief ditherer, Imre Nagy, as prime minister; a cloth-hearted liberal if ever there was one.

Donath had decided to act and was now poised to speak to the mob, loud hailer in hand, his rubbery skin as red as the beetroots the farmers were smuggling into the city. 'You boys ready?' he shouted to his teams of machine gunners on either side of him. Satisfied that everything was in place and to his liking, he lifted the hailer to his lips.

'This is the police,' said Donath, his crackly voice cutting through the drone of chanting drifting up from the square. 'This is the police,' he repeated, ensuring he had their attention. Twenty thousand Hungarians listened. He hesitated, perhaps aware of the magnitude of responsibility that lay with him. His fingers rubbed the metal of his Order of Lenin medal. 'This is an unauthorised demonstration…' A howl of jeers thundered up. Donath cleared his throat. 'I repeat, this is an unauthorised demonstration. You are to disperse immediately.'

'This is a peaceful demonstration,' came the reply from a few voices amongst the thousands.

'What did they say?' asked Donath.

The voices from below continued. 'We are unarmed… we carry no weapons… this is a peaceful demonstration…'

'Peaceful or not,' Donath replied through the inhaler, 'it is still unauthorised and illegal. You are hereby ordered to…'

But his voice was lost, drowned out by the mass of responses. 'Assassins, murderers! Death to the AVO…'

Donath paced up and down the rooftop behind his men, 'How dare they?' he seethed. 'How dare they?' He raised the inhaler but the jeers and insults intensified. He lowered it again.

'Pigs, down with the AVO, out with the Russians…'

The sweat was pouring off Donath's face now as the speed of his pacing quickened. Zoltan knew what was coming next and knew also that whatever happened, they, the AVO were going to suffer for it.

But first, Donath tried again. 'You are to disperse,' he yelled through the inhaler. 'Immediately.'

The insults bounced straight back, louder still. 'Bastards, killers, death to the AVO!'

Donath threw the inhaler down. 'Right, that's it. We've got our orders, you know what to do.'

Zoltan and Paul exchanged nervous glances. Yes, thought Zoltan, we know what to do, but we didn't expect to have to do it.

'OK, men, I expect you to do your duty, unpleasant as it may be. Remember your loyalty lies not with this counter-revolutionary mob but with our masters, the government, and their worthy fight for socialism. If we don't show these bastards who's boss around here, things will only get worse. We fight now, for what we believe in, for the real workers of this country, not these renegades down there who masquerade behind the proletariat mask, these sons of the bourgeois, these capitalist offspring, whose veins run with blue blood.' He paused, allowing his words to take hold while the noise from below intensified by the moment. 'We do this for Hungary, for communism, for the advance of socialism. Gentlemen, and ladies, engage…'

Zoltan stiffened as his finger pressed against the trigger, the barrel of his rifle pointing down at the swirling body of demonstrators below.

'Fire!' The command seemed to provoke the end of the world. And the end of the world started with a scream; a communal scream that arose from the square, the like of which Zoltan had never heard before; a scream that encompassed every octave and each note between to produce a single sound so terrifying, he knew he would carry it within him for evermore.

Zoltan closed his eyes and pressed. No chance of missing, no hope of a single bullet being wasted. The consolation was that he didn't have to man the huge machine guns on either side of him, both now spurting their continuous and vile discharge into the crowd.

But as the screams crescendo, it was of scant consolation.

*

Zoltan is running. Again. How long did it last? Five minutes, two hours? He doesn't know. It doesn't take too long to kill so many so quickly. The Hungarian tanks had moved in – but on the side of the rebels. The army had gone over, as had the regular police force. They'd all deserted the regime, merrily gone over to the insurgents, handing out their guns like lollipops, raiding the arsenals, the ammo dumps. There was no time to lose, not with the tanks there. Some of the tanks were Soviet – T-54s and T-34s, but who was shooting at whom? Donath, fortunately, wasn't prepared to hang about to find out. They, the AVOs, knew when it was time to go. A last look down onto the square. It was like peering down into Hell. Bodies prostate, huddled, torn apart. The place was almost empty now, like a swarm of flies caught in a funnel of smoke, they'd panicked and battled and eventually escaped. Now only the dead and the dying remained. And a few others, those unable to pull themselves away from their fallen brothers and sisters. The dying who begged not to be left alone to face the darkness by themselves; to have someone to hold their hands for those few last moments in that solitary region between dying and death.

How they'd got down the stairs, Zoltan didn't know, nor did he know what had happened to Paul. What their orders were, he didn't know that either. There was a truck waiting for them, thirty yards away. Some made a run for it, their guns still in their hands, but the insurgents came from nowhere, hundreds of them. Shots were fired but not for long. Zoltan didn't wait. He ran and he was running still. They'd been lynching the AVOs. Boys he'd known, informers he knew but pretended not to, strung up, beaten to death. Or burnt.

People were dangerous now. That first day, that was still largely confined to the students and a few sympathetic workers. Now, it was the whole bloody lot of them. Bare-handed assassins, every one of them. Right now, tears marked every face, people hugging one another, seeking comfort, contact. Whatever they sought, Zoltan didn't care, as long as their grief saved him and allowed him to escape. A boy in a roll-neck pullover holds a machine gun so big he can hardly lift it. But attempt it, he does. He wants to make a name for himself. But not from me, thinks Zoltan, as he picks up speed and disappears round the corner.

And now he too is crying, his heart pleading for the warmth of her touch, the silkiness of her voice, the way she strokes Roza's hair and talks gently into her ear, a voice capable of keeping away the worst of monsters.

'Zoltan, Zoltan, speak to me, what's happened?'

But he can't talk, his throat too dry, his mind filled with too many images; diabolic images he helped to create. She doesn't realise it, his dear wife, but this time the worst of all monsters is in her arms.

'I'm sorry, I'm sorry.' He repeats it again and again; no other words come to him. 'I'm sorry.'

Slowly, Petra comes to understand the meaning of his story merely by listening to him uttering the same word repeatedly.

'My God, Zoltan, what have you done?

'I'm… I'm sorry…'

'We're dead. They catch us here, we're as good as dead.'

The words permeate. He looks up at her, his head nestled in her bosom. It's been a long time since they've had such physical contact. He knows it's meaningless, but he's grateful nonetheless. 'What do we do?' The very sentence signifies his final submission. All his working life, he's tried. Tried to be the man he wasn't, tried to be the hard bastard, tried to do his best for his family. But no more. No more. But Petra… she'll know what to do; she'll save them. 'What do we do?'

'Get you out of this uniform for one thing.'

Yes, she knows what to do; she'll save them, all three of them.

Chapter 23
Day Four – Friday, 26 October

1.

They'd smashed the windows and doors, and broken into the *Horizon* bookshop. I watched as about a dozen men, including George and Milan, trailed in and out, carrying armfuls of books and dropping them ceremoniously onto the street. The shop's stock of books was exclusively Soviet or Hungarian communist, dusty books no one wanted to read and that no one but the seller had touched for years. It was, after all, a Soviet bookshop. George, Milan and the others looked like boys playing a game they knew was forbidden, and enjoying it – the risk merely adding to the joy. But for now, there was no risk, yet the knowledge that what they were doing was, until last week, inconceivable more than made up for it. Many others crowded around and watched. I skirted around the edge of the spectators; fearful in case a convoy of Soviet tanks should appear. I half-listened to the gossip, the rumours and counter-rumours. *Nagy's gone to Moscow, Gero is dead, Gero is holding Nagy hostage, the Soviets are withdrawing, the Soviets are coming in greater number*. It was a time of half-truths and untruths. President Eisenhower had apparently spoken, sending a message of support to the Hungarian people. Did it mean the US would act? Probably not, they thought, not with the presidential elections only a week away. Delegations had gone to the US and British legations, demanding that Hungary's plight be brought to the attention of the United Nations. The world had to know what was happening – that we, the repressed, were standing up for ourselves, and for freedom.

George came to find me. 'It just gets better and better.'

'You be careful,' I said in return. Ignoring my advice, as I knew he would, he returned to his work as the burner of books. The pile of books and pamphlets had now built up to a pyramid simply waiting to become a bonfire. The titles, in Russian or Hungarian, and the familiar portraits adorning the book covers stared up from the street – Stalin, Lenin, Marx, Khrushchev, and our own puppet versions – Rakosi, Gero, Kadar and their ilk. I wondered who on earth would want to buy a book of essays written by Ernest Gero? The thought was ludicrous. I guessed the shop must have survived on a subsidy because I was damned if I could see how it could make a profit – in all the years I passed it, I never once saw anyone go in or come out.

Finally, came the posters – thrown on top of the pile, the largest saved to last – a huge portrait of Stalin in his military jacket, the medals, a supercilious smile, his determined eyes daring the viewer to dissent.

'Are we ready to burn?' asked Milan, a diabolic look in his eyes.

The small gathering cheered as George unscrewed the top of the petrol can and held it aloft like a trophy before pouring it over and around the Soviet pyramid. Milan produced a box of matches from his back pocket, lit one and threw it on the pyre. The flame caught and quickly spread through the posters, Stalin's gaze disappearing inch by inch. People approached with sticks, prodding the fire, encouraging it to take, removing books and throwing them back on top.

'Lenin,' shouted out Milan. '*Will the Bolsheviks Retain State Power?*'

'Rakosi – *Moscow Education*,' added George. Together, they ripped up the books, tearing out large chunks of paper, and threw them into the fire with a cheer.

It was then that I saw it – fallen to the side, as yet unnoticed by either the gathering or the flames – a book in Hungarian entitled *Famous Soviet Footballers, 1947 – 1953*. I tried to ignore it but the more I tried, the more I was drawn to it. Apart from the gold writing the cover was plain, dark green in colour, nothing to attract the eye. And I wanted it. How famous was Valentin? Probably not that famous at all, but the book was thick, and he had played for Moscow Lokomotiv, and the years coincided. There was a chance he might be listed or referred to. I had to check, I couldn't leave this book to burn.

'Stalin – *Collected Works, Volume Ten*.'

'Marx – *Das Capital*.'

'Hey, George,' shouted Milan. 'Why did Lenin wear normal-sized shoes while Stalin wore boots?'

'I don't know.'

'In Lenin's time, Russia was still only ankle-high in shit.'

I kicked the book free from the rest and quickly bent down to scoop it up and picked another at the same time and held them both behind my back.

But I wasn't quick enough. 'What have you got there, Miss?' asked a hard-faced youngster wearing a quilted jacket.

He had two cartridge belts zigzagged across his chest and a rifle over his shoulder.

I tried to move away, pretending I hadn't heard him, slipping the two volumes into my coat pocket, edging around the now huge bonfire, the heat scratching my face.

This time, he shouted at me, drawing the attention of many others. 'Can't you hear me, Miss? I said what book have you got there?'

He'd said *book* not books. I felt inside my pocket and drew out the thinner title. By now I was being watched, some half dozen pairs of eyes strangely interested in me. But not George or Milan, they were still busy on the opposite side of the fire, their outlines visible only as blurred figures.

'*Recipes for the Proletariat Housewife*,' I said triumphantly. It was a title I'd recently got to know well. The dishes, in theory, looked delicious but in practice were impossible to make – few of the ingredients were ever available for us to buy.

But my heart sank, as his voice came back to me again, edged now with undisguised menace. 'And what about the other book?' he said.

'Other book?' I was playing for time, hoping George would come to my aid.

'Yeah, come on, what about the other book?'

I drew it out knowing I didn't want to lose it, convinced now that Valentin's name would appear within these untouched pages. 'Only a book on football.'

'You can't keep it, you can't keep nothing from this place – it's all scum. Throw it on the fire.'

The few people nearest me echoed his words. 'Go on, throw it,' they said, not realising the torment they were causing me. I lobbed the cookery book into the heart of the flames and watched it disappear instantaneously.

'George! Milan!' They heard me and through the haze of flames. I saw them looking around for me. 'The other book is for them,' I said firmly.

'They can't have it,' said the youth.

'You OK, Eva?'

'I've got you a book, George – on football.'

'Didn't know you were browsing.'

'She's trying to keep it.'

'I thought you might like it.'

George went to take it from my hand but I gripped it firmly, not willing to let it out of my reach. 'Soviet players, forty-seven to fifty-three, your era, George, it might have some of the Lokomotiv players you played against.' Please, just accept it; don't make me burn it.

But the youth interrupted. 'You can't keep anything from this shop, you know that.' Others around him consented through a chorus of jeers.

'I don't even think about those times now; anyway, the boy's right, burn it.'

'Then I'll have it.' Milan put his hand out. Oh, thank you, Milan. I tried to pass it to him but the youth tried to grab it. It fell, landing on a smattering of dying embers. I scrambled down, forgetting all show of decency, and plucked it off knowing I had just made matters worse by my inelegant haste.

'You're a sympathiser, aren't you?' The boy placed both his hands on his rifle strap.

'She's AVO,' shouted an ugly female voice from somewhere. Someone laughed. My head throbbed; an accusation was as fatal as a judgement. I stepped back, my eyes fixed on his filthy hands toying with the strap, threatening to slip the rifle from his shoulder.

'Don't be ridiculous, she's with me,' said George, inching towards the youth.

Milan joined him. 'You keep your twitchy fingers to yourself, pal.' The two of them together were enough to calm the boy. He stepped back but the indignation in his eyes still burned on me. 'I'd say she's AVO,' he said, playing to his audience.

'Russian whore…'

George spun round, his fists already clenched. Milan grabbed his arm. 'Leave it, George,' he said; the youth slipped the rifle off his shoulder.

'George, help me.'

They were closing in, the three of us, trapped in an increasing circle of hate, the heat of the fire sucking the breath out of me, the flames reflecting in their eyes, giving them each a demonic look. Under the noise of the fire, no one had noticed the Soviet tank poised at the end of the street. The thunderous boom of the shell smashing into the building behind us took all by surprise. The glass in the windows sucked out in slow motion, followed by the whooshing sound of a million glass arrows.

The flash of pain tore through my right hand as a shard of glass embedded itself. My mind blank, I yanked it out, the glass burning my flesh as it withdrew. The pain dulled; my mind tottered between two worlds.

Many of the crowd, which moments before had threatened to lynch me, now shrieked and scrambled to their feet. Others lay prostrate, pierced by glass. A cloud of black smoke, dust and masonry descended on us, dampening the intensity of the flames. The woman, who first accused me of being AVO, lost her footing as she tried to get up and burnt herself on the edge of the fire. Shots fired back, the bullets pinging off the metal hulk of the tank. A machine gun rattled in return, but their aim was poor. I felt myself being dragged to my feet. 'Get up, Eva, for God's sake, get up.' It was George, his face black with heat and sweat.

I saw the small groups of men, crouching behind a tree or pressed against the building, firing at the tank, their faces contorted in concentration, their boots crunching on the carpet of broken glass and masonry. The youth with the quilted jacket lay on the pavement, a hole in his neck, his eyes that had viewed me with such hostility now facing skywards. But where was George now? Or Milan? I was by myself – standing to the left of the fire, the side of my face feeling like it would melt in the blaze, my right hand stabbing me with pain. But I couldn't move. The tank drifted in and out of view behind the cloud of smoke and dust. The air filled with gunfire and screams.

'Get down,' shouted a strangulated voice nearby but whether it was aimed at me, I couldn't say.

I didn't know anything any more; my mind had ceased to operate, numbing me of pain or fear or any sense of self-preservation.

But in the depths of my consciousness, there was something I was certain of. In the Soviet tank that now bore down on me sat a man, a Russian, whose name appeared on the pages of the book in my coat pocket.

2.

'There, there – to your right, two o'clock, fire!'

The machine gun clattered, the noise bouncing within the confines of the metal hulk. They had them running, scurrying away like rats.

'What are they burning?' asked Vladimir.

'Don't know,' replied Valentin, 'but the smoke's getting everywhere.'

'Fire!' Another round brought down a couple more.

'That's a Russian bookshop there, they're burning all the books, the bastards.'

'We'll teach them to burn our books – fire,' said Petrov, the driver.

Valentin peered at the scene in front of them, the bonfire, the spiralling smoke, the insurgents shooting at them, the women hiding behind those with guns, some scurrying away, others hit, writhing on the ground. But he envied their freedom, to be able to roam about the streets, to breathe the air, to have circulation in the legs. After almost a week in a claustrophobic tank, tempers were frayed, the conditions inside hideous, the noise unceasing, the smell of excrement, dirt and fumes so thick you could bite it, their clothes rank, their food limited and obnoxious.

'Unit forty-two, unit forty-two, come in, come in.' The radio crackled into life, the distant voice belonging to Andropov, the divisional commander.

Vladimir answered it. 'Sir? Over.'

'Calling for assistance, what's your position? Over.'

Vladimir held his hand over the radio. 'What's our position?' he mouthed.

'Fuck knows,' came the reply.

'I can't tell him we've got lost down some side street.'

'Tell him anything then,' said Petrov.

'Unit forty-two, are you still there? Over.'

'Sorry, sir; lost you for a bit there. We're uncertain of our exact position but we're in the district of the British Legation, not far from the Interior Ministry building. Over.'

'We need support. Report to the southern end of Lenin Boulevard immediately. Over and out.'

'He's calling us back. Come on, let's go.'

Petrov manoeuvred the gears into reverse, the tank coming to life, the heavy engine stirring. 'We shouldn't have come down here alone anyway,' he said between gritted teeth.

He was right, of course, thought Valentin, it was too dangerous to patrol alone; solitary units were too exposed and vulnerable to attack. Bitter experience had taught them too to avoid the narrow streets where insurgents could readily drop petrol bombs on them from the higher floors.

'The smoke's clearing,' said Valentin, returning his attention to the bookshop as the tank inched backwards. It was then that he saw her. A woman standing next to the fire, bright red hair, the smoke dancing around her. 'Christ.'

'What's up, comrade?'

'That woman.'

Vladimir took the machine gun. 'Look at her, stupid cow, just asking for it.'

'No!' Valentin slammed his hand down on the gun.

'What the hell are you doing?'

'Leave her. She reminds me of someone.'

Vladimir laughed. 'Well, in that case, we wouldn't want her to come to any harm, now would we? Is it her?'

The tank had reversed to the end of the street, and Petrov was clumsily manoeuvring the metallic beast around. The woman faded out of view as people gathered around her and yelled unheard obscenities at the tank and fired defiant shots into the air. 'No, it can't be,' he said, 'too many years ago.'

Too many years ago.

Chapter 24
Day Five – Saturday, 27 October

1.

'We're winning, we're winning!' Milan hugged George with such ferocity, George feared his lungs would burst; instead, they were bursting with happiness.

'The future is ours, George; there's no turning back now.'

'Not with Nagy back on our side.'

'Three cheers for Imre Nagy!'

The friends were preparing to go out for the morning, wrapping themselves in coats, scarves and hats for the weather had turned cold. But the new dawn had banished old fears – Nagy had pronounced: the revolution was theirs; the government had admitted that the insurgents were not counter-revolutionaries but had risen out of legitimate grievances against the regime. He announced too that the AVO was to be disbanded, Soviet troops withdrawn, and the Soviet Star replaced by the traditional Hungarian emblem of Kossuth. In the meantime, he said, there would be a ceasefire.

'Eva not getting up?'

George sighed. 'No, I don't think so.' His joy was tempered by Eva's behaviour the day before. He'd been embarrassed by it, and by the fact he had been forced to defend her from those who eyed her suspiciously. The way she behaved was peculiar, the way she stood there defiantly in front of the Russian tank, refusing to take cover. Some may have thought it courageous but George knew differently. How she survived while so many around her fell, no one could fathom. It was nothing less than miraculous. Afterwards, when he tried to speak to her, she snapped at him, 'Some things, George, you'll never know about me.' Of course, he'd never know if she never said. But something wasn't right.

'How's her hand?'

'All right, just a scratch really.'

'She was lucky not to have been mowed down. What was it about that book? She's crazy.'

George shook his head despairingly.

'Let's go.'

2.

'I need to go out to get some clothes and food. We can't be seen in these clothes; we stick out.'

Zoltan was lying in bed, his daughter sitting next to him reading a magazine he didn't believe she could read. The room was surprisingly intact considering the amount of bombardment the street had suffered at the hands of the Soviet tanks. A couple of window panes had crashed through and all the others were cracked. But inside, apart from a layer of dust everywhere, everything looked almost normal. Petra had swept up the shards of glass, squared the pictures, put back up the curtain rail.

She now stood in the doorway. He didn't want her to go; he needed her next to him, needed his wife's reassuring presence near him. 'Do you have to go?'

'Yes.'

'Can't it wait?'

'No, it can't. Roza will stay with you.'

'Mama, no.'

'Roza, come here a minute.' Roza left his side and went to her mother, who took her hand and led her into the living room. Zoltan groaned. Petra would be telling her that she needed to stay with her father, and not to complain. Roza and he were almost strangers, hence his daughter's reluctance to be left alone with him. He sympathised, for he had no idea what to say to her, had no idea what her hobbies were, how she was doing at school. He remembered how, when she was much younger, he could entertain her with a few magic tricks. She was too old for that now. When he asked how things were, all he got was a lot of shrugging of shoulders and noncommittal responses he didn't understand. He couldn't remember when they'd last spent time alone together. Petra never fully trusted him with her and always preferred to be around when he and Roza occupied the same space. Occasionally, when he slept, he could still see Roza in her pink coat and matching hat face down in the water. She was a different girl now, ten years old with a self-assurance he found alarming. But in the last four days, she'd regressed years, clinging to her mother, blaming again her AVO father for all the trouble in the world.

Roza returned to the bedroom, glancing at him from under her fringe, circling by the wall, unwilling to commit herself again to his company.

'Come, Roza, why don't you sit back here and tell me what you're reading about in your magazine.'

*

Petra wanted to run, to get it over and done with, but she forced herself to walk. She needed to find some proletariat clothes. It was the first time she'd ventured outdoors since the start of this frightful rebellion and she felt as if everyone was staring at her. She knew she wore her guilt like a badge, guilty for her marriage to an AVO, guilty for the finer clothes she'd worn, the make-up she could afford to buy, for the annual holidays on the coast, for the plentiful daily delivery of Western-style food. She wore the closest she had to scruffy clothes but she knew it was only the overcoat that disguised her. Stripped of her coat and the world would see her for what she was. Privileged. They would lynch her.

The outside world had changed since she last saw it five days ago. Electric cables hung down, tram lines ripped up, once beautiful buildings now scarred with gaping holes, trees uprooted, walls collapsed. Was this the work of man or God? Hand in hand, perhaps both. And the bodies – many covered with the Hungarian flag. Every few yards a loose limb, another bloated victim. She couldn't bear to look. How could she possibly hope to do what she knew had to be done?

'Morning.' The old lady's voice made her jump.

'Morning, comrade,' she replied automatically.

The old woman peered up at her from beneath her shawl, eyeing her from head to foot, her toothless mouth open. 'Don't comrade me, you silly cow.' She spat on the ground, turned and hurried off up the street.

The old woman could tell, and not simply from the misplaced 'comrade'. Down the hill, she could see a group of children and to her amazement, they carried guns. She shivered. It wasn't worth the risk, she was going back. She pulled her headscarf further down her forehead and, gripping her coat tightly, walked briskly up the hill and back towards the apartment.

It was only as she ascended the stairs that the idea came to her.

Tiptoeing down the corridor on the first floor, one floor below her apartment, she pressed her ear to the first door. Silence. Not daring to breathe, she gently turned the doorknob. Locked. She breathed out and realised how hot she felt. But the coat had to remain. She could hear voices behind the second door and so moved to the third. Silent again. This time, however, the door was not locked. Inside, the lights were on but the place was bitterly cold – more chance of it being empty. Two plates of blackened food on the living room table brought a sigh of relief – no one lived here now. She went to the bedroom, determined now to complete the task and get home. The bed was made, pillows plumped but felt like stone such was the cold. She pulled open the wardrobe door and found what she'd come for. Using the chair from the corner, she also found a suitcase on top of the wardrobe. She thanked her luck and began piling in the limited number of trousers, skirts and jackets, male and female, everything old and black. The sizes didn't matter; as long as the appearance deceived.

She desperately wanted to get back now. Only one floor away but she'd never felt so vulnerable, so far from home. From the clothes, the pictures, the furniture, she guessed they'd been a middle-aged couple. She wondered what had happened to them.

As she walked back into the living room, she turned the light switch on. His eyes burnt into her. She screamed. Jumping back, she dropped the suitcase. She slammed into the wall and couldn't stop screaming. But he didn't move. 'Please, don't…' She couldn't talk, her heart beat too violently to think the words. She was crying now, her head felt light, dizzy.

And still he hadn't moved.

'Hello?' How small her voice sounded. 'Are you…'

He sat upright on the armchair, a black suit, his square-shaped head fixed to his square shoulders like two blocks of wood. His face was white, his lips blue, a large red hole camouflaged within the blackness of his jacket.

Without taking her eyes off him, Petra knelt down, her fingers reaching out, and picked up the suitcase. Taking slow, large steps, she stalked out of the room, her eyes fixed on his – terrified lest they might move.

The living room door, as in her own apartment, was only a step away from the front door. With a leap, she slammed both doors and found herself in the corridor, her hand clasped against her mouth, trying to hold back the vomit in her throat.

But in her hand – the clothes she had come for.

3.

Gyűjtőfogház: an ugly name for an ugly place.

Josef Horvath had spent five days short of six years incarcerated within its thick wet walls, the first two in solitary. Now, at least, he had company – an old Jewish chemistry lecturer by the name of Hentz and a young farmhand called Laurence. In age, intelligence and upbringing, Hentz and Laurence represented the opposite ends of the spectrum with Josef as the halfway point. Socially and intellectually, they were as divided as they could be, but they shared similar AVO-inflicted scars, and here, in this hellhole, men put aside their differences, their prejudices, and stood together, united by circumstance – and matching pyjama-like grey prison uniforms.

For weeks now, the inmates knew something was happening, but what exactly no one could say. Rumours abounded, gossip circulated, and hearsay spread like a contamination of false hope. Things had started changing almost imperceptibly – the AVO guards behaved with a little more decency; their food rations improved gradually, both in the quality and the amount they received; they were allowed to receive letters, parcels and even visits. It improved everyone's morale and benefited all. Josef's only contact with the outside world was Eva. It'd been seven months since her last visit; five months to the next. She'd believed his story that he'd divorced her to protect her. It was true, but there *had* been another woman, a woman who had failed to stand by him. As soon as she realised that his arrest was imminent, she disappeared, never to be seen again.

Then, following Rakosi's downfall a few months before, almost half of the prisoners had been freed. It was a pure chance whether you were one of the lucky ones or not. Josef, the chemistry lecturer and the farmhand were not. But their hopes had been ignited.

Then, nine days previously, on 18th October, something extraordinary happened – something that made the smouldering of hope blow even stronger. Someone (no one knew who) had broken into the prison compound, made it to the prison wall, and shouted up, 'Prisoners, don't worry; you'll all be free within a fortnight!' Now there was real excitement. Talking was banned, as always, but the whisperings and gentle tapping on pipes lasted all night. What did the message mean, what was going to happen to free them, who was the messenger? It seemed too wonderful to be true; it had to be a hoax, or worse, some AVO machination.

But on 24th October, instead of hope, came further despair – the AVO guard doubled, and the prisoners' rights of exercise withdrawn without notice. The guards themselves became tense and twitchy, lashing out at the slightest digression.

However, it was the guards, Josef noticed, who gave away the next clue – they suddenly appeared with the Soviet stars removed from their caps and, further still, most had swapped their AVO uniforms for regular blue police ones. You could taste the excitement. Why, everyone asked, were the AVOs disguising themselves?

And now, today, 27th October, the next piece of the puzzle raised the temperature still further – someone had spotted the Hungarian tricolour with the Soviet hammer and sickle removed. No more whisperings, no more tapping, now the prisoners bellowed at each other through their cell walls – spreading the news, speculating loudly on its meaning.

Josef, Hentz and Laurence talked at once. 'The food, the visits,' bawled Hentz. 'The message –'

'The messenger,' added Laurence excitedly.

'Yes, the messenger, the caps and now *this*.'

'They've kicked the Russians out,' yelled Josef.

'Perhaps they've kicked the Commies out with them, sent them all back to Moscow.'

They were all talking loudly, relishing the freedom to do so.

The door swung open, an AVO appeared briefly in an ill-fitting police uniform. 'Gentlemen, please, keep the noise down.' The door slammed shut.

The three of them, standing in a circle, looked from one to the other. 'Did you hear that?' said Hentz quietly.

'He *asked* us to keep the noise down.'

Josef almost had to sit down. 'I can't remember the last time someone used the word *please*.'

'And he called us *gentlemen*,' said Laurence.

'Is that why we're talking in hushed tones now?' asked Hentz. 'Because he asked us so nicely?'

Josef began to laugh.

'I suppose it is quite funny,' said Hentz.

'Funniest thing I've ever heard,' added Laurence.

The three of them laughed with total abandon, making up for years without humour, choking and doubling up with laughter.

But then Hentz stopped as abruptly as he'd started. 'Shush,' he urged. 'Shush now, listen.'

'What? What is it?' asked Laurence, wiping his eyes.

'Can't you hear?'

Josef strained his ears. 'No, what?'

'For goodness sake, and I'm the old man around here, what's the matter with you two, can't you hear it?'

'Is that someone singing?' asked Laurence, his hand cupped to his ear.

'Good God, yes,' said Josef. 'So it is.'

Straightening his back, Hentz said, 'I never thought I'd hear that again.'

The singing they could hear belonged to one man. Even through the cell walls, Josef could hear it, the voice clear and proud; for he was singing the national anthem, not the communist *Internationale*, but the Hungarian National Anthem of old, the slow melody, full of melancholy, the words stirring and poignant. Another voice joined in, then another and another. Like a huge wave it gained strength and momentum as it advanced until, unstoppable, the whole complex was awash with voices, a thousand voices, singing as they'd never sung before. Hentz, Laurence and Josef, representatives of the social spectrum, held hands as their voices rang out, tears streaming down their faces, united as only the tortured can be.

As the anthem ended, the spontaneous cry went up: 'Give us our freedom, give us our freedom…', a thousand feet stamping the ground, a thousand hands hitting their prison bars, a thousand voices, deadened for so many years, now chanting for the freedom they knew was theirs.

The cell door opened, this time a different AVO, but still disguised as an ordinary policeman, a look of desperation on his face. 'Please, please, you can't keep this up.' His hand delved into his pocket. Josef stepped back; surely they wouldn't be so foolish to start killing now. But in his hand, a fresh packet of cigarettes. 'Here,' he said. 'Take them, I'll get you more, only stop the noise, please.'

Down the corridor, Josef could hear more cell doors being opened, more desperate AVOs pleading with their captives. The world was turning upside down and how glorious the feeling was.

Laurence grabbed the cigarettes and pushed the guard to the side. The man fell back against the damp wall, his eyes shocked and frightened. Standing in the doorway, Laurence looked back at his fellow inmates. 'Well, are you two coming or what?'

'What? Now?' asked Josef, realising what a ridiculous question it was but it all seemed too easy, too perfect. Behind Laurence, he saw men running down the corridor, a flood of humanity in grey pyjamas, shouting with joy, pure, ecstatic joy.

With one foot in the cell, the other out, Laurence grinned. 'I suppose if you want,' he said, 'we could hang around for another year or two.'

Hentz laughed, slapping Josef's back. 'The boy's right; what are we waiting for? After you, Josef, my friend, after you.'

Chapter 25
Day Six – Sunday, 28 October

1.

Petra and Roza had been queuing for over an hour. Petra only hoped they wouldn't run out by the time she got to the front. Gone were the days when she could simply walk into a closed-access store, flash her pass and take her pick from an opulent range of foodstuffs and be served by polite, subservient staff. But the queue of women was cheerful, strangers brought together by atrocity, able to talk for the first time without fear of their words being reported to the likes of her husband. Despite the chaos around them, these women felt free. Petra was pleased for them, and listened to their tales and their gossip, but said little, speaking only to agree or show astonishment; for she feared if she spoke, her words might betray her, her tongue might slip a nugget of information exposing her AVO connection. Twice Roza made to speak; twice Petra shot her a glance that silenced her daughter.

Nearby, outside a pawnbroker, another line of women queued. It was a Hungarian housewife's habit to pawn the family's winter clothes during summer and the summer clothes in winter. But they remembered too well how in '45, the Russians had looted every pawnbroker they came across. No one was taking any chances this time. Whilst the women queued for food or clothes, a small gathering of men ambled nearby, each armed with a rifle. They stopped, offered each other cigarettes and lit up. She didn't know why but something made Petra turn round to look at them. One of them, a man with long thick sideburns wearing a black beret and a short jerkin jacket, was staring straight at her. He winked at her and touched his beret by way of a greeting. She shuddered and turned her back on him.

On the baker's window, someone had daubed *Russians go home* in bright red paint. Plastered up on the windows and the walls of the neighbouring shops and the pawnbrokers, a whole series of revolutionary newspapers displayed for people's consumption – news, theories, poems, jokes and cartoons. Rakosi with his bald head was a favourite target of the cartoonists. After years of silence, people simply wrote and read whatever they wanted to. Nearby, the carcass of a Soviet tank blocked the pavement, its burnt-out shell still smouldering. The women ignored it, preferring to concentrate on the newspapers while waiting for their share of the next food delivery. Food was coming in from the provinces, trucks laden with bread, milk, flour and vegetables bearing banners that read *For our friends in Budapest from the village of…* Oranges and bananas had become forgotten treats to ordinary citizens. But it was the supply of chicken and duck that caused the most excitement – plentiful supplies of trussed-up poultry, labelled *For Export to U.S.S.R.* These women hadn't had chicken or duck for years, believing the government line that they were in short supply. Instead, they realised now, the government had been packing it all off to the Russians.

The women talked excitedly of Nagy's announcement of the ceasefire – no more Russian interference, no more AVO – they couldn't believe it was for real, it seemed too far-fetched. The AVO were running sacred, hunted down and ferreted out of their hiding places and lynched by insurgents determined to make them pay for their years of brutality. Never again would the population be at the mercy of the AVO.

Petra smiled weakly and ignored Roza's inquisitive expression. Roza had been unable to disguise her amusement, seeing her father in the clothes of a proletariat. They were nearing the front of the queue now. The men in the lorry handed out strict amounts per person but refused payment. 'True communism at work,' said one.

Petra thought of Zoltan cowering at home, clinging to the bed, waking up covered in sweat. He was known to too many people in this city; known for his loyal and long-time work as an AVO officer. How long could she hide him there, how long before they came for him? Somehow, they had to escape. But where? And how?

Twenty minutes later, with her string bag full, Petra took Roza's hand and made her leave.

The gruff voice took her by surprise. 'Good morning, Mrs Beke.'

She looked up and the man with the sideburns and black beret was standing behind her, acting out an exaggerated bow.

'Come, Roza, quickly,' she said, pulling on her daughter's hand, the panic rising fast within her. Roza, sensing her mother's anxiety, obeyed without murmur.

She told herself not to turn around; to do so would only

betray her guilt. But as she reached the end of the street, she did turn around. He was still there, still watching her. He waved a lazy wave. Like a statue of salt, she felt rooted to the spot. Roza saw him too. 'Do you know that man?'

'No,' said Petra, turning, wanting to hurry away.

'He seems to know you.'

'He's mistaken then, isn't he?' she snapped. 'I've never seen him before.'

She only hoped she'd never see him again.

2.

Famous Soviet Footballers, 1947 – 1953. The book remained in my pocket. But I'd been wrong; there was no mention or photo of a Valentin Ivanov, midfielder for Moscow Lokomotiv at the turn of the decade. I'd scanned the index and skimmed the whole thing, all two hundred and eighty-two pages, and not a single mention. He hadn't been as famous or noteworthy as I'd hoped. No matter, the book was still a reminder and I had no intention of letting go of it. I thought of Valentin; I couldn't imagine how dreadful it could be, holed up in one of those tanks, mobile coffins as Milan called them, for days on end, a moving target for petrol bombers and a population intent on destroying anything remotely Russian. I imagined him safely in Moscow, strolling hand in hand with a beautiful young Russian girl, hundreds of miles away from this turmoil. I didn't know how much longer I could stand it. Yes, we all wanted freedom but I didn't want this. George and Milan, in the meantime, were having the time of their lives. Every morning, they were up early, intent on playing their own part in these 'wondrous days' that forever more would be recorded in the history books. Somehow, they were able to

206

distance themselves from the carnage, from the bodies piling up, the brutality of it all. But I couldn't.

Today, I nervously stepped outside with them; afraid of what images might confront me. George had insisted on my coming, as I hadn't left the apartment since the day of the bonfire. I'd used the injury to my hand as an excuse. Doused in white spirit and securely wrapped in a bandage it did, occasionally, throb but the pain, if truth be told, was nothing.

A cold veil of snow drifted through the streets. Immediately, we met a good-looking boy, a teenager, who stopped to speak to Milan. He wore a trilby and carried what, George told me later, was a bolt-action rifle.

Milan and the boy shook hands. 'Apparently,' said Milan, 'the communist HQ is the place to be. Whole lot of AVOs holed up, should be quite a spectacle.'

George rubbed his hands. 'Let's go then.'

'Wait,' I said. 'What do you mean by spectacle? I don't want to see any lynching, thank you very much.'

'Eva, come on…'

'No, George, I know what you're going to say, they're AVO, they deserve it, but they're still human and I don't want anything to do with it.'

'Keep your voice down, people will get the wrong idea.'

Milan interrupted. 'Well, couldn't I go anyway and leave you two to go towards the park instead?'

I sighed theatrically. 'If you must…'

*

A large crowd had assembled in and around the City Park. Families gathered with picnics, undeterred by the gentle fall of snow, children rummaged around playing with empty cartridge shells, their parents and grandparents watching from a distance, sitting on blankets or foldable chairs. How strange it all looked; a light, almost-carnival atmosphere; a summer scene transposed into early winter, halcyon days transposed onto a battle-scarred landscape. Milan had gone off with his teenage friend to the communist HQ but George, ever-loyal George, had stayed with me. He was trying his best to disguise his frustration.

A suitcase caught my eye – it'd been left open on a chair and was full of banknotes. People passed by and dropped more into it but no one, as far as I could see, was actively guarding it.

'It's to aid those who're in most desperate need,' said George, reading my thoughts.

'And no one takes from it?'

He shot me a look suggesting my question was as ridiculous as it was unnecessary.

Towards the centre of the park, near the statue of Stalin's boots, a large meeting was taking place, rows of people on chairs, a speaker standing on a box, shouting, waving his arms about, a Hungarian flag wrapped around his wrist.

'What's going on?' I asked.

'Ah, those happy souls. Would you believe it, it's a meeting of the prisoners who forced their way out of *Gyűjtőfogház* the other day.'

My hand went to my mouth. 'The prison? I didn't know they had.'

'Eva, I despair sometimes. We're living through the greatest upheaval since the war and you're not aware of anything that's happening around you.'

'But that's the one Josef is in.'

'You mean – *was* in. The prisons are empty – all over Hungary. The only prisoners left are the insane ones.'

'Josef could be here.'

'Well, let's go and have a look.'

'No. Not yet. But don't you want to join them?'

He thought for a moment. 'No, it's not for me; I've been out for three years. I'm OK now.' He looked at me tenderly and, feeling momentarily awkward, I knew I was part of the reason that George was OK. We strolled towards the meeting, my heart pumping furiously. The speaker had said something that had made his audience laugh. He bowed in appreciation as his audience cheered and clapped.

'You go,' I said.

'Go? Go where?'

'Go join Milan. It's your revolution; it's unfair of me to hold you back. If you're quick, you'll catch him up.'

I could see his expression, torn between excitement and reluctance. 'Are you sure?' he said, and I knew he meant it; he would have stayed had I wished it but if Josef was there, and there was a possibility, surely, then I wanted to face it alone.

'Yes. Go on, you go.'

His eyes flashed with excitement. He kissed me on the cheek and managed to walk off without breaking into a skip.

I turned my attention to the gathering of liberated prisoners – so many men, and a few women, of all ages, of all classes; a cross-section of society; all different but all tainted by the same shared experience.

'Our personal liberation is a reflection of the nation's liberation,' the speaker was saying, still waving his arms about. 'Too long we have lived in a prison called Hungary, too long at the mercy of our guards, the Soviet Union.' His audience clapped enthusiastically. 'Too long we've lived in a sealed tin, hermetically sealed from the outside world. And what happens if you lift the lid and allow some fresh air into the tin?

Everything inside goes rotten. You can never seal it shut again and expect things to remain the same inside. We, my friends, have breathed that fresh air, and we have exposed this regime to be rotten to its very core. We will not be sealed in again.' This time, as they clapped and cheered, a few rose from their seats to give the speaker a standing ovation. And that's when I saw him.

'Oh, my God,' I said aloud, my knees giving way.

He was there, standing up, clapping, his eyes wet with emotion, or was it the cold? Needing to sit down, I staggered to a nearby bench, fearful that I should faint. The voice continued in the background. 'Mr Nagy promises us free elections based on secret ballot; he promises us a new government founded not just on the communist party but an all-party coalition…'

'Are you all right, love?' The voice, nearby, seemed distant.

'She looks ill.'

'Has she fainted?'

I hadn't realised I'd closed my eyes but on opening them again, I was surrounded by a group of elderly ladies, leaning over me, blocking out the sky.

'The old parties are reforming and clamouring for their spot on the political stage; they too want a popular front…'

'Welcome back to the land of living, love; we thought you'd fainted.'

'She needs a doctor.'

'Smelling salts, that's what she needs.'

I didn't want their suffocating concern; I needed air, I needed space, but didn't have the heart to push them away.

'What's come over you, dear, are you OK?' More people had gathered behind them. How could a fainting woman on a park bench cause so much interest at a time like this, I wondered. 'But what they don't seem to realise is that all this talk and posturing will amount to nothing unless we can garner world opinion on our side. Without it, we are lost, without support, the Russians will say we've gone too far, and they'll bang the iron fist and we'll be back where we started…'

'Yes, yes, I'm all right.' My voice sounded weak and far away. 'I just need a few minutes.'

'For goodness sake, give the poor woman some air.'

'She's fine.'

'Wrap yourself up, love, it's cold now.'

And as suddenly as they had appeared, they were gone; the dreary sky of grey visible now, pressing down on me, snowflakes melting on my face.

'But will the world listen to us? Will the United Nations take seriously our plight when the world's attention is focussed on the unfolding events taking place right this minute in Suez…?' I'd laid down on the bench and realised I was sprawled across it like an old tramp. People passed by, glancing disdainfully at me, young and old, carrying either picnic baskets or rifles, sometimes both. 'The world holds its breath and watches as British and French troops amass in the Middle East; the United States turns inwards as Eisenhower and Stevenson fight it out for votes. So where, ladies and gentlemen, does it leave us? I'll tell you where – at the mercy of Khrushchev and his henchmen…'

I pulled myself up and readjusted my skirt, wanting to appear more ladylike. And then, like a biblical parting of the waves, the crowds dispersed and there, not more than ten yards from me, his eyes fixed on me, standing as still as Stalin's statue that used to dominate the park, was my ex-husband.

Chapter 26
Day Seven – Monday, 29 October

1.

I woke up this morning with my ex-husband sleeping only a few feet away.

I stared at him for a while trying to equate this crumpled figure with the man who'd once been a constant in my life. Yesterday afternoon, in the park, we sat for what seemed like hours with his head in my lap, the two of us sobbing.

I asked him where he was staying but he couldn't speak, he seemed totally helpless. I needed to act for him, to make his decisions. He was too weak to walk the distance back to the apartment but I managed to catch us a lift on a truck full of men with guns. Josef hesitated before climbing aboard, his attention caught by the large Kossuth emblem someone had painted on the side of the truck. I knew the feeling, no one had ever thought we'd see it again, the symbol of our country, the emblem of our patriotism. But now it was everywhere, crudely painted on vehicles, on shop fronts, on signs. He stared at it, his eyes wide, the emotion stifled by surprise, when a pair of arms, strong patriotic arms, reached down and physically hoisted him onto the truck.

On this late Monday morning, the sun made an effort to brighten the living room as we ate our breakfast of bread and jam, with cups of black and unsweetened coffee. Basic foodstuffs that both of us, but especially Josef, thought were the pinnacle of luxury. But hungry as I was, I couldn't eat, too worried about George, about how to explain the reappearance of my past. Josef ate slowly, savouring each mouthful; a habit, he told me, from his time in prison. The cherry flavour of the jam was almost too much for him, his senses not used to such an assault on his taste buds; and the coffee made him feel heady, so unaccustomed was he to its strength. Ordeal by luxury.

Mid-morning. Josef and I sat quietly at the table, the shared breakfast plate empty. Still no sign of George or Milan but it wasn't the first time they'd disappeared for a couple of days, revelling in the joy of chaos and the chaos of liberty. Occasionally, Josef asked me a flurry of questions – what had happened during his time away; what had caused this sudden uprising; what had happened to the old Stalinists like Rakosi and Gero; where did Imre Nagy fit into it all? I answered as best as I could, often leaving him with more questions. I longed for Josef to talk without peppering me with questions, longed for him to mention Anastasia, but our past was not a subject we broached, nor the future. Both seemed too far away. For now, we concentrated on the present. And all the time I kept a watch on the door. At some point, George would be back. How would I explain this stranger in his space, this dishevelled man with baggy eyes and long, witch-like fingers? Josef was a weakened man. I remembered him as a man of some eighty kilos. He now weighed little more than fifty-five. I dreaded to think what deprivations he endured.

'How strange everything feels,' he said. 'It's odd but after a while life in a cell becomes your only reality. You give up on dreaming of freedom and your past begins to feel as if it belongs to someone else. So you're left with this stretch of meaningless time. After months of solitude, you crave company, for a pair of friendly eyes, a sympathetic ear, and when it happens you love your fellow inmates with an intensity that is frightening and then, after months of living on top of one another, one longs for solitude.'

2.

'I'm cold, Mama.'

'I know, Roza, here, let me rub your back.' Petra knelt down, wrapped her arms around her daughter and squeezed her tightly. 'Papa's going to get us away from here soon, aren't you, dear?'

Zoltan, sitting upright in the armchair, made no attempt to answer, instead kept his eyes fixed on a portrait photograph of Rakosi on the opposite wall. He hadn't shaved for days, his 'dead man's clothes', as he called them, fitted poorly and were of such dreadful quality it was a wonder they didn't fall to pieces whenever he moved. He still wore his AVO regulation boots, solidly made from black leather; and in his pocket, he kept his AVO service revolver; the only remnants from eight years of service. Zoltan's career, which had been gradually grinding to a halt, was finally over. But right now, that was the least of their worries.

Their surroundings were unfamiliar, having abandoned their upstairs apartment and come to a vacant basement one instead. The block had survived relatively intact, but the building next to it had been pummelled by Soviet shells, and they felt safer being nearer to the ground. The place was also covered in a heavy layer of dust; many of the windows smashed and, despite the gas fire, he had never felt so cold.

'Zoltan? Zoltan, we can't stay here.'

214

Slowly, he turned his head, his eyes red, his face etched with symmetrical lines – years of age accumulated in seven days. 'We can't go out there; I'd be recognised.' He looked back at Rakosi's rounded and deceptively jocular features and his shiny bald head. 'Lynched,' he said, spitting the word out.

'You have to go back to them and fight,' she said.

'What?'

'To the AVO.'

'The AVO's dead.'

'No. There's still enough of you to take control of the city. Find Donath and fight, Zoltan. If you don't, they'll take over completely. The city and the whole country will be in the hands of barbarians. You owe it to us.'

Roza nestled in closer to Petra's bosom. 'I'm hungry.'

'I know, sweetheart, I'm going out soon to find something. You can come too, if you like.'

*

It could be that simple, thought Petra. She and Roza could leave the apartment and not come back. While they remained with him, they too were marked but not if they simply walked out on him. Most people wouldn't know; wouldn't associate them with Zoltan or the AVO. Ten years they'd been married, thrown together, like so many couples of their age, after the defeat of the Nazis. Did she love him; had she ever loved him? In 1946 it wasn't a matter of love, it was a matter of survival, and a massive effort to start life again while adjusting to the ever-perpetual presence of the Russians. Love didn't come into it, but ideals did. Zoltan was an idealist; they both were. A dedicated fighter against fascism, he became a communist, determined to root out those who threatened its early survival in Hungary. Stepping into the AVO boots seemed a logical progression. But ideals and logic had lost all meaning many years ago.

A fine layer of snow covered the streets, mirroring the white dust inside. Petra walked quickly, holding Roza's hand, encouraging her to keep up and get warm. Everywhere, people swarmed about or huddled in groups, youngsters with cigarettes and guns, men reading revolutionary newspapers, women carrying string bags half-full of vegetables, people in bandages, nursing their wounds, somewhere a dog barking. But still, she thought, how quiet everything seemed. No more crackle of machine guns, no screams of battle, no rumbling of tanks. But the evidence lay all around them; the debris of revolution all the more visible in the silence: disjointed corpses covered in lime to disguise the stench of death, burnt-out tanks, hanging cables and uprooted tram lines, collapsed buildings and gaping craters, and smashed cars, abandoned trucks and empty trams. Everything around her in need of an adjective because normal things had lost all sense of their normality. Roza squeaked and hid her face in a gloved hand – hanging upside down from a tree, a man stripped bare, his body gently swaying in the wind, his torso red, black and raw, his mouth stuffed full with bank notes. Petra tightened her grip on her daughter's hand and pulled her along, regretting the need of having to drag her along, exposing her to such sights.

The queue was mercifully short but she soon realised it was because she was late. There was nothing left, said a robust middle-aged woman in a battered apron, come back tomorrow when they were expecting fresh supplies from the country. The look on Roza's face reflected how Petra felt. But here, said the woman, have a couple of beetroots. It was of little consolation but Petra thanked her.

She started walking towards the City Park, the opposite direction from the apartment. Roza asked where they were going and Petra palmed her off with something about needing exercise. She wasn't going back; she'd made up her mind, she wasn't going back.

At first, she walked as if on golden pavements. She grinned at passers-by, believing that she shared in their victory – the Russians had gone, democracy was around the corner and she was free of Zoltan and the death sentence he carried on him like a label. But after almost half an hour, Roza's occasional moan had become constant; the cold seeped into their bones and Petra, when she thought about it, had no idea where to go. In living a life of relative luxury as an AVO's wife, she had, one by one, lost all her friends. Until this moment it had never bothered her. But it bothered her now.

'Good morning, again, Mrs Beke.'

She spun round. He was there, standing casually behind her, as if he'd been expecting her, as if he'd been standing there all the time, wearing his quilted jacket and beret, smoking a handmade cigarette. He must've been following them. The faint smile on his face made her shudder.

She turned her back on him. 'Come on, Roza, we're going home.'

'Back to Mr Beke?'

Roza glanced inquisitively up at her mother. 'Mama, isn't that—'

'Yes, come on,' she said, pulling on her hand, desperate to get away from him as quickly as possible.

'Mr Zoltan Beke, officer of the AVO,' he said, the voice behind her quiet but piercing.

She stopped but didn't turn around – too frightened to do so, too frightened to carry on walking. But Roza did turn around.

'Hello, you must be his daughter.' His familiarity towards Roza repulsed her.

She listened as his footsteps approached slowly, deliberately. He drew level but still she couldn't bear to look at him. 'What do you want?' she said, her voice edged with guilt more than fear.

'Your husband and me go back a long way, Mrs Beke.' He drew on his cigarette. 'A long way.' She wanted to deny him, to say she hadn't seen him for weeks, but she couldn't, not in front of Roza. 'Guess he must be out of a job these days.'

'Roza,' she said, firmly. 'Please, wait for me on the corner there.'

'But why—'

'Roza.' Her daughter looked at her and at the stranger, opened her mouth but then decided to do as she was told.

'What a considerate mother you are. So, tell me, how is he these days? Still alive? So many AVOs now taking their own lives, you never know.'

'I said what do you want?'

'I'd like to see your husband get the justice he deserves.'

'He was only doing his job.'

'His job cost me six years of my life and my fingernails.' He fanned his fingers out in front of her face and, sure enough, a layer of skin had grown where his fingernails should have been. 'Cost me half my cock too, want to see that as well? No? Can't say I blame you, it's not a nice sight but hey, it's still functional in every way, if you know what I mean.'

'I'm pleased for you.' Immediately, she regretted the patronising tone.

He pushed his face into hers. 'Oh, are you, Mrs Beke, you AVO whore?' She twisted her head, the smell of tobacco and garlic filling her nostrils. 'I followed him for months, got to know where he lived, got to know you, your daughter. But I didn't have the nerve to do anything. Didn't even have the means. Then all this shit takes off and someone puts a gun in my hand. I go to find him. But of course, everyone's gone. Imagine my delight in seeing you yesterday. Meet me tomorrow,' he growled, thrusting a scrap of paper into her hand. It was an address but she didn't read it, not wanting to know it. 'After dusk. Don't bring the kid. I'll be waiting for you.' He made to leave, throwing the cigarette on the road.

'I won't come.' Her heartbeat stopped.

He laughed. 'Your daughter – pretty little thing. It's Roza, isn't it?' Lifting his voice, he shouted, 'How old are you, Roza? Nine, ten?'

Roza nodded back, her eyes checking for her mother's permission.

'OK, OK,' said Petra. 'After dusk.'

'I look forward to it.' He tipped his beret. 'Nice seeing you again, Mrs Beke. Goodbye, Roza.'

She watched him leave for a few moments, then glanced at her daughter, still waiting obediently on the corner of the street. She walked up to her, her feet heavy and awkward. 'Shall we go home?' she said.

'Why are you crying, Mummy?'

'Oh, it's nothing.' She wanted to kiss her, to hug her, but something held her back. She knew if she did, she'd never let go.

3.

The column of a dozen tanks rolled across the Hungarian countryside, Budapest already an hour behind them. Following in the rear came the motorcycles and trucks. The T-54 in front of them had placed a gruesome mascot on the back of their tank – a dead comrade, propped up and held in place by ropes. The dead soldier watched Budapest fade into the distance. Petrov had complained, saying it wasn't right that they were being subjected to a dead man's vacant gaze from here back to Moscow. A dead Hungarian he could have coped with, perhaps, but not one of their own, too close for comfort. But the team in front said they were taking him home in dignity; not for their colleague the trucks full of stiffs thrown in haphazardly without any respect.

The locals certainly lacked respect. The whole route seemed lined with peasants, silent and angry, wanting to see with their own eyes the departing Russians. Many jumped out to spit at the tanks and yell Russian obscenities at the soldiers. Vladimir, who spent most of his time leaning out of the turret, remarked that at least the Russian language lessons weren't for nothing. At first, he yelled back at them but soon lost interest as the line seemed to stretch ahead continually.

How lovely it was to feel the cool air chasing away the nauseous smells of grime and diesel fumes inside the tank. Vladimir, still leaning out of the turret, started singing a bawdy song, too loudly for Valentin's liking. He resisted the temptation to pull his friend down by the legs and tell him to shut the fuck up. Why upset the locals even more? Part of him was impressed, however, amazed at how cheerful Vladimir could remain after living on their nerves for six days with very little sleep. But they were going home and that was excuse enough for Vladimir to sing his songs. The relief at leaving Hungary was tangible but Valentin felt too exhausted to appreciate it. Never had he been so tired, and so unable to sleep. But there was more to it than that. For the second time in his life, he was leaving Budapest with a knot in his stomach.

He remembered the first time. In some ways it wasn't too dissimilar, together with a bunch of men, a team united in their objectives and by their experiences, relieved to be leaving and talking of what they'd do when they got back home. But last time, they were on a plane; last time they didn't stink, nor salivate at the sight of a cow in the field. But at least this time he didn't feel as if his heart was breaking.

He remembered the flight so well – the face he forced himself to adapt not to give himself away, the food he forced himself to eat, the jokes he forced himself to laugh at. And all the while he recalled every moment and detail of the previous day, wishing he could relive it a thousand times.

It'd been seven years. How many permutations can a person's life take in seven years, even within a country with closed borders and limited choices? The more he thought about the woman in front of the bonfire, the more he realised it couldn't have been Eva. All he had to go on was the red hair and a strange feeling that pricked his heart. She was too far away, too obscured by smoke and the chaos around her. But why had she remained so resolutely calm when a 100-millimetre tank canon bore down on her? His colleagues had dismissed her as a crazy woman but, at the time, he thought them wrong. Fanciful thoughts that defied logic and clouded reality. It wasn't her; it was ridiculous to think it was. But in his tired, tired mind, he allowed his imagination to indulge the fantasy.

Chapter 27
Day Eight – Tuesday, 30 October

1.

Josef and I had more physical contact in those two days than we had had in the last three years of our marriage. I fed him, bathed him and helped him to sleep. I gave him some of George's clothes and lent him George's razor. He slept little but often. One of the joys of being free, he said, was being able to sleep without a dazzling light bulb perpetually on, constantly penetrating through the eyelids. Once, he remembered, there'd been a power cut and the men cried for joy, so relieved to escape the intensity of false light. Sometimes he cried for no apparent reason. Not the huge sobs of the park, but quiet, rather dignified tears. I'd offer my hand and he either took it or waved me away. Either way, I didn't mind, I was only pleased that he was coming to terms with the misery dealt him by the AVO.

I went out twice and obtained more food and an extra blanket, each time hoping George wouldn't return during my brief absences. But all the time, I couldn't equate this man I was tending to as my husband. His mind as well as his physical being had been permanently changed. Gone was the man I married, the man of principles; gone too the man who dedicated his life to work for fear of doing otherwise.

How I enjoyed these couple of peaceful days together. This man I once knew vaguely as a husband playing the part of the perfect guest, polite, undemanding and unassuming. The care I lavished on him was not of his asking but purely from my want. Between us, we perfected an isolated existence, divorced from the world outside.

After breakfast, Josef excused himself, saying he needed a shave. He felt the desire to shave twice a day, although he had no need to. But after so long with a beard, he said, he simply enjoyed the process and the sensation of clean, shaved skin. So many ordinary things he appreciated.

I cleared away the plates and breakfast things and busied myself with the washing up. It amused me to occupy my time with domestic chores while half the apartment looked as if a Soviet bomb had hit it.

Finished in the bathroom, Josef hovered and seemed awkward. Finally, he declared that he had to meet a few friends but would it be OK if he came back to stay for a while longer. Yes, I said, that'd be fine; he could stay as long as he needed. He looked relieved and thanked me. Taking George's coat I'd lent him, Josef hesitated before leaving. Perhaps he wanted to tell me how grateful he was, how he never forgot me during his time away, how he knew now what a neglectful husband he'd been, how selfish his behaviour after Anastasia's death; I could see it all in his eyes but he said nothing, the words stayed imprisoned within him.

I couldn't decide whether I minded not being asked to accompany him but obviously, he had things to do, things that didn't concern me, things that perhaps he thought I wouldn't understand. I sat down with another coffee wanting to reflect, wanting to be overcome with a guiding emotion. But for a long time, nothing came. I simply sat there, my mind empty. Josef's return, I knew, was going to change me. Too long I'd spent looking backwards, wishing that things had been different. Anastasia is always there, I wouldn't wish it differently, but after so many years I knew it was finally time to bury her in my mind, to let go of the physical being that lived still in my dreams. And Valentin, who'd occupied so little time in my life but took up so much space in my emotions, had to leave. In my mind, I kissed Valentin one last time and bade him goodbye. No more would I wonder where he was, or what he was doing. I picked up the book of famous Soviet footballers, and threw it out of the window – quickly, not allowing myself a second thought. How ridiculous to attach such importance to something that reminded me of him by his very omission. My future belonged in the present; I could no longer afford to suffocate myself with the past. Josef was back; Josef, I hoped, was my future.

Of course, I still had to tell George. George who had rescued me, who had given my life a direction at a time when his own life veered precariously left and right. Mutual rescue.

*

George, when he finally returned, came back alone, looking dishevelled and tired but happy. Josef was still out doing whatever he had to do. George told me in great detail the places he'd gone – with or without Milan. It seemed as if not one part of Budapest had been spared his presence at some point over the previous couple of days. I was pleased for him;

the uprising had rejuvenated and changed him. I was seeing a different George now, a more animated George, one ready to embrace life and whatever it held, not the man I was accustomed to, the one who silently suffered, who, like the rest of us, wore his blinkers, hoping the world would go away and leave him alone.

I'd been washing up when George walked in. Having half-listened to his adventures, I resumed my work, picking up a tea towel to dry the plates, and at the same time, deciding that I had to tell him about Josef. 'George...'

'How's your hand now?'

'Oh, it's fine.'

'Have you heard – it's confirmed; they've cancelled Sunday's Hungarian–Sweden game. No surprise there. Pity though.'

'George, I need to speak to you.'

He caught the tone in my voice and sat down slowly at the table. 'Are you all right?'

'Yes, I'm fine, really, but there's something I have to tell you.' I was still drying a side plate, wiping in a continuous circle. His eye caught it. I placed the plate to one side and, still holding the green checked tea towel, sat down opposite him. 'George, I've been thinking about... well, about you and me.'

'Go on.'

'When you think about it, we only know the edges of each other's past and yet it is our pasts that brought us together. And we carry on living without plans and with no idea where we're going or what to do with our futures.'

'Not any more. Everything's changed now; it's changing as we speak, we have a future more glorious than any of us could ever have hoped for.'

'People can start making plans now.'

'Yes, absolutely. What was the use of plans when we had no future? We, the proletariat, worked for the benefit of everyone, but only the Party benefited from the work we did. But things have changed and perhaps now we do have a future to look forward to. Once a National Assembly is in place, and we have a new government that truly acts in accordance to the people's will and not to Moscow's whim, then everything we've fought for in the last week will have been worth it, and those who died will not have done so in vain. Then, we really will have a future.'

I picked at the tea towel, unthreading a strand of green cotton. 'And the past? Our past?'

'The past will always be there, as a reminder of how we let ourselves be manipulated and tortured, of how we lived in fear of the State and how that fear infected our daily life like a cancer. But it is to the future we need to focus our energies on.'

'George, you sound like a politician.'

'We all have to be politicians now – our future depends on it.'

The intense look of sincerity in his eyes squashed me. I knew that he loved me. But I loved George as a woman loves her brother. I had to tell him about Josef but the words wouldn't come; it would have to wait.

Later, I thought, I'd tell him later.

2.

The outside of the building was pockmarked with bullet holes; every window smashed; the front door blasted into pieces. She had to force the fragments of the door to one side. The dark stairway reeked of filth and urine. She looked at the scrap of paper – first floor, it read, number three. She climbed the stairs, strewn with rubble, her heart beating like a platoon of marching soldiers. From outside, she heard a round of laughter and felt as if it was aimed at her. She felt inside her pocket for the money. Almost five hundred florins, most of what they had left. The loose cash Zoltan kept about his person was as much as a factory worker took home in a month. Maybe more. Carrying it now only brought to mind the wads of banknotes stuffed into the mouths of lynched AVOs. She too would be lynched if anyone knew how much she had on her.

A cool breeze whistled down the corridor, the light bulb swung ominously from the ceiling. Number Three. She knocked softly. No answer. She turned to leave, pretending to be satisfied – she'd come as told and knocked, not her fault if no one was there. But then she thought of Roza and knew it didn't count – a mouse wouldn't have heard that knock. She turned to try again and this time noticed that the door was slightly ajar. Slowly, nervously, she pushed the door open and gingerly stepped inside. *I'm doing this for my daughter*, she thought to herself. A shaft of light blasted through the window illuminating a simple table and chair in the middle of the room. Above the table, a chandelier dangled by a single wire, bits of plaster and masonry littered the floor, dry dust everywhere.

'Hello,' she said, quietly, praying not to hear an answer. As her eyes adjusted to the dark, she noticed the bed to her left in the corner behind the door, equally coated in dust and bits of wood. Above the bed a portrait of Rakosi, without the glass, his features distorted by graffiti into a caricature. Any other time, she may have laughed. She stepped carefully across the floor and saw, under the bed, a teddy bear, ragged and coated in dirt. She ran her finger over the table, leaving a line of wood exposed between the expanse of dust like an aerial view of a river cutting through a plain. It was then she heard the crunch of shoes behind her.

She spun round. Silhouetted in the door, the now-familiar quilted jacket and beret, the scent of handmade cigarettes. 'Mrs Beke,' he said. 'Nice of you to show. Apologies for the state of this place but you know how things are.'

'Shall we get this over and done with?'

'Do you know, I know your name but you don't know mine. You must think me very rude. Tamas, at your service, ma'am.' He clicked his heels and bowed. 'I suppose that's how you expect people to greet you, eh, in this great society of equals?'

'OK, how much do you want?'

'Want?'

'You can have it all.' She'd come prepared to bargain, to play the game. Start at three hundred and rise when needed. But she didn't want to play now, she was frightened and simply wanted to get it over and done with and get out. She fished in her pocket and pulled out the notes, rolled up and held in place by an elastic band. 'Here, five hundred.' She tossed it on the bed where it threw up a small cloud of dust. 'That's it, I have nothing more.'

He looked at the money, kept looking at it as if he'd never seen so much (which, Petra knew, he wouldn't have), then looked back at her. She stepped back, knowing immediately from the glare in his eyes, she'd made a mistake. 'You stupid bitch, your sort thinks money will buy you out of anything. I don't want your fucking money but I'll take it, I'll stuff it up your husband's arse.' Outside a truck speeded past. He glanced at the window, as if he was expecting someone to appear, then back at Petra. 'Please, take your skirt off.'

It sounded more like a request, the host offering to relieve his guest of her coat. 'No.' The refusal may have slipped out but inside her throat, it had traversed mountains of fear to emerge.

He laughed. From inside his jacket, he pulled out a revolver, clicked it open, inspected it and closed it again. She noticed his fingers without fingernails. 'Your skirt, Mrs Beke, if you please.'

'You don't have to do this –'

'You'll be my first in six years – you know that? OK, perhaps there was the odd whore here and there but we won't count them.'

'No, please, not me…'

'You don't remember, I told you, your husband ordered my cock to be chopped in half. Your sod of a husband. I almost bled to death. Couldn't piss without pain for years. I swore I'd get my own back, I'd kill the bastard. But this, this is so much sweeter, to fuck his wife with the remaining half. So, blame it on him, it's his fault, you hear? And you'll go home and tell him. Tamas Kopacsi, he'll remember. Fucked his wife with half a cock. Ask him if he's still got the other half. Perhaps, he kept it as a souvenir, eh?'

'I'm sorry for what he did, really I am, but you can't –'

'Can't I?' He took a step towards her, his thumbs hooked in his belt. 'Your skirt.'

She glanced at the window. The left shutter hung on one hinge. She wanted to scream but who would come to help an AVO wife? How far up were they? First floor, too far to jump. How silent the street, how empty her heart. She'd never felt so alone, so at the mercy of another. She wondered whether she'd prefer the bullet but the thought of Roza waiting for her, wanting her to come back, filled her mind. She thought of

Zoltan and realised for the first time in years, she loved him and had never told him. How she wanted to tell him now, to shrink in his arms and disappear, engulfed in his warmth, his smell. The tears tickled her cheeks.

'You're keeping me waiting, Mrs Beke.'

How absurd his politeness, his use of her name.

With fingers shaking, she unhitched the hook on her skirt.

Chapter 28
Day Nine – Wednesday, 31 October

Zoltan gazed out of the broken window onto Republic Square and the scurrying figures below. The morning mist hung heavily, the square carpeted in places by autumn leaves. Armed insurgents, men and women, had positioned themselves behind trees and burnt-out cars.

Wearing only his 'dead man's' civilian clothes, Zoltan had rejoined his company the evening before and felt better for having done so. Petra was right; there was still a chance, a fighting chance. Better to die fighting than caged up in that hole, frightened of every unfamiliar noise.

Donath had welcomed him back with a raised eyebrow.

Young Paul joined him at the window. 'It doesn't look good, does it?' he said.

'No. But we'll be OK.'

Behind them, other AVOs smoked and waited, their rifles and guns propped up against the wall. A long mahogany table decorated with wilted flowers and blotting pads dominated the conference room, surrounded by high-backed chairs. From the ceiling, hung three lavish chandeliers and, along the walls, a veritable gallery of portraits of great leaders, past and present, Hungarian and Russian. A large clock above the double doors at the far end showed ten o'clock. Men positioned themselves at each of the many windows looking down on the square.

A burst of gunfire splattered the building. The two men ducked as glass shattered around them. Everywhere, men crouched on the floor as bits of plaster fell on them, segments of chandelier glass tinkled to the floor and a cloud of dust floated down.

Donath strode in from the anteroom next door where the regional commander had set up office, surrounded by phones and yes-men (Donath, thought Zoltan, being one of them). 'Get up, you fools,' he bellowed. 'They're not going to hit you while they're firing upwards.' Zoltan looked up and saw the fresh sprinkling of holes in the ceiling. 'The commander's on the phone, we should be getting reinforcements soon. Now get up and return fire. Lieutenant, I leave it to you.' With a click of his heels, he swung round and returned to his master.

The men gathered up their Kalashnikovs and crawled to the windows. Zoltan found himself sharing a window with Paul but another round of fire kept them down. A portrait of Gero clattered to the floor. 'Fire,' shouted the lieutenant from the far side of the long room. Zoltan peeked out of the window, only shards of glass remaining, steadied his rifle and fired aimlessly into the square. Paul followed his example. The insurgents fired back. The whole room reverberated to the sound of gunfire from all directions, ricochets pinged, glass shattered, the walls thudded with bullets. To Zoltan's left, the AVO machine gun rattled continuously while the assistant frantically fed the belt with more bullets. A piercing scream rose above the noise; someone to Zoltan's far left had been hit. Colleagues pulled him back as he writhed in pain, clutching his shoulder. The returning fire was coming at them vertically now, the insurgents had occupied the building opposite. The wounded man yelped helplessly as someone tried to check the spray of blood with a tourniquet.

Saturated in sweat, Zoltan fired and kept firing, ducking occasionally, his teeth clenched solidly. He saw a rebel take a bullet down in Republic Square, someone ran to his aid. Zoltan held his breath, aimed and fired. The rescuer went down in a heap and Zoltan felt the surge of ecstasy rise up within him. He wanted to kill, to pluck the bastards off one by one. An AVO to his right fell backwards silently and landed with a thud, his shirt ruined by the spurt of blood from his neck.

Zoltan reloaded. Outside, the rebels were dropping, sustaining casualties at a fantastic rate. A bullet hit the window frame inches from his face. He looked up and saw a figure duck down behind a window in the building opposite. The figure reappeared. Zoltan fired and the man slumped forward as if trying to escape from the building. 'Got him,' exclaimed Paul. For a moment, Zoltan was about to argue the case but then a T-54 lumbered into the square followed by dozens of more rebels using it for cover. Seconds later, two ambulances appeared. Men and women with Red Cross armbands jumped out. The AVO machine gun sprayed the newcomers. A nurse fell lifeless, her white uniform doused in crimson red.

A haze of smoke had descended over the square but the gunfire maintained its tortuous momentum. Every few minutes, another AVO fell. The room heaved with their groans and shouts. More AVOs ran in; some to replace their fallen colleagues, others to carry the wounded away for patching up. The dead, they left where they fell.

More rebels crowded into the square, zigzagging across the open space, firing up at the AVOs. Every tree, every vehicle used for cover; every window in the opposing building occupied. Paul ducked down to catch his breath, 'Christ,' he said, 'for everyone that goes down, another ten spring up in their place.'

Those in the square were getting closer; soon they'd be storming the building. The insurgents were close enough now to throw their home-made Molotov cocktails. Zoltan heard the screams from the floor below as the petrol bombs exploded.

The T-54 fired its first salvo. It shot high. No damage — this time. The AVO machine gun fired back, but a bullet in the head of its AVO operator caused it to pause. Before the replacement had a chance to take his place, another volley from the tank smashed into the building two or three floors above them. For a moment, Zoltan feared the ceiling was about to collapse on them.

The far door opened. It was Donath again, a wet cloth around his mouth against the dust, crawling in on his hands and knees. Above him, the clock read eleven. Through the cloth, he shouted something out but the noise trampled on his words. He disappeared again. But his message spread along the room from one window to the next; it didn't take long, there weren't that many of them left now. Zoltan hoped the message would survive intact by the time it reached him. This was no time for Chinese Whispers. Finally it reached Zoltan and Paul: 'No reinforcements coming.'

The two men gawked at each other, absorbing its significance. Someone, somewhere, had decided against helping them, had decided to leave them to their fates. They were on their own.

'We're not going to get out of this, are we?' said Paul, close to tears.

'Yes, of course we are,' replied Zoltan, not bothering to hide the lie betrayed in the tone of his voice. 'Keep firing.'

Huge cracks appeared in the ceiling and the wall behind them, the whole building creaked as another tank shell smashed into it.

'Come on, let's get out of here.' As they dashed for the door, Zoltan realised the room was awash with dead and dying colleagues.

'Comrade…' A uniformed AVO Zoltan knew only by sight had grabbed his trouser leg, 'get me down to the basement.' The side of his head had caved in, coagulated in blood and shattered bone.

Paul waited a few steps away, 'Fuck sake, leave him,' he implored.

'No, comrade, please…' The grip on his trousers tightened as another shell tore into the wall next to the window where only moments before he and Paul were positioned. Zoltan clenched shut his eyes and pulled his leg away. He wanted to apologise but what was the point? The injured AVO was still screaming at them as they made their way down one of the two stairways, his screams eventually obliterated by the noise of mayhem coming at them from every direction.

AVOs seemed to come from every direction, scrambling down the stairs but as they approached the ground floor, they realised that with the huge front doors blasted away, they could not reach the basement stairs without exposing themselves to gunfire. Voices above them told them to come back up to the first floor.

The room was filled with uniformed AVOs, most of whom Zoltan knew only by sight, if at all. Donath was amongst them. 'My boys, my boys,' he said, approaching Zoltan and Paul. 'You're my only ones to survive.'

'What's happening, boss?'

'We're surrendering. The commander's sending out a forward party under a white flag.' He looked at each of them in turn. 'Thank you, boys. We've come a long way together, eh? A long way.'

It seemed ridiculous, thought Zoltan, but he couldn't help but bristle with pride; proud that at this last hour, his boss was finally acknowledging his worth.

The surrendering party consisted of three women and a white flag. Good idea, thought Zoltan, the insurgents wouldn't harm unarmed women. The women waited for their orders. How strange, he thought, the one at the front, holding the flag, had eyes of different colours. It gave her a strange look, but certainly not unattractive. Quite the opposite. The three women passed through the crowd of AVOs, the flag above them, setting out on their fateful journey onto the street and into the hands of the insurgents and the unknown. Shouts of good luck followed the trio as they marched bravely down the main stairway. The men and women left behind stood awkwardly in silence, no one sure of their place, like unfamiliar guests at a party.

They heard the shouts outside. 'They're surrendering; don't shoot.' They listened as the guns ceased their work, and as the shouts and yells died away.

'It's working,' whispered Paul, his eyes as wide as a child's.

Donath nodded authoritatively.

The atmosphere lightened as the guests familiarised themselves with their surroundings.

Then, outside, a single shot rang out, followed moments later by another and then the third.

The burst of cheering outside chilled those inside. For a few stilled moments, they remained motionless, each of them coming to terms with God's decision. The seconds stretched as their lives closed in. Their last chance had just passed them by; death was coming to greet them like an invisible friend, its arm around their shoulders, showing them the way to the eternal darkness that lay ahead.

Then, as one, everyone propelled themselves in different directions. Amidst confusion and screams they collided, pushed and elbowed their way out, each for himself, each opting for a different route to escape, to flee for their lives. The insurgents' footsteps were audible now on the main stairway, intensifying the panic. Those who had elected to go that way were soon dragged out and shot.

Zoltan found himself charging down the second staircase, surrounded by others, amazed to see Paul and Donath still beside him, not sure who was following whom. As they passed the ground floor, a group of insurgents poured in like a tidal wave crashing over a fragile boat. The narrow space filled with screams and yells as the forces clashed and clamoured. In a matter of seconds, he saw a rifle butt smash into a head, a knife plunge into a stomach. Wherever he tried to move, a uniform blocked his way. The stench of blood and fear soaked into him. He saw two insurgents pull Paul out by his arms and hair, the high-pitched screams disintegrating into helpless sobs. A flash of courage pierced him, he wanted to save him, but something knocked Zoltan to the ground.

A hand pulled him up, the hand of a young insurgent, his eyes, behind broken glasses, full of fire. 'You OK, friend?' said the boyish voice before disappearing into the tumult.

It took a few seconds to understand the significance – they thought he was one of them, without his uniform, he was one of the insurgents. The fight in the stairway dissolved as quickly as it had started. The insurgents moved out, taking with them their screaming prisoners, leaving behind their bloodied victims. Zoltan followed them, joining in with the shouts of 'death to the AVO' with apparent ease because inside, his heart felt numb.

The scene outside knocked his heart back into frantic activity – the burning cars and distant bodies registered only briefly, but he retched at the sight of Paul's lynched carcass, his body twisting grotesquely by his ankles. Around him still, the insurgents pummelled their victims before carrying them off to their places of death. An arm slapped him round the shoulder. 'Don't waste your tears for these bastards,' said a voice in his ear. He turned round but the man had already gone, instead what he saw jolted his heart.

Donath's white face eyed him steadily as they stripped him of his jacket, the tunic he'd donned for so many years, and threw away his medal, the Order of Lenin that he'd worn so proudly. Only yards apart, the two men locked eyes. *Don't give me away now, boss; don't give me away.* The men around him tore off Donath's shirt, exposing his flabby chest and bulging stomach but still his eyes remained sharply focussed on his former pupil. Unnoticed by all but Donath, Zoltan shook his head, pleading with his eyes to be spared. His own death wouldn't save Donath's; his old boss knew that. Suddenly, Donath was upside down and within seconds was hanging by his feet to a nearby tree. How quickly the insurgents had mastered their art. But Donath didn't scream, didn't plead for his life as the executioners soaked him in petrol.

It was only as the flames engulfed him that his eyes closed.

Chapter 29
Day Ten – Thursday, 1 November

1.

George was fast asleep when Josef returned early to the apartment. I had so wanted to tell George of the husband who'd been forced to divorce me, to tell him of my past, but the moment never came, never seemed the right time. I wondered whether there'd ever be a right time. The last thing I wanted was for the two men to meet before I had had the chance to explain but when Josef knocked on the door at ten in the morning, it was too late, the chance had gone; the meeting was now inevitable.

Josef lingered on the threshold and for a moment I felt I could have sent him away. Part of me wanted to, part of me wanted to confine him to the past where I felt he belonged. Instead, I gave in and invited him in. He apologised (unnecessarily) for his absence and told me that people were going back to work, the strike was as good as over but the mood still swung between hope and fear – the Russians were leaving / the Russians were coming back. No one, he said, seemed to know.

I offered to make coffee and as I waited for the pan of water to boil I found myself smiling, almost laughing, at the ridiculous situation I'd put myself in. Here, in the apartment, were the two men of my life, one current, the other past, each unaware of the other's presence. But the saddest part of all was that I loved one as a brother and I wasn't sure how I felt about the other.

'Something amuses you, Eva?'

'No, it's nothing.'

'I picked up one of these new newspapers. There's so many to choose from now.'

'It was easier when there was only the *Free People*.'

'Eva, you can't mean that. That mouthpiece of the Party served no one but itself.'

'You used to digest it every day.'

'It helped me survive. But these new ones, they speak the truth; they have opinions of their own. OK, the writing leaves something to be desired but you can't fault the sentiment. Some of them are only a page or two.'

'Your coffee.'

'Thank you.'

'What do we do, Josef?'

'What do you mean?'

'You and me. The future. Our future.'

'I don't know.' He stirred three spoonfuls of sugar into his coffee. 'I guess we'll have to see how the dust settles and decide from there.'

'Aren't you frightened of the future?'

'I'm more frightened of my past.'

'The past.' I felt my stomach tighten. 'We don't really go

there, do we? We never talk of the past.'

'You know I'd rather not.'

'But I do.'

'There's no point, woman. You tell me, what would be the point?'

'I suffered, Josef. And yet, seven years on, we've never discussed it.'

'I've never wanted to.'

'But have you never thought of what I might want? No, more than want – need. We lost a baby, Josef, yet I've never been able to talk to you about it.'

'For goodness sake, Eva, it was a long time ago. Surely you've got over it by now.'

'How can you say that?'

'I'm sorry.'

'You've never said how it affected you, you never told me —'

'OK, if you must know, it didn't affect me very much at all. There – I've said it. Eva, it's not as if I got to know her. She didn't make it and I'm sorry about that but we've lived through war, oppression and now, by the looks of it, a revolution as we speak. I've been tortured, had my dignity thrown out the window and was locked up for six years in conditions I wouldn't keep a pig in. And yet we always have to come back to a person who never was.'

'Our daughter.'

'Yes, our daughter.'

'You never think of her?'

He shook his head.

'I thought…'

'You thought what, Eva?'

'I don't know. I just don't know any more.'

I don't know how long George had been there, standing in his dressing gown, his hair eschew, examining the stranger sitting at the table. I felt my stomach tighten. 'George, I didn't see you.'

'Who's this?' he asked.

Josef rose to his feet, glancing at both George and me.

'George, I'm sorry, let me introduce you, this is… this is Josef, my husband.'

'Your husband?' George walked over in slow deliberate strides, his shoelaces undone, his eyes fixed on Josef.

'Josef's been away for a few years,' I said, using the familiar euphemism.

'How long?'

'Six years.'

'Long enough.'

'Yes.'

'*Gyűjtőfogház* Prison?'

Josef nodded.

George spun on his heels and said to me, 'Is that what you were trying to tell me yesterday, when you talked about knowing only the edges of each other's past?'

'Yes. It was.' I felt drained. I didn't want another confrontation.

Josef looked awkward. 'I'm sorry but do you… you both live here?'

'Yes,' said George.

'We're flatmates,' I said. 'There're three of us. There used to be many more but they've all gone one by one.'

'I see.' He paused, looking from George to me. 'The last thing I want is to…' he grappled for the word, 'to upset your arrangements. Perhaps, it'd be best if I left.'

'Perhaps it would be,' said George. 'How long have you been married?'

'Well, technically we're divorced but we got married in forty-six,' said Josef.

George stared through him, absorbing the situation, pondering his next move. 'Ten years.' He turned to me, shaking his head. 'You never said it was that long.'

'I tried to – yesterday.'

'I don't know what… If you excuse me, I think I need some air.'

'George, you don't have to go.' I didn't want him to leave, not now.

'I won't be long but I…' He looked at me and then at Josef. He tried to smile.

'Are you OK, George?'

'I'm sorry,' he said. 'Sorry for everything.'

2.

They'd been out in the forests for five days now, fighting off the cold and living on meagre rations; waiting for orders that never came while the Soviet Politburo made up their mind. Rumour followed counter-rumour: they were withdrawing; they were going back in; more tank divisions were pouring into Hungary; a final push was only a matter of days away. No one knew for sure, least of all the colonel. The Hungarians, surely, had gone beyond the point of compromise. If Khrushchev had truly accepted the Hungarians' position, they would have been ordered out by now. But still, no order came, one way or the other.

Their presence was no secret and the locals routinely came up to see them and ask what they were still doing in their country. Even these peasants seemed convinced that more

Russian tanks were coming in than going out. Valentin heard the colonel tell them that the soldiers were still there in order to ensure the safe evacuation of Soviet citizens living in Hungary. So, they asked, why are you hiding away in the forest? The colonel had no answer. Waiting for orders was his only retort.

But at least they were away from the insurgents. How many people had he killed out there in Budapest? He couldn't say, not because he'd lost count but because it was impossible to estimate while stuck in the dark coffin of a T-54. He hadn't given it any thought until now; too wrapped up in the thrill and the fright of battle, too concerned for his own skin to worry about the enemy's. Valentin had narrowly missed out on going to Korea so this was his first experience of armed combat. In his mind, he referred to it as armed combat because he couldn't, in all consciousness, call it war. Not when the enemy consisted of ordinary citizens, women and children – so many children, many as young as nine or ten. He couldn't have credited children with such valour, such a keen disregard for their own lives. What were they fighting for? Did they truly believe in their cause or was it, for them, simply a grand adventure? They all admired the way the kids attacked the tanks with their ingenious methods – pouring petrol in the paths of the tanks and then setting alight to it; jam on the tank windscreens; the hanging saucepans impersonating anti-tank guns, their highly effective petrol bombs. (He often wondered whether Vyacheslav Molotov, high ranking dignitary of the Soviet Politburo, saw it as a compliment that his name was so associated with homemade petrol bombs.) The tank crews soon scratched away the word 'petrol' from the petrol caps. But the admiration for the children's courage came only with the safety of time and distance. At the time they were considered as rats – small, lethal and unpredictable; and, like vermin, they sought any way to exterminate them. The thought made him shudder with shame now – he saw too many dead children, too many bearing unimaginable wounds.

And the women too. But when Valentin thought of the female fighters, his only thought was of the redhead at the bonfire, valiantly standing her ground while her comrades fell. (Although he tended now to think his colleagues right – it was not so much valour but the act of a woman demented by battle).

The whole city, the whole country, had been activated by the Soviet presence and the justice of their cause. He saw it more with each passing day. At first, only the young men and the fearless street kids carried their fight, but then, as the days progressed, more and more seemed prepared to join the affray – men and women of all walks of life flocked to the cause, the young and the old joining together. From the neutral man's point of view, it was an inspiring sight – only he wasn't neutral.

The general consensus of the Russian soldiers was that they, the tank regiments, were engaged in the wrong type of war. It wasn't the place for tanks patrolling the streets, providing easy targets for snipers and ambushes; what they needed was infantry, soldiers on foot and in mass, able to face the enemy on equal terms. However the Soviet military authorities were not ones who listened to the voices of their soldiers.

Did he want to go back in? No, of course not. Who'd want to relive that experience; to kill the children, the ordinary citizens, or face death at their hands? He wanted to get back to Moscow, collect a medal, and return to the routine he'd wanted to escape from.

But a part of him did want to go back; a part that however hard he tried to repress, was always there, the romantic in him, the part lacking any sense of reality, lurking, keeping him awake at night, telling him things might turn out all right when he knew damn well that it was an impossibility. But the thought was still there, entrenched in his mind that there was always the chance, a small chance, he might see her again – just one last time.

3.

George had known, of course, he'd always known. But that didn't make anything easier. Why, like a locked diary, had she kept her past hidden from him; why, when he'd known it to be there, had he not insisted she told him? She knew all there was to know of him – his father, his football, the years of incarceration – but he knew so little of her. Their knowledge of each other swung unfairly to her advantage.

George found himself in City Park and wondered how he'd managed to walk so far in such a daze. It felt like a state holiday – despite the cold the park was again full of families with picnics, children playing, people walking their dogs. He found a bench and sat down. A toy boomerang landed next to him. Picking it up, he saw two girls of about ten waving to him, asking for it back. He threw it but of course, it went in totally the wrong direction and the girl had to run further to retrieve it. He sat back down feeling self-conscious and slightly embarrassed.

So, this Josef was Eva's husband. With that certain fact came a hundred questions – what did this man's reappearance mean? What did it mean to Eva? Had theirs been a happy marriage, was it to continue? Did she love him? Somehow, he thought not. But equally, George knew she didn't love him either. Although somehow it worked. They'd floated together, the flotsam of wrecked lives, clinging onto each other. Love was not a necessity. But companionship was.

And now her husband was back, and Eva had accepted him back. He regretted now his hasty departure – he knew it'd been motivated in part by a sense of melodrama. And what good had it done him, save leave him with a cauldron of questions, and a heart perturbed more by this downturn in events than by Soviet tanks? And now, here he was, feeling somewhat foolish, sitting in a park waiting and wishing things were as they were, whilst, around him, people passed by, celebrating their victory and talking excitedly of a liberated future. He felt a fraud – embarrassed that such a minor distraction in his domestic life had so vehemently diminished his revolutionary fervour. He stood up and the world returned into focus – the park, the picnics, Stalin's boots, the revolution. As he left, George glanced back. The girls had resumed their game of boomerang.

He walked the streets, gawking at the post-revolution chaos that scarred the city, occasionally stopping to read one of the many new newspapers plastered up on walls or shop fronts. A weak sun filtered through the haze of clouds; people were out on the streets, a whole city trying to make sense of the past few days, trying to fathom what the future held for them. The optimists clapped each other on the back, and talked excitedly of elections and democracy; the pessimists shook their heads at their light-headed friends, predicting an imminent return of the Russian tanks (600 or more, some said). He saw a queue of people outside a Post Office – people waiting to withdraw their life savings. A few isolated tank crews remained but no one paid them much attention save asking the soldiers why they were still there, the evasiveness of their answers taken as ignorance. Some Russians still thought they were in Berlin or Prague. Nagy, some reckoned, was already negotiating Hungary's withdrawal from the Warsaw Pact. It seemed too good to be true; he couldn't equate the scenes of misery that lay at every corner with the bright new, Soviet-free society that so many enthused about.

No street was free of corpses; bodies lay statuesque, covered in coats or Hungarian flags, or sprinkled with lime. People strolled from one to another, their hands clasped over their mouths, lifting the coats, looking for a loved one. The dead AVOs or pro-Soviets who had the fortune to die from a bullet rather than suffer at the hands of the lynch mob had their chests skewered with pictures of Stalin or Rakosi.

He was now back in the street of the apartment, having walked a huge circle. So, this husband of Eva's must have been among those released from the city jails a few days before – the much-feted release of the totalitarian victims. Josef was one of them. The two men had much in common. It irked him when he recalled the expression on the man's face as he sat there in *his* apartment, at *his* table, being waited on by Eva, drinking what was left of *his* coffee. *Who's been sleeping in my bed?* At the time he hadn't really noticed it but when he relived the scene in his mind (as he'd done so many times already), he could almost feel the smug triumph in Josef's eyes, the radiance of irritating satisfaction. And what was upsetting him was that Eva failed to see it. The man was manipulating her.

So immersed was George in his role of self-pitying victim that it took him a few seconds to register that the object of his resentment was walking briskly towards him wearing one of his coats.

Not wanting to appear as if he'd been waiting on the street, he made to move but hesitated, not sure of what direction to go in. It'd seemed more natural, he thought, to look as though he was walking away from the apartment – no, towards it. In his indecision, he spun around and virtually collided with Josef. Josef glanced up, muttered an apology, and took a few steps before halting in, what George considered later, a rather exaggerated fashion. He turned slowly, his wizard-like finger pointing accusingly at George, his eyes flashing with delighted recognition, 'It's you, the usurper.'

Usurper? The word sliced through him with its mocking sharpness. 'I was…'

'Yes?'

'Going home.' he said firmly, hoping the quiver in his voice didn't sound as clearly as he feared.

'Going home, indeed!' For a man so thin and fragile after his years locked away, he possessed a brittle bitterness that George found unnerving. 'Going home to my wife, perhaps?'

'You're divorced.'

'Only in the eyes of the authorities. But listen…' He stepped closer, an artificial smile spreading across his face. 'I wanted to thank you.'

'What d'you mean?'

He quickly looked left and right as if frightened of being overheard and said, 'For looking after Eva – you know, while I was detained.'

'I don't –'

'It must've been difficult for her but you took her on, gave her shelter, so to speak, and that took guts, I'm sure. I don't mean you harm, calling you usurper, that was wicked of me, I'm sorry. But listen, George – it is George, isn't it? – Go home now, back to your own life if it still exists amongst all of this. I can take over from here.'

'You don't understand –'

'But I do, though, George. You're fond of her, I appreciate that, she's a lovely woman. But now that I'm back – she and I, well, we need time together, you know, get to know each other again as man and wife.'

'She no longer wants you.'

'How can you say that? How do you know – have you asked?'

'Not in so many –'

'Exactly. I mean, how well do you actually know this woman, George? We met in forty-five, Eva and I, and together we fought the Nazis, together we lived through communism. Together we survived the baby…'

'The baby?' The words fell like heavy stones.

'Yes, the baby. She never told you? No, she wouldn't have. No one knew really, just us.' The words so pitifully said, could not disguise the sparkle of renewed triumph in Josef's eyes.

A couple walked by, arm in arm, rifles slung casually over shoulders, her laugh reaching to the sky. 'You're lying,' said George.

Josef, this delicate man, seemed possessed of an anger that dwarfed George's own sense of injured disbelief. 'You truly think I would lie about such a thing?' he said. 'You think I would make up such a story in order to score petty points over you? Go away, you silly boy, come back when you're a proper man, when you know something of life.'

George stared at him, at Josef's hard detached expression, desperately wanting to articulate something to diminish this man but with his mind suddenly numb, nothing came. He looked up briefly at the apartment window and wondered what Eva was doing at that moment, whether she was aware of him and Josef together so close to her. He looked back at Josef, whose expression had remained exactly the same.

Involuntarily, he found himself taking a step back, then another, and a third. With the word, baby, echoing in his mind, George withdrew, his dignity in tatters.

Chapter 30
Day Eleven – Friday, 2 November

1.

'Was it really ten years?'

They were both sitting at the kitchen table at right angles, neither catching the eye of the other. She was toying with a packet of cigarettes, twisting it one way and another. But Eva didn't smoke, had never smoked to his knowledge but then… his knowledge didn't stretch back that far. 'Yes, George. Ten years.'

'Where has he gone now, this husband of yours?'

'Ex-husband.'

'Are you truly divorced?'

She'd placed a box of matches on the packet of cigarettes and, from the box, poked out a match, so that it looked like a tank. 'Yes. No. I don't know.'

Having never been one for conversations of this sort, he found it difficult and had to summon up strength to probe her with these questions. But he knew the question he really wanted to ask was too far beyond him. Instead, he asked, 'Where is he?'

'I don't know; I think he goes off to meet his fellow jailbirds.'

He thought back to the time of his own release and could understand the need to connect with others who'd undergone the same experience. But then, back in fifty-three, it had been impossible.

She pushed the tank across the table and stupidly, he watched it. It provided them both with a distraction during the period of prolonged silence. She looked up at him. Instinctively, he knew and caught her eye. A flicker of a smile, an acknowledgement, crossed her face. 'OK,' she said, 'I'll tell you.'

A moment's relief was replaced by a more sustained feeling of dread.

'I should've told you a long time ago but… Josef and I had a daughter.' The words came out quickly, taking them both by surprise. 'Her name,' she said more slowly, 'was Anastasia. She died. She lived sixteen days.'

George stared at her, his eyes agog as if everything and nothing made sense. 'Sixteen days. I'm sorry, I had no idea,' he said in a whisper. 'Why didn't you…'

'I supposed I'd learnt to live with it. But Josef's return, it's brought it all back, those horrible, dark days, those sixteen days in the hospital, praying for her, desperate for her to live, I would have given anything.'

'Yes, I can imagine.'

'Since his return, I've been waiting for him to mention it, to say her name, but he doesn't. It's as if he can't bring himself to say it. He refuses. And now I feel so confused. I don't know what I want any more.'

'Anastasia.'

'Yes.' She snapped the match in half.

'A pretty name.'

'Yes. God, it's so nice to tell someone. I had a friend once – Agnes. I've no idea where she is now but she was the only one who ever knew. I was with her the night you and I met. For so long I felt such a failure. I needed Josef to say I wasn't, and I still do. I just wish he'd say something, to speak of her but his silence is as oppressive as it ever was. I don't think her name has ever crossed his lips. I've waited all this time. The times I visited him in prison, he never mentioned her and I thought it best not to make an issue of it. After all, five minutes; what can you say in five minutes? But now… surely, now, I thought. But I was wrong. I was wrong to think he'd be different. I've realised I've waited all this time for a different person. But he hasn't changed; prison hasn't changed him at all. I need him to share the burden and in refusing to do so, I feel as if I can't get on with my life. It's almost as if I need his permission to let go of the past.'

'I see,' said George, not understanding a thing.

The tears she so resolutely held back now came, her face crumpling in front of him, her frame shaking. He wanted to take her hand but knew he couldn't; she seemed too far away, too remote. 'I see,' he repeated. 'I see…'

2.

The battle of Republic Square, as they called it, had scared the shit out of him but conversely Zoltan now felt better and more confident than he'd done for weeks, months even. He'd survived because they'd mistaken him for one of them. He was able to go out now and wander the streets, find shops to buy food and be part of this post-apocalyptic city. Sprawled in an armchair, he realised it was time to go out now – to get some bread, perhaps some vegetables and, if lucky, some meat. It all depended on what supplies had come through from the surrounding countryside. It was a relief to be thinking of such ordinary things – to feel *normal*.

Petra sat on the side of the bed with Roza behind her, playing with her mother's hair. It was virtually the first time Petra had emerged from under the blankets since her 'encounter' – as he referred to it. He couldn't bring himself to use the words she screamed at him during her darkest moments – raped, she said, sodomised, violated – a whole string of words each one thrown as an accusation, each one intended to diminish him. He hadn't told her of his own encounter – of how they'd murdered Paul and strung Donath up and burnt him alive, how they slapped him on the back and took him as one of theirs. He didn't think she'd acknowledge his trauma at the same time as coming to terms with her own. And, more to the point, if he'd failed her in the past (as she made quite plain) then he felt it incumbent upon him to be strong for her now, for her and for Roza. Poor Roza – the one in the middle, caught between their experiences of violence with no means to equip herself against its fallout. How vulnerable she looked now, plaiting Petra's hair, clinging onto her mother, frightened to let go.

'How you're feeling?' he asked nervously.

'We have to leave.'

He nodded in agreement although he had only the slightest idea why she should want to leave when the apartment had proved such a secure hiding place. So many AVOs had been rooted out of their homes and dragged away from their families. 'Where do you want to go?' he said as if they were planning a holiday.

'New Zealand – where d'you think? Austria, of course, where else?'

'But why? I blend in now.'

'No, Zoltan, you may think you blend in but there must be hundreds who've passed through your offices –'

'Yes, I know. I know.' He didn't want her to carry on, he was conscious enough already of the ghosts astir in his memory. He sighed. 'OK, you're right but how on earth do you propose –'

'I don't know – you're the man, you fix it. We can't stay here, it's not safe, we *have* to get away while we can.' Zoltan tried to imagine it, the three of them, a bag each, hitching a lift out of the city. Although only one hundred miles to the west, Austria might as well have been on the moon. He tried to think of a tactful way to point out the absurdity of it but before he had a chance she continued, 'You have to find someone who'll take us.'

'It'll cost us.' He said it so quietly he barely heard it himself. The last of their money had gone into *his* pocket – the rapist, the sodomizer, her violator.

'There is some left,' she said. 'You could use that.'

He wasn't convinced; the idea seemed as dangerous as it was preposterous but the two of them, his wife and his daughter, looked at him with such expectation that he felt he had no choice but to try. He collected his coat and pulled on his boots, ready to leave, to embark on this foolish errand for the sake of them both. He leaned down to quickly kiss Petra goodbye but she grabbed the lapels of his coat and holding him there, kissed him with unexpected affection. From such a small display of tenderness, Zoltan felt his muscles tighten, his pride expand. She let him go, a gentle smile on her lips. He cupped his hand on the side of Roza's face and kissed her cheek. As he reached for the door, he turned to look at them – his wife, his daughter. And they were both smiling at him.

He left with tears in his eyes and a rush of love through his soul.

Perhaps, in his heart, he knew he'd never see them again.

3.

George kept on walking. Where to and to what purpose, he had no idea and didn't care, as long as he kept walking. Black flags hung from balconies side by side with the Hungarian tricolour. Today was All Souls Day, the Day of the Dead. Church bells rang out in remembrance of those who had died. How strange it was to hear the bells – it had been years since anyone had last heard them. How lovely it was to hear them again.

He noticed that the trams were back in action, that people were returning to work, shops and cafés were open, and that not a single Soviet soldier could be seen on the streets. Yet, the uprising that had so transformed him, so absorbed his energies had overnight become a side issue. He overheard a group of women in a queue talk of 'crossroads'. He assumed they meant Hungary but the word seemed right – he was at a crossroads.

Anastasia.

He wondered how old this daughter of Eva's would be now. It explained so much. Like she said, they knew so little of each other's past but there was nothing unusual about that. Everyone had a past; a family untouched by the far-reaching tendrils of the state was a rare thing in Hungary. If you hadn't suffered personally, then you knew someone close who had. Everyone understood but few talked of it. People didn't have to know the details to understand that their sufferings had run similar courses – a roadmap of torment.

Tightening his scarf, he stopped on the corner of Andrassy Street and Lenin Boulevard. The cold sun shone weakly, radiating nothing but uncertainty on this poor nation which for so long had groaned under the pressure of totalitarianism and now stood falteringly on the brink between freedom and further bloodshed. The Soviets were coming back in greater force. The rumours were too strong now to be denied. People passed him, blank faces with blank pasts who, having tasted freedom, now feared it was about to be snatched from their grip. And suddenly, amongst them, a face he recognised with a jolt. No vague recollection was this, but a face from his past he knew as sure as the face he saw each morning in the mirror.

'Mr Beke,' he called out.

The man turned, his eyes wide with panic, 'No, sorry, friend, not me.'

How strange it felt, reaching out his hand, offering his declaration of good intent. 'George Lorenc, don't you remember?'

Beke had made to walk away. Instead, he stood rooted and glared at the proffered hand as if it were a rose that hid the thorn. 'You must be mistaken,' he said politely, tonelessly.

The sound of the AVO's voice echoed back through the years. *You're the sort of man that this country needs. Strong, talented, forward-thinking. Are you forward-thinking, George?* His eyes scanned the man who, more than anyone, had ruined his life, the man who asked for so much and took everything. *Sometimes one has to sacrifice a little personal glory for the sake of the common good.* If only it had stopped with the personal glory. He wanted to feel something akin to anger, to feel the fury he was entitled to feel. But nothing came apart from a well of emptiness in the pit of his stomach. He heard himself say the words, 'I wish you well,' and then questioned whether he'd really said it.

A flicker of recognition crossed the AVO's face, a flicker too of a grateful smile. 'Thank you.'

'You still wear the boots, I see.'

The man looked down at his footwear. 'Yes,' he said, 'perhaps I shouldn't.'

'No, probably not.' And with that, George turned and resumed walking, conscious of each step, knowing he was walking away from a conversation he would replay in his mind for the rest of his life and wonder why he hadn't made more of it. Whether Beke watched him leave, he didn't know and pretended to himself that he didn't care. He walked as if walking through the thickest mist, not knowing where he was going or where he'd come from.

Something about the encounter made him continue walking for miles. He walked to the point he began to limp, as was often the case when he was tired. He ended up at a place he'd never wanted to see again. But cloaked in mist, he was powerless to stop and soon he found himself in front of where his parents had lived, or at least the space his parents' apartment block had occupied because little remained of it but a pile of crumpled stones and burnt bricks in the midst of which lay his crumpled memories. And the memories were bitter. The devotion his mother had shown for his passion for football came not from maternal love but from her love for another man. It was something he tried to forget but it was always there dishonouring the memory of his father, his sad, broken father. One goal in a football game changed everything – for him, for his parents. And when he thought of the forces of the state pitted against him, it wasn't a dehumanised adversary he saw but one single man – Zoltan Beke. The man he'd just offered his hand and wished well, the man he'd just walked away from. It wasn't how he imagined it to be during the one thousand, three hundred and seventy days.

He remembered his return from prison, coming here and finding his parents gone, the new occupants too frightened to speak to him lest they compromise their own survival. His parents had not left a single trace of their existence; no souvenir to counter the memories embittered by his mother's infidelity.

It seemed like such a long, long time ago.

4.

Zoltan's newfound confidence had seeped away like oil through a colander. Now, as he trod through the wounded city, he felt like an accidental gatecrasher, not wanting to make a sound, frightened in case he was spotted by the hostess. Petra was right – even without the uniform he was still recognisable to those who had crossed his path over the years; so many, he'd long lost count. Each face was a threat. He daren't catch anyone's eyes and kept his gaze focused on the pavement directly in front of him. He didn't want to be out here any longer; he had to get back to his wife and daughter, even if it meant returning empty-handed, for he had no idea how to organise transport out of the country and now he was too afraid to approach people. He felt hungry, afraid and very alone.

He'd liked to have jumped on a streetcar but with so few working and those that were so jam-packed he couldn't bear to see all those faces. It'd only need one recognition. He'd been lucky with George Lorenc. Of course, he remembered him, remembered the football game, every minute of it, the fluctuating extremes of emotion – Ivanov's goal, the minutes that crept by until Lorenc's equaliser, the fury on Donath's face, the barely-disguised glee on Fischer's.

The smell of roasted chestnuts wafted on the breeze, reminding him how hungry he felt. On the corner, stood a vendor selling paper cones of warm nuts. He joined the short queue and dug in his pocket for loose change. He felt the presence of someone behind him but took little notice until the voice, laced with menace, spoke to him, 'You're AVO.'

The world ground to a halt. The coins fell from his hand and tinkled on the pavement; the people in front turned to stare. 'No,' he replied quickly, turning to catch the leering face of a boy, no more than twenty, but tall and broad-shouldered.

The boy pushed him hard in the chest. Zoltan fell back into the person ahead of him in the queue. 'Hey, Miklos,' the boy called out. 'I found an AVO.'

The queue broke up and quickly formed an impromptu circle around him. The chestnut seller, upset at the commotion round his stand, yelled at him: 'What's going on? Get away from here.'

'Fucking AVO.'

'No, please, I'm a worker.' Zoltan saw the man called Miklos approach, a short, hard-looking man with one arm in a sling stained by dirt and dried blood. 'A worker like you,' Zoltan added as Miklos bared down on him.

It felt as if the whole street had stopped in its tracks to stare. Miklos laughed. 'A worker, eh? With hands like those? Nice boots.'

Zoltan ran. He ran so that everything passed him in a blur, the buildings, children playing on a tank, the pavement beneath his feet; he ran for his life. And behind him the feet of others, chasing after him, catching him up. Tears poured from his eyes, the breeze, the blind panic, his ears deafened by his heart pounding furiously, as his brain urged him to keep running, to keep going, to keep living. It was the sudden inexplicable pain in the back of his left leg that brought him down, collapsing awkwardly onto the pavement. He knew instinctively they'd shot him but not to kill. A moment later, they were on him, and the lead sky disappeared from view as the kicks pummelled him from every angle and pain throbbed from every part of him and the blood blinded his eyes.

'Wait! Wait a minute.' The voice came from far away but quickly became louder as it approached. 'Wait, wait,' the word repeated until its authority brought an end to the trouncing. Zoltan didn't understand what was happening, didn't know the voice, but loved it all the same. His eyes too inflamed to open, he was aware of a face next to his, rough bony fingers on his chin. 'It's him all right, twice we've met.'

Something in its tone frightened him anew. Willing his eyes open, he caught sight of the unfocused face looming down into his, inches away, the drifting clouds behind. A hand waved about in front of his face, blurry at first but then the hand came into focus. And then he knew – the misshapen fingers, the crescent-shaped scar above the right eyebrow. The name jumped up from his memory – Jasper Szabo.

'I just wanted to make sure,' said Szabo, his eyes fixed on Zoltan.

Zoltan wanted to speak but the pulsating pain in his leg wouldn't let him. Helplessly, he watched as Jasper Szabo rose to his haunches, made to leave but then, turning round, spat at him. 'Take him,' he heard him say, *take him, take him* – the words echoed through his mind. His time was at an end now and with the realisation, the pain evaporated as the numbness took over. No longer frightened, no longer regretful, the end approached like the night – as inevitable and as final.

The sky disappeared again as Zoltan felt the rope tighten around his ankles.

Chapter 31
Day Twelve – Saturday, 3 November

The rumbling noise seeped its way into my consciousness, slowly forcing me awake. I lay there for a while wondering if what I could hear was true or if perhaps I was still asleep. Then with sudden clarity, I sat bolt upright. 'Oh my dear Lord, they're back.'

Josef, next to me, muttered something.

Running to the window, I screamed, 'They've come back.'

'Who?'

'The tanks, of course, Russians.' I pulled aside the curtains. It was still dark but above the deep growl of the tanks, I could hear screams and shouts. I could smell smoke drifting through the air.

Josef joined me at the window. 'Bastards,' he said. 'God, it's only five.'

An explosion nearby made me jump. 'They lied to us.'

'The Soviets?' Josef was already pulling on a jumper over his pyjama top. 'Of course, they lied to us; you didn't expect them not to try again? They'll kill every fucking one of us before they're through.'

'What are you doing?'

'We're leaving. Hurry up and get dressed.' A whole series of explosions shook the apartment block. 'Goodness sake, Eva, come away from the window.'

'But where are you going?'

'Me? Both of us. Out of this city. Out of this country. Austria. That's where I'm going – Austria.'

'But… Austria? How will you get there?'

Tying his shoelaces, he spoke without looking at me. 'I've no idea. But we'll find a way. It's either that or get killed. As an escaped prisoner, I stand no chance. And there's no way I'm going back to jail; I'd rather die than go back. Hurry up; put some clothes on.'

'What do we do about George?'

'George? He's not our concern; leave him.'

'But he is *my* concern.'

A rattle of machine gun fire sounded in the near distance making us both duck unnecessarily. 'He doesn't have to be. You don't love him.'

'That's not the point; I can't leave without him.'

'So where's he now, this friend of yours? He's not here. He's out in the streets again still thinking it's all one big adventure. He could be dead by now.'

'Then I won't leave at all.'

'No, you can't stay, you have to come. Get some food together. Come on, Eva, I need you.'

I need you. I think perhaps it was the most revealing thing Josef had said in years. Yet I could only shudder at the extent of how much a stranger he'd become to me. For a day or so, I dismissed the squalor around us and tried to re-live the dream of forty-five when we believed we could take on the world, when communism offered us all we'd ever hoped for. But in those three small words, *I need you*, Josef again had forgotten the other half of the equation – *me*. Everything in our relationship had been based on what he wanted, on what he needed; never did he stop to think or to ask what I wanted. Always the assumption that our desires coincided; an invisible harmony of wishes.

'I can't leave. I can't leave Anastasia.'

His mouth gaped open. 'What on earth are you talking about?'

I sat down on a chair. I felt weak. 'I can't leave Anastasia.'

'Don't be ridiculous,' he said as he put on his coat.

'I'm not leaving.'

'For Christ's sake, Eva, she's dead. She's always been dead. You're obsessed.' He grabbed my arm and tried to yank me to my feet.

I gripped the chair. 'Leave me alone; let go of me. You never even tried to understand me.'

The pain stung my cheek. I put my hand to where he'd made contact.

'OK, I'm sorry,' he said. 'I didn't mean to do that. But, Eva, I beg you – we have to go *now*.'

'You go.'

The apartment door swung open with a flourish. George charged in. 'It's murder out there,' he said, catching his breath. 'The Soviets are everywhere. They're storming Parliament and shooting at everything in sight.'

'What about the government?' asked Josef.

'No one knows for sure but it's over. They say Nagy is going to take refuge in the Yugoslav embassy. What… what's been going on here?'

'Josef thinks we should leave.'

'He's right. Why's your cheek so red?'

'No,' said Josef. 'I'm not going with him. Two jailbirds together – we'd be a liability to each other.' He was pacing frantically, desperate to leave. 'You have to decide, Eva.'

'Decide?' There was nothing to decide.

'You can't stay with him to die in this shithole; you're my wife.' Again, he took my hand in a pounding grip, pulling me towards him.

'Let go of her,' yelled George, trying to prise his fingers from mine.

'Josef, stop,' I cried. 'Just stop.' I thought I was yelling but the words emerged as barely a whisper.

I heard the dulled thud. Josef was on the floor, sitting upright as if he had chosen to sit there, looking slightly bemused, rubbing his jaw. He jumped to his feet, his whole face distorted with panic and anger. 'You stupid, stupid –'

'Get out,' seethed George through clenched teeth.

'I'm going; I'm going, all right.' He caught his breath, his eyes darting from George to me, his mind whirling for something suitably final to say. 'This time tomorrow, I'll be in Austria. This country can die for all I care.' He spun round with a melodramatic twist and headed for the door. There, he paused, turned and looked at me one final time. 'You never did deserve that baby.'

And then he was gone.

*

Despite the roar outside, inside the silence descended on the apartment like a blanket. George put an arm around me and squeezed my shoulder. How strange, I thought, that one's whole relationship with a person can change with the utterance of one sentence; years of knowledge fall apart in seconds. I hated him with a rage that left me feeling enervated. I thought that prison had changed him but I was wrong – Josef was still the same man, nothing had altered.

I stared at the door, George's arm still around me. 'You'll need a wash, George; I'll boil up some water,' I said, trying not to let my voice betray the shame simmering inside me.

'You would've made a wonderful mother.'

I tried to smile. 'Thank you, George.'

'She's buried here, in Budapest, isn't she, and you don't want to leave her?'

I nodded many times, unable to speak. I thought of the wooden cross, the name barely visible now in the weathered wood. Of course, I couldn't leave her, my poor little girl, my darling girl.

'But you have to move on.'

'I can't do it; I can't do it to her.'

George took my hand. How small it felt in his. 'You sound like a communist but you know better than that.'

'I don't understand.'

'If the communists are right and there is no God, then it is only the mortal remains that matter. They can't allow for the soul, for our souls are the one thing they can't control. But we know them to be wrong. There is a God, we do have souls, and what remains in the soil is neither here nor there. It is what's here, in our hearts, that matters. And wherever you go in this life, your daughter's soul will be within you. If you stay you're letting them win, you're allowing them to beat you down with their indoctrination. Don't let them beat you, Eva. Come with me now. We'll build a new life out there somewhere away from all this and then you'll see I was right.

Anastasia will be with you and always will because you did deserve her and you still do.'

I felt weak. My hand almost disappeared into his strength. Yes, I thought, it was that simple. Yet it took a simple man to provide the answer I'd been looking for all along. A simple and lovely man.

Chapter 32
Day Thirteen – Sunday, 4 November

1.

Petra felt as if she was walking into Armageddon. Fires raging, the ceaseless noise, the chaos of panic. Fighting the urge to go straight back home, she took Roza's hand and with a suitcase in the other, pushed herself on. She convinced herself that being at home was no safer than dodging the shells outdoors. Roza trembled next to her, repeatedly asking where they were going. Petra had no idea but it made sense to her to head for the western outskirts of Buda, the side nearest the Austrian border.

The wreckage left in the wake of the tanks shocked her, and she realised the previous onslaught had been nothing but a warm-up in comparison. Bodies lay where they fell, the wounded yelled out for help that never came. The stench of blood and dust from shattered stones was tangible; the thunderous noise intensifying, clouds of black smoke blocking out the sky. Buildings, already damaged, now collapsed or destroyed by flames, burying or burning whole families in the process. Above them, planes skimmed across the rooftops so low Petra felt the urge to duck, huge shadows following in their wake. The bombs dropped only a few streets away from her, more explosions, more slaughter.

After twenty minutes, she took a wild chance and asked two complete strangers, white with dust, cowering in a doorway, if they might know someone willing to take her and her daughter across the border. She asked a couple because she didn't think a woman would know and she was too worried to ask a man by himself. But they didn't know and if they did, they yelled back, they'd be heading that way themselves. Petra kept going, the suitcase heavy, the burden of Roza heavier still.

She came across a row of bodies outside a bakery, torsos cut in half by cannon fire, a lagoon of blood, the stink of death. She tried to cover Roza's eyes but she'd already looked away, her hand clasped over her mouth. In the hand of an elderly victim, half a loaf of bread, now splattered with blood.

As they edged away from the centre, away from Buda and beyond Rose Mount, the damage receded, the devastation became less marked. They sat on a doorstep halfway up a steep hill and caught their breaths. Above them, a Russian helicopter hovered as the skies darkened. She looked back at the view and felt sickened by the inferno of fire destroying their beautiful city and its people. She wanted to feel something akin to anger but exhaustion defeated all else within her.

Roza leant against her, the eyes still wet, her skin deathly pale. When she spoke, her voice quivered with shock. 'We'll never find Papa now.'

Petra wondered whether to continue lying, promising Zoltan's imminent return. 'We might see him,' she said feebly.

'Yes.' Both absorbed the other's attempt to placate. Petra stroked her hair. What a horrible way to grow up, she thought.

It'd been two days since Zoltan left in order to find them transport. As those first hours passed, she expected him to come back any moment, successful in his mission. She carried on saying it to Roza long after she stopped believing it herself. But as she fell asleep that night, a flicker of hope remained. It'd been the quietest night since the start of the uprising – the lull before the storm. Next morning, the flicker was extinguished; she knew him to be dead. She only prayed that his end had come quickly, that he'd been spared the humiliating ritual so relished by the mob. Did she miss him? She didn't know, every moment was too wrought with dread to think about it but she missed him for Roza's sake.

A man in his thirties came jogging up the hill towards them. By the time he reached them, he'd slowed down to a walk. Petra asked him quickly, before she lost her nerve, 'Where can I find someone who'll take my daughter across the border?' She realised she'd said "my daughter", and realised she'd be happy to send Roza on alone if it meant saving her.

The man looked at Roza. 'You can follow me if you… like,' he said breathlessly.

She knew he was about to say 'if you *trust me*' but that might have sounded too threatening. It was his hesitation that decided her. 'I'd be so grateful. How far is it?'

He pointed up the hill. 'Five minutes. But hurry.'

'Oh, thank you,' she said, rising to her feet with her suitcase. 'Come on, Roza.'

'No, I can't, not yet.'

'Roza, we must, please, the man's waiting.'

Another helicopter passed overhead. Not too far in the distance, the noise of destruction continued with increasing ferocity. A slight drizzle began to fall. The man took Petra's case and smiled encouragingly at Roza. 'It's not far, I assure you.'

As they followed the man up the hill, he turned and asked, 'Forgive me but I have to ask this, how much cash have you got on you?'

Petra hesitated a moment, wondering whether to downplay her last pool of money. 'Two hundred florins,' she said, surprising herself with her honesty.

'We'll say a hundred and fifty. Fifty to pay my cousin to get you out of the city, and a hundred for the ride to the border. That leaves you with fifty for negotiation.'

Ten minutes later, Petra and Roza found themselves leaning against a Skoda in a dark shed lit only by torches. What a relief to have avoided the bombs, the tanks and the impending rain. Their guide talked to another man, an older man with a trimmed beard and glasses. The sound of bombs persisted in the distance.

'Antony, my cousin, can take you to a village three miles from the border now but it will cost you fifty florins.' He winked at her, acknowledging that the haggle over money had worked.

'That'll be fine, thank you.' She squeezed Roza's hand. 'Thank you,' she said to the cousin who also winked at her.

2.

Some kind of animal instinct had taken over. It was different to before; they felt different – more primaeval, more basic. During the moments when his mind reached out into civility, Valentin recognised it for what it was, but mostly, he too became swallowed up in the mindset of an automaton, brutal and merciless.

Perhaps because they'd so expected to be quartered out and back home, or perhaps because they'd believed the lie that any further duties would only concern escorting Soviet citizens out of the country and nothing else. They hadn't expected to be thrown back into the battle under orders to 'conquer and exterminate'. Vladimir especially had regressed into an all-out assassin of the innocent. Hunger too played its part – one daily slice of black bread and a rasher of bacon each hardly sufficed for hard-working, hard-killing men.

Valentin was astonished at how the Hungarians kept going – the elderly determinedly queuing for food, motivated more by the certainty of hunger than the mere possibility of death; the youngsters still sniping and throwing petrol bombs. But this time the insurgents were fighting against the tide. The sheer number of Soviet tanks and Soviet manpower was proving impossible for the street fighters. A solitary shot from a building and the tank would throw everything at it until nothing but a pile of rubble remained.

Everywhere fires raged, buildings collapsed and all the time the corpses mounted up.

Three p.m., the sky was black with smoke. Valentin and the crew had just destroyed a huge milk lorry parked outside the hospital on Bela Bartok Street. As the milk flowed like a stream into the drains, they pulled away; Vladimir punching the air with delight that they'd managed to deprive the hospital patients of their supply of milk. They swung off the main road and poked their noses into a narrower side street. Valentin wanted to turn back but Vladimir, pulling rank, ordered the tank forward. Valentin felt uneasy; this was too much like the first days when solitary tanks ventured down these tight alleyways and found themselves surrounded and pounced on by homicidal kids. But not much was left of this street; not one building remained unscathed.

It was then he saw her again – the blaze of red hair, the purposeful walk. He couldn't see her face but he knew it was her. This time he knew. 'Stop,' he shouted at Petrov at the wheel.

'Why, what's up?' said Petrov.

Vladimir barked at him. 'We can't stop now.'

'I take full responsibility for my actions but give me a couple of minutes, there's someone out there I know.'

'What – *here*? You mad? You'll get sniped.'

For a moment Valentin hesitated; Vladimir was right, it'd be a stupidly risky thing to do. 'I'll take that chance.'

'You're mad.'

'Please. One minute.'

With a sigh, Vladimir ordered Petrov to stop.

Valentin unbolted the hatch as the tank slowed down. The cold, fresh air hit him. He could still see her, no more than a hundred yards away. He shouted, 'Eva,' but knew she'd never hear him over the cacophony of noise coming from all around. Half expecting each moment to be his last, he jumped down from the tank and ran steadily towards her. Flashes of Budapest '49 skimmed across his mind; a left-footed shot, a goal, a café, an old man with a walrus moustache, a bedroom, the longing eyes of a woman he knew he'd love forever. 'Eva, Eva!' Still, she didn't hear.

He could almost touch her. 'Eva,' he shouted again. 'Eva, it's me, Valentin. Valentin Ivanov, *Eva*.'

This time she heard, she spun around, a hand pointing out. The face – it was young, attractive even – but it wasn't hers.

A lifetime's worth of disappointment crashed through him in a second – the realisation he'd spent seven years remembering one afternoon, seven years of expectation, of hope both unrealistic and unreal, and that the hope had finally died. 'Sorry,' he said knowing that he'd be saying sorry for the rest of his life. 'I'm sorry, I thought…'

He realised then that the hand pointing at him gripped a revolver. It fired once, twice. With the sound still thumping through his head, she turned and fled. Seizing his stomach, trying to stem the spray of blood, he didn't see her scurry away. 'Sorry,' he said again as he fell to his knees. 'Eva, I'm sorry…'

3.

I could hardly think; my mind whirled with jumbled thoughts and distorted images. I allowed George to lead the way, dragging me through the streets by the hand. I shivered in the November drizzle. 'We've got to get to the station,' he urged. 'They've got the trains running again. We're meeting Milan there. For God's sake, Eva, hurry.' Before leaving, I grabbed every bit of food I could find and stuffed it into a small suitcase. Not much, I thought, but hopefully enough. I packed a few clothes. But nothing else.

'What's the point, the place will be teaming with AVOs.'

'Not necessarily; they're too busy reclaiming the streets. Anyway, we'll see when we get there. Just come on. We haven't got much time; there's a train heading west due to leave at eleven.'

The central station, when we got there, was a mass of people crowding the length of the platform, clambering onto the train. People were pushing and barging, shouting, yelling, a ceaseless flow of desperate faces. Children were crying, parents pleading with them to find the strength to fight and board the waiting train. The train's engine was running, a thick pall of steam rising above the hoards towards the station canopy. 'We'll never find Milan in all this,' said George. 'Let's get on.' The carriages inside seemed packed, a seething bulk of people.

'Don't we need tickets?'

'It's too late, we'll miss it.' He was right – I spotted a couple of guards trying to keep order, demanding tickets but their task, against such a volume of people, was impossible. George gripped my hand and I held on, frightened of letting him go in the density of the crowd. A young couple ahead of us on the steps of the train were trying to collect their children. The man was about to jump off to gather a child. George, picking up the child, passed it to him. In return, the man pulled George up onto the train, who, in turn, offered his hand and pulled me aboard. A whistle blew; the train was ready to go. Two conductors ran up and down the platform, slamming shut the doors only for them to immediately re-open as more people tried to scramble on. George and I were squeezed together. Every seat was taken, people sitting on each other's laps; every inch of the aisles, toilets and doorways crammed with people and baggage. The train lurched forward, the door nearest to us still swinging open. The crowd surged forward as one, then back again as the train picked up speed. Finally, someone managed to close the door. We were on our way.

After half an hour, the train made its first stop. A few passengers alighted but the relief was only temporary as others took their place and forced their way on. Despite the number of people, the carriage was silent – no one talked for fear that among them might be AVO. But after another twenty minutes, rumours filtered down from one carriage to the next – every station would be brimming with AVOs, ready to detain all those suspected of trying to escape. Surely, I thought, that would mean virtually everyone. Another rumour reached us –

that before the next stop, a village only a couple of miles before the border, the driver would slow down to allow people to jump off the train. It was a nice thought but no one believed it.

But sure enough, thirty minutes later, the train did slow right down. 'He's done it,' said George. The doors opened, and people took the plunge and jumped. Again, George led the way. With the grassy bank below us, he looked at me. 'OK?'

I hesitated, fearing the drop.

'Don't worry, he can't be doing more than ten miles per hour.'

'Hurry up, lad,' came a voice behind me. George jumped, rolled over and immediately sprung to his feet.

'Go on, miss, you can do it,' urged the man, almost pushing me off the train.

I jumped. I tumbled through the wet grass but George was right – I was fine. As we found our feet, our coats wet, I almost laughed. 'Bless the driver,' I said aloud.

George smiled and together we watched the train disappear leaving a trail of smoke in its wake. I looked around – there were perhaps forty of us that had made the jump. Near me, a woman and a child, the child waving at the receding train. And there, among them, flapping his arms at us, was Milan. 'Well, fancy meeting you here,' he called out as he made his way towards us.

I felt reassured by his presence.

'Guess what – about three miles over there,' he said, pointing vaguely over the horizon, 'is Austria. And I, my friends, have come prepared – I have in my possession not only a map but a compass and even a torch.'

'Milan,' I said, 'you think of everything.'

'I have my military training to thank.'

'And we've brought some food. Hard-boiled eggs, sausage and a couple of onions – pickled, and a couple of apples. George has got water.'

'Well, this is going to prove to be one hell of a picnic.'

'Ending with Austria and freedom,' added George, beaming.

'Yes, sir. All we have to do is keep walking westwards. We'll have to avoid the roads; it wouldn't be safe. It's two o'clock. We could be there in a couple of hours, before nightfall if we're lucky. You two ready? Let us go. Remember, the road to freedom starts with a single step.'

'Thanks for that, Chairman Mao,' said George.

'Excuse me,' said a voice. 'Can we join you?' It was the woman with the child. 'I've also brought some food. Not much, but enough to share.'

I could see Milan hesitating. 'How old is she?' he asked, glancing at the child.

'Ten. But she won't be a hindrance; will you, Roza?'

The girl shook her head without conviction. Milan sighed.

It was George who spoke. 'Of course; the more the merrier.'

The woman's face broke into a smile, such was her relief. 'My name is Petra,' she said. 'And this is my daughter, Roza.'

We all made our introductions, shaking hands as if meeting at a party. She looked at me fondly, as if relieved that she wasn't the only woman.

And so the five of us set out, buttoning our coats against the icy wind. The thick clouds moved quickly. Nearby, our fellow passengers had spread out but all walking in the same direction – towards the border and freedom.

Milan's "couple of hours" turned out to be twice as long.

Traipsing through unending fields, mud and soggy ground hindered our progress. The group of forty had dispersed. The five of us were on our own. It was dark but for the light of the moon. My fingers felt numb but the ground was too precarious to allow the luxury of putting one's hands into one's coat pockets. Although shivering with cold and my shoes soaked through, I felt no undue concern, as long as we had Milan to guide the way with his compass and map and his eternal optimism.

'I think we're getting close,' said Milan quietly. 'Soon we should be coming across a canal on the other side of which is the border. But we can't wade through the water; it could be deep in places and dangerously cold. But according to the map, there should be some bridges further up.'

'And then Austria?' asked the woman, Petra.

'I know – it seems too easy. We just walk across the bridge and into another country, another world.'

'As long as there are no trolls beneath the bridge,' I said, wrapping my arms around myself.

'You're right. We should be OK but we can't be sure when those bastards might spring up. Someone on the train was saying that since the wire was cut they've reinforced the border controls. As long as we stay away from any watchtowers, we should be OK. Shall we feast?'

'A feast it is not but yes, I'm starving,' I said. 'Are you hungry, Roza?'

She nodded shyly. Petra and I shared our provisions of food.

'Bloody typical that we should have a full moon,' said Milan, biting into a slice of bread and salami.

'At least we can see where we're going,' said Petra.

'Yeah but it makes us more visible to the AVOs.'

'Yes,' she said quietly. 'Those damned AVOs.'

*

Twenty minutes later, the last of our provisions consumed, we were still walking with no end in sight. Roza lost her balance in the mire and stumbled exhausted onto the ground. She started to cry. We all turned on her, silently beseeching her to remain quiet. Her mother knelt down and whispered words of encouragement in her ear. I helped Petra gently pull her up from the earth. Slowly, we picked our way forward.

We entered an area of waist-height reeds. Milan carried the girl on his back. The soggy terrain sucked on our shoes, soaking our socks and the bottom of our legs. 'George,' I whispered, 'I'm so cold.'

'I know, but it can't be much further now.'

I blew on my fingers. I so wished I'd remembered to bring gloves.

'It's ironic when you think about it,' said Milan, as we trudged forward under the light of the moon.

'What's that?' said George.

'We fought so hard to get rid of the fucking Soviets out of our country and instead, it's us that's leaving.'

'Milan,' I said, 'don't swear in front of the girl.'

The girl's mother smiled at me.

We trudged forward through ploughed fields, our feet sinking into the soft earth, our trousers soaked with wet mud, one slow step at a time. The enormity of what I was doing, of what we were doing, hadn't hit me until this moment. We were leaving. We had embarked on a course of action that, if it failed, would certainly have us arrested and imprisoned. Or worse. Yet success seemed almost as daunting – here I was, trying to escape from my country, to bid it farewell, perhaps forever. To leave behind everything that I knew; a lifetime of memories, of familiar places, of familiar people. I pushed myself on, trampling through the reeds, so tired but not wanting to fall behind the boys, not wanting to appear a burden to them. I tried to think more positive thoughts – I could settle in a place where the church was allowed to exist without persecution; where I need not guard my every word. Freedom with a small suitcase of clothes. I offered a prayer. I wanted to exchange sometime in return for giving me the means to push myself on, for delivering us safely over the border. But I had nothing to offer except perhaps myself. Yes, that was it; it is what He would want – My Dear Lord, please help us. Deliver us from the evil we live in. In return, I offer you my devotion. I can offer no more; no less.

Ahead of us in the distance, the shimmering lights of a town. I stopped to catch my breath. Looking up at the moon I realised it had begun snowing. Snowflakes fell on my face. The wind cut through me. 'You OK, Eva?' said George. My feet felt so cold with the wet, so heavy.

'I don't think I can go on. I'm cold, George, so cold.'

George put his arm around me and squeezed my shoulder. 'You can do it, Eva. Think of what lies ahead.'

'It can't be far now,' added Milan, readjusting the weight of the girl on his back.

'Here, let me have a go,' said George.

Roza slid off Milan. Her mother knelt down and kissed her, whispering encouragement in her ear. She helped lift her daughter onto George's back.

'Where are we?' she said, her voice rising in panic. 'We seem to be stuck in a swamp. It's coming up to our knees. There's nothing as far as the eye can see.'

'Oh, but there is,' said Milan. 'Can't you see what I can see?'

With a renewed purpose, he strode forward, taking huge steps, sludging through the reeds.

George and I glanced at each other and then followed, the girl on his back, her mother behind us. Sure enough, after about twenty yards, we were at the canal. We all stared at it silently, contemplating the slow flow of water between the steep banks. But it was wide – perhaps twenty metres. Hope mixed with despair. We were so close, so tantalisingly close, but the obstacle that lay between us and freedom seemed so daunting.

'We have to find a bridge,' said George.

'Yes, there'll be one at some point,' said Milan. 'Shall we go?'

The sight of the canal to our left gave us all a renewed sense of determination. Surely, we thought, we'd find a bridge soon.

For forty minutes or more, we walked silently with the wind blowing the sleet into our faces. The snow had given way to rain. Milan stopped short. We caught up. Roza slipped off George's back. Her mother took her hand and rubbed it. At least they each remembered to bring gloves.

'What's wrong?' asked George.

'Look…' There, on the opposite side of the canal, at the top of the bank, a flag hoisted on a flagpole. Red and white, the flag of Austria. Just a small stretch of water between us and freedom; my insides almost collapsed within me. I felt like crying.

'And look what's over there,' said George, lowering his voice. Our eyes followed his, and what we saw frightened me so much I felt as if someone had punched me in the stomach – silhouetted on the horizon was the foreboding sight of a watchtower.

'I think I'm standing on planks of wood,' said Petra.

George stamped his feet next to where she was standing. 'This was the start of a bridge,' he said. 'There was a bridge here.'

'Bastards,' muttered Milan. 'They've blown it up. We're going to have to risk the water. I'll take the child.'

Roza gripped onto her mother still tighter. 'Roza, do as the nice man says; he'll carry you across the water to the other side. You have to trust him. Look… look at how tall he is.'

'As tall as a goalkeeper,' said Milan, stretching back his shoulders. He knelt down. Roza, keeping her eyes fixed on her mother, reluctantly climbed onto his back.

A flare shoots up, illuminating the sky. Instinctively, we all crouch down. Just as we straighten ourselves, the sudden sound of machine-gun fire blasts out. As one, we throw ourselves down, happy to taste the wet earth on our lips. But the blast is distant, aimed somewhere else, perhaps at others like us trying to escape. Cautiously, George gets up first. The landscape seems even quieter now as the echo of gunfire fades into the wind. We all rise, looking at each other for reassurance. The watchtowers loom high above us like huge black monsters. I'm convinced the guards will hear my heart beating.

Petra, I notice, is crying. 'I shouldn't have done this,' she says, wiping her eyes with a gloved hand. 'Poor Roza. It would have been better if I stayed and taken my chances in Budapest.'

George sees them first. 'Get down,' he urges, taking my hand. I see them too – moving shadows beyond the watchtower, running rapidly towards the canal. Suddenly, the shadows are exposed in a huge bright light. The machine guns fire furiously as the searchlights beam down on them.

'Now!' said Milan in a sort of subdued yell. With the guards' attention diverted to their right, we had a chance.

George took my hand as we slid down the bank, leaving a trail of mud in our wake. Behind us Milan, with Roza clinging onto his back, and her mother holding her hand, glancing nervously towards the watchtower. I gasped as the water cut through my clothes like a thousand shards of ice, clasping my hand over my mouth to smother a shriek of pain. I'd lost contact with George. Where was he? I heard him swear. I glimpsed Milan struggling to maintain balance. Petra, her face creased with pain, tried to steady him. I could hear Roza crying, calling for her mother. 'I'm here, my love, just a few more steps.' The water, so cold, was soon up to my waist. I could no longer feel my legs but my bones felt brittle with cold. The distance between George and me surprises me. His arms flail as he beats back the water. My heartbeat quickens as I hear another rattle of machine-gun fire. Somewhere, far away, I hear a scream. Someone yells, a man. The water is receding; I'm over halfway there. A light flicks on; it's as bright as day. The watchtower has seen us. I can't see; everything is but a white light. Machine guns crackle, their bullets thudding into the earth behind us. My time has come. My mind is blank with terror. Roza screams. Petra screams. Another fearful round of fire; this time little jets of water splash up around us as the bullets land so close. Some anguished cry frightens me further still. I realise it is me, sobbing uncontrollably but still, I wade through, my legs fighting against the weight of water. But it's getting easier. Another few steps, I'm on the bank. Glancing back, peering through the light, I see George has retraced his steps to help Milan buckling under the weight of the child. I scramble up the bank, my breaths coming in short, panicked grunts. More bullets, more splashes. I look heavenwards and realise I have fallen next to the flagpole. The others are on the bank, a huddle of figures, but they are not safe yet; they need to climb up. They're too close to each other; they need to separate. George has taken Roza, holding her to his chest. Another round of gunfire. Halfway up the bank, George falls. Roza tumbles out from his arms. George clutches his thigh as the hot blood oozes through his fingers. Roza scrambles to her feet. George cries out urging the others forward but his voice is cut short as another bullet rips into his chest.

Milan scoops the child up and scrabbles up the bank. Petra slips and slides back down. She screams at Roza to keep going, to keep going. I stretch my arms out for the girl. Roza falls into my embrace as Milan collapses next to me. Another burst of machine gun fire cuts her mother down as she screams at her daughter to keep going…

The machine guns stop their deadly work as suddenly as they'd started, the clattering rhythm fading into the night. The searchlights are switched off plunging the world into pitch-blackness.

Only yards separate us but on one side lie George and Petra, their bodies engulfed in mud; their lives extinguished on Hungarian soil. Lying next to me, fighting for breath, is Milan, and, huddled in my lap, shivering, is Roza. The rain falls heavily, the sound of the wind broken only by our heavy breaths and the sobbing of a little girl. Our journey is at an end; a new journey awaits us. But for now, we stare back into the blackness, our eyes blind with the abrupt switch from light to dark, our hearts breaking.

Above us, the Austrian flag flaps in the breeze.

Epilogue

Thirty-three years later

Friday, 16 June 1989

I vowed never to return to my country. I am English now –
and proud of it. But I, along with thousands of other refugees,
have returned to the nation of our birth for this solemn and
symbolic ceremony. For today, almost thirty-three years after
the Revolution, Imre Nagy is to be honoured with a funeral
befitting a man of his stature. There must be tens of thousands
lining the routes, and here in Heroes' Square, paying our last
respects to the great man who, more than anyone, symbolised
the hope and the ultimate defeat of the Uprising. Alongside
him, four other coffins of leading participants from those far-
flung days, and next to them, a further coffin – an empty one
to commemorate the three hundred or more victims of state
retribution during the chaotic days following 4 November
1956. Today, the whole country stands and remembers. Shops
and businesses are closed, schools have been given the day off.
In the Square, flowers and wreaths everywhere, Corinthian
pillars decked in black and white, Hungarian flags with the
central Soviet emblem removed, bowed heads united by grief
and ingrained memories.

Yet, Imre Nagy died exactly thirty-one years ago on 16 June
1958, less than two years after the communists, with their

Soviet masters, had quashed the uprising and re-established one-party rule. By this time, I was in London, in Camden with my 'daughter', Roza.

After that fateful night of the 4th November, we stayed in Austria until the following year, helped financially and emotionally by the Red Cross and other sterling organisations. We lost contact with Milan within hours of being taken in and never saw him again.

It was a time of recuperation, of assessment, it was a time when our emotions felt numb, each one of us coming to terms with the horrors we'd seen, the friends and homes we'd lost, and the freedom that lay ahead of us. At the time, a future of freedom seemed no less daunting than the totalitarian past we'd escaped from. But it was the children separated from their parents who suffered most, unable to comprehend the new world around them. Roza fell into a silent, dark world of her own. For months, she didn't talk, didn't smile, barely ate. I was never asked whether Roza was my child; it was simply taken for granted. By the time we arrived in England, we'd both slipped into the assumed roles of mother and daughter, and neither of us ever sought to correct the mistake.

Meanwhile, in Hungary, the communists returned, the AVO re-emerged in their uniforms and, with their Soviet friends, plucked out leading insurgents for execution and scores more for deportation to Russia. They exhumed the bodies of their fallen colleagues and reburied them with full military honours. By the end of the year, the Iron Curtain was back in place but not before over 200,000 men, women and children had escaped into Austria. Nagy had found asylum in the Yugoslavian embassy but was kidnapped and held by the Hungarian communists for almost two years before they put him on trial which was as secret as it was pointless. In June

1958, they executed him and his 'fascist counter-revolutionary' followers and unceremoniously dumped the bodies. He was 62. (Only last year, on the thirtieth anniversary of Nagy's death, the police used terrible violence to break up a ceremony in honour of his memory.) In November 1958, the communists won 99.8% in a single-party election. Everything in Hungary was back to normal.

In January 1959, in London, I met James, my future husband. Roza, by this time an Anglophile thirteen-year-old, accepted him as the perfect stepfather and she more than made up for our own lack of children. In 1976, Roza married a quiet Scotsman called Robert. It took me six months before I understood a word he said. Four years later, they presented us with a grandson – George. James and I had twenty-five happy years together before cancer took him away from me a week before our silver anniversary in 1985.

When last year, Roza became pregnant for the second time, she told me the doctors had said it would be a girl. She asked me for a suggestion for a name. Idly, I offered the name closest to my heart. Roza immediately pounced on the idea and Robert, always too timid to contradict his wife, readily agreed. Despite my best efforts to disincline them, the name stuck. And hence, forty years later, Anastasia was re-born.

When news reached us of today's ceremony, we returned to our country, something we'd never dared hope for. And now, in Heroes' Square, we stand and remember – Roza, her baby, nine-year-old George, and me. Roza, I know, is thinking of her parents, Zoltan and Petra, and I can't help but feel a slight stab of jealousy – even after all these years.

As we listen to the eulogies and watch the solemn laying of flowers, we feel for perhaps only the second time in our lives proud to be Hungarian. We listen to the speeches – words criticising the government and the continued interference of the Soviet Union, and demands for multi-party elections – echoes of 1956; words inconceivable even a few weeks ago.

And now the minute silence.

I remember the two men of my youth – both footballers who once played opposite each other. I remember the afternoon in the Hotel Astoria; the Café of the Revolution; the boy, Tibor, who denounced his parents for their own salvation; the night I stepped on George's foot; the silhouetted watchtowers on that final night, Roza in my arms, her mother lying dead next to George only yards away in a different country, another world.

And I remember my little girl. Sixteen days. I am sixty-three now; Anastasia would be forty, three years younger than Roza. Roza is not my daughter, her children not my grandchildren, but my love for them is as real as any mother or grandmother. Through tragedy, God brought us together and together we found our salvation and made our future. Thirty-three years on, Roza is with me still, her baby, Anastasia, not yet one, in her arms.

I don't believe in reincarnation but sometimes I wonder. I used to believe that my Anastasia lived only in my memory and that once I die, her brief spell on this Earth would be swept away with the wind, her existence forever obliterated.

But now, at last, I'm not so sure.

THE END

Novels by **R.P.G. Colley:**

The Love and War Series
Song of Sorrow
The Lost Daughter
The Woman on the Train
The White Venus
The Black Maria
My Brother the Enemy
Anastasia
Elean
The Mist Before Our Eyes
The Darkness We Leave Behind

The Searight Saga
This Time Tomorrow
The Unforgiving Sea
The Red Oak

Rupertcolley.com

9 781999 721121